ABOUT THE AUTHOR

Elizabeth O'Roark spent many years as a medical writer before publishing her first novel in 2013. She holds two bachelor's degrees from the University of Texas, and a master's degree from Notre Dame. She lives in Washington, D.C. with her three children. Join her book group, Elizabeth O'Roark Books, on Facebook for updates, book talk and lots of complaints about her children.

ALSO BY ELIZABETH O'ROARK

The Devil Series:
A Deal with the Devil
The Devil and the Deep Blue Sea
The Devil You Know
The Devil Gets His Due

The Summer Series:
The Summer We Fell
The Summer I Saved You
The Summer You Found Me

1

NOW

It wasn't that long ago that I could get through an airport without being recognized. I miss that.

Today my sunglasses will remain on. It's one of those obnoxious *"I'm a celebrity!"* moves I've always hated, but that's better than a bunch of commentary about my current appearance. I slept most of the way from Lisbon to San Francisco, thanks to my handy stash of Ambien, but I'm still fucked in the head from the call I received just before I got on the flight...and it shows.

Donna has always been a ball of energy, cheerful and indefatigable. I can't imagine her any other way. Of all the people in the world, why does it have to be *her*? Why is it that the people who most deserve to live seem to be taken too soon, and the ones who deserve it least, like me, seem to flourish?

I've been promising myself that I just need to hold it together a little longer, when the truth is that I've got three straight weeks ahead of holding it together with no end in sight. But if I think nothing of lying to everyone else, I'm certainly not going to quibble over lies to myself.

I duck into the bathroom to clean up before I head for my

luggage. My hazel eyes are bruised with fatigue, my skin is sallow. The sun-kissed streaks the colorist added to my brown hair won't fool anyone into thinking I've spent time in the sun lately, especially Donna. Every time she's visited me in LA, she has said the same thing: "*Oh, honey, you look so tired. I wish you'd come home*", as if returning to Rhodes could ever improve anything.

I step back from the mirror just in time to catch a woman taking a picture of me from the side.

She shrugs, completely unashamed. "Sorry. You're not my taste," she says, "but my niece likes you."

I used to think fame would solve everything. What I didn't realize is that you're still every bit as sad. You just have the whole fucking world there to watch and remind you you've got no right to be.

I walk out before I say something I'll regret and head down the escalator to baggage claim. It wasn't until I started to date Cash that I understood the kind of chaos that can descend when the public thinks they know you—but today there's no crowd. Just Donna waiting near the base of the escalator, a little too thin but otherwise completely fine.

She pulls me into her arms, and the scent of her rose perfume reminds me of her home—a place where some of my best moments occurred. And some of my worst.

"You didn't need to pick me up. I was gonna Uber."

"That would cost a fortune," she says, forgetting or not caring that I'm no longer the broke kid she was once forced to take in. "And when my girl comes home, I'm going to be the one to greet her. Besides...I had company."

My gaze follows hers, past her shoulder.

I don't know how I didn't see him, when he stands a foot taller and a foot broader than anyone else in the room. Some big guys go out of their way to seem less so—they slouch, they smile, they joke around. Luke has never done any of those things. He is unapologetically his unsmiling self, size and all.

He looks older, but it's been seven years, so I guess he would. He's even bigger now, harder and less penetrable. His messy brown hair still glints gold from all those hours he spends on the water, but there's a full week's beard on a face that's normally clean-shaven. I wish I'd been prepared, at least. I wish someone had said, *"Luke will be there. And he'll still feel like the tide, sucking you out to sea."*

We don't hug. It would be too much. I can't imagine he'd be willing to do it anyway, under the circumstances.

He doesn't even smile, but simply tips his chin. "Juliet."

He's all grown up, even his voice is grown up—lower, more confident than it was. And it was always low, always confident. Always capable of bringing me to my knees.

It feels intentional, the fact that I'm only learning he's here *now*. Donna knows we never got along. But she's dying, which means I'm not allowed to resent her for this tiny manipulation.

"He offered to drive," Donna adds.

He raises a brow at the word *"offered"*, arms still folded across his broad chest, making it clear that's not *exactly* the way it happened. It's so like Donna to attribute far kinder qualities to us than actually exist.

"How many bags do you have?" He's already turning toward the carousel, manning up to do the right thing, no matter how much he hates me.

I move in front of him. "I can get it."

It irks me that he walks to the carousel anyway. I press a finger to my right temple. My head is splitting, finally coming off everything I took yesterday. And I just don't feel up to polite conversation, especially with him.

I swallow. "I didn't know you'd be here."

"Sorry to disappoint."

I see my bag coming and move forward. "That's not what I

meant." What I really meant was *"This is the worst possible situation, and I don't see how I'm going to weather three weeks of it."* I guess that's not much better.

I glance over my shoulder. "How is she?"

His eyes darken. "I just got in this morning, but...you saw her. A strong wind could knock her over."

And with that there's really nothing left to be said. Not easily or comfortably, anyway. The silence stretches on.

We both reach for my bag at the same time, our hands brushing for a moment.

I snatch mine back but it's too late. Luke is already in my bloodstream, already poisoning me. Making me want all the wrong things, just like he always did.

2

THEN

MAY, 2013

It's nearly the end of the school year, and the road outside the diner looks like a poorly organized parade—Jeeps and pickup trucks full of kids and surfboards, blasting music that flashes to life and fades just as fast. This marks the start of the high season, and for the next three months, Rhodes will be flooded with surfers and families buying ice cream and t-shirts, burgers and gas. It's when most of the local businesses actually turn a profit, when the town and its residents seem to wake from a long slumber.

Me, especially, though it's doing more harm than good at the moment.

"If we weren't so busy, you'd be fired by now," grouses Charlie, the line cook.

If he were someone else, I'd tell him my boyfriend is coming home at last, but Charlie is not that guy. I could tell him I'd just gotten a terminal diagnosis, and he *still* wouldn't be that guy.

"I know. I'm sorry." I push my hair back from my face and grab two plates from underneath the heat lamp.

"Don't be sorry," he replies, pitiless as ever, turning to remake the order I wrote down wrong. "Just stop fucking up."

Stacy takes the two plates from my grasp. "Church types, section two. They're yours."

She always sticks me with the older women who come here after Bible study because they are shitty tippers. For me, it's their attitude that's hardest to bear: the smug, self-satisfied way they'll remind me how lucky I am to have this job. How lucky I am that the pastor and his wife—Danny's parents—took me in.

"Surprised to see you here," says Mrs. Poffsteader. "Doesn't Danny come home today?"

The question—so innocent. The tone—not so much. I should be too excited to work today, she thinks. I should be getting ready. And if I *wasn't* working, she'd probably imply I was lazy. There's no winning with them.

"Tonight," I reply. "I've got plenty of time."

"Miss Donna said he's bringing a friend home."

I force a smile. "Yeah, Luke. I think they're going to surf." Luke Taylor, Danny's teammate, seemed like a perfectly nice guy the one time we spoke, and I know his scholarship doesn't cover housing over the summer, but I really don't want my summer with Danny hijacked by some college friend with different priorities. My social life this past year has revolved entirely around church—singing in the choir, helping Donna with the events—so it doesn't seem like it's asking too much, wanting a little of Danny's time to myself. I really hope Luke doesn't plan to stay.

"I figured he'd have found himself a college girl by now," Mrs. Miles says. "But I guess it's good for you it's still working out. Such a kind thing the pastor did, taking you in like that."

I don't care that she's implied Danny could do better than me—it's a sentiment I agree with. It's the *subtext* I tire of: *"Be more grateful, Juliet. You'd be nowhere without them, Juliet. Prove to us that you're worthy of the favor they've shown you, Juliet."*

"It was." I pull out my notepad. "What can I get you to drink?"

They look disappointed in me as they order their iced tea. I know what they wanted: some avowal of gratitude on my part. They wanted me to gush, to prostrate myself, to admit I'm trash and will always be trash who doesn't deserve anything I've received. People only want to see charity going to those who know their place.

And I *am* grateful—a little over a year ago, I couldn't make a sandwich without having my shoulder dislocated. I couldn't count on having ingredients for a sandwich in the first place.

But there's something about this constant demand for displays of gratitude from people who've never lifted a finger on my behalf that makes me miserly with it. I thank Donna every single night. These bitches from church? I hope they're not holding their breath.

I bring them their drinks and take their orders. They quiet every time I approach the table, which is no surprise. Even with their Bibles sitting out, their favorite topic remains the same: how Danny could have done so much better than me and how the situation will come to no good. It's a relief when they finally leave.

I clear their table—one-dollar tip on a twenty-five-dollar tab, naturally. I'm about to lift my tray when the bell over the door rings again, and a dreamily handsome guy—blonde and square-jawed and smiling at me like I'm his favorite thing in the world—walks in. The posh private school blazer has been replaced with shorts and a UCSD Football t-shirt, but he remains just as Teen Disney perfect as he was when I first met him during my sophomore year. He still looks too good for me. Yet somehow, he's mine.

"Danny!" I screech, dropping the tray with a clatter and running across the restaurant to throw my arms around his neck.

He squeezes me tight for only a second before gently detaching himself. He's not quite as comfortable with displays of affection, but it's hard to blame him. As the pastor's son in a small town, his every move will be discussed at length...Most likely with his parents.

"How are you here so early?" I ask breathlessly.

"Because—" He glances over his shoulder with a grin. "—I wasn't the one driving."

It's only then that I look past him, at the guy who's now walking in. I blink. Once, twice. I had an image of who Luke would be: cute, all-American, the boy you bring home to Mom. Just like Danny.

But Luke is not *cute*. He is not the boy you bring home. He isn't even a boy—he's six and a half feet of lean muscle, in need of a shave, taut and tan and...dangerous, somehow. As different from Danny as anyone I've ever known.

The smile on my face flickers out. My mouth goes dry and my heart thuds in my ears. He isn't smiling either. I can't tell if he is uncomfortable or angry, but the nice guy I met by phone has completely vanished, and the one in his place already appears to not like me much.

"Hi," I whisper, my voice uneven. There is something about his face that makes me feel compelled to stare: the odd color of his eyes—brown with a hint of green to them, the hollows beneath his cheeks, the unexpectedly soft mouth.

Danny throws an arm around my shoulders. "Told you she was the prettiest girl alive, didn't I?"

Luke glances at me as if weighing Danny's words. "You told everyone that, yeah." It's as close as he could come to arguing the point without doing so, yet here I stand, still staring at him and trying to ignore this insistent flutter that's suddenly bloomed to life, low in my gut.

I swallow hard, shifting my gaze back to Danny. "I'm not off until five."

He places a gentle kiss on my forehead. "Take your time. We're driving up to Kirkpatrick to show Luke why he should stay for the summer."

I force a smile to cover the unease I can't even explain to myself. And based on Luke's scowl, I'm guessing he feels it too.

∼

THE SUN IS STARTING to slip by the time I arrive at the Allens' tidy home, with its welcoming front porch and well-tended rose bushes in pale pink bloom.

Last year, all I wanted in the world was a cute house like this to come home to, a place where I'd be safe. I arrived here right after my stepbrother pulled my shoulder out of the socket, and I thought I'd be happy forever if I could call it mine.

It's funny, the way you get what you want and just start wanting something else.

Tonight, I wish I could face-plant in bed for five minutes, or at least rinse the stink of the diner out of my hair. When you're someone's guest, though, you don't get to be tired. You don't get to have a bad day.

"Juliet?" Donna calls from the kitchen. "Come give me a hand with the potatoes, won't you?"

Donna doesn't mean any harm—she legitimately enjoys cooking and creating a nice home, and she always wanted a daughter to help in the kitchen, to pass these things on to. But being here often just feels like an extension of my workday— even in my dreams I'm refilling someone's coffee or rushing off to find ketchup.

Luke and Danny are sitting at the table, glowing from an afternoon in the sun, hair still damp from the shower. Luke is sitting on the far side, in Danny's normal seat. When he came into the diner, his height made him seem almost lanky. Seated, though, he's too large for the table, for the room. We were four normal-sized people, perfectly balanced, without him. He's thrown off our equilibrium, and it feels dangerous somehow.

Danny asks how work was while I drain the potatoes Donna boiled. If I could speak freely, I'd mention the church ladies who spent their entire lunch badmouthing me and saying they were surprised Danny hadn't found someone else. I'd mention Mr. Kennedy put his hand on my ass again, or that some teens glued their tip to the table with ketchup.

"It was okay," I reply instead, because the pastor got me the job, and I don't want to seem unappreciative. The Allens think I'm quiet, but I'm not sure that's true. There's just so much I can't say that it's easier not to talk.

I mash the potatoes while the conversation quickly reverts back to surfing, the thing Luke and Danny bonded over last year. There are a thousand ways to describe a wave: bumpy or mushy or glassy or heavy, and they seem to be using all of them. I don't know what any of it means, but when I glance over, I'm struck by the way Luke has come alive, talking about it. His eyes are bright, his smile is wide, and I think I've never seen anyone quite so magnetic in my entire life. I don't even *like* him and I want to stare; I want to smile when he does.

The pastor's car pulls into the driveway, and we move a little faster because he likes dinner served right away. He hugs his son and shakes Luke's hand before he takes his place at the head of the table. I help Donna carry over the food and then slide onto the bench beside Danny, who presses his lips to the top of my head before his nose wrinkles.

"You smell like a cheeseburger," he says with a grin.

Luke, across from us both, glances at me a moment too long, as if he's waiting for me to explain myself. Perhaps he's thinking the same things Mrs. Poffsteader did: that if I cared enough, I'd have taken the day off. That I'm some predatory girl using his friend for a free place to stay.

I'm not. I know I'm not. But I have no idea where I'd go if

Danny and I broke up. I've got very little saved from the diner, and it's been made clear to me I'm no longer welcome home. Not that I'd go back there anyway.

"Is there any pepper?" asks the pastor.

Donna's eyes go wide in surprise. I have no idea why she's startled—the pastor will always decide something's missing, no matter how hard she tries. I rise without being asked, and Luke's brow furrows. He's still watching as I return with the pepper, something hard in his gaze.

"Can you get the tea while you're up, Juliet?" the pastor adds before launching into a long story about a woman and her baby who came in looking for help. He often does this at dinner—discusses the events of his day, seeking something in them he can use during Sunday's sermon. Maybe the theme will be *God helps those who help themselves*. Maybe the theme will be *Charity begins at home*. He hasn't figured it out yet.

Through it all, Luke remains silent, but he still sucks the air out of the room. Danny's house has been a haven for me for the past year and a half, but with Luke here...it no longer is. I really hope he doesn't decide to stay.

Donna and I rise to clear the table, and Luke begins to rise as well, but Donna waves him down with a fond smile.

"Sit, sit," she urges as if he's some visiting dignitary.

I run out to the garage for a tub of ice cream from the freezer while Donna brews coffee. I put out cream and sugar while she cuts the pie. These are tasks I complete every single night, but suddenly I feel conspicuous, as if I'm pantomiming them on a stage, because Luke is watching, and his judgment is a tangible thing, making every action I take feel forced and false.

They eat their pie while I start scrubbing pans, and when my gaze catches his by accident, his eyes flicking from my face to the dishtowel with disdain, his thoughts are so obvious it's as if he's said them aloud: *"I see through you, Juliet, and you don't fucking belong."*

I've tried my best this past year to be kind, gentle, and forgiving like the Allens, but I can't be that person with Luke. I just can't.

I narrow my eyes at him. *Maybe I don't belong here, Luke Taylor. But neither do you.*

A pleased gleam lights his eyes as if it was the reaction he wanted from me all along.

AFTER DINNER, we go to a party in a gated community, thrown by one of the kids from Westside—the snotty private school Danny attended on scholarship. Danny does his best to include me.

"You remember my girlfriend, Juliet," he says, and most of them do, but act as if they don't. That's what they're like.

We're offered beers, which Danny refuses on both my behalf and his. That's okay, though. What I want more than a regular high school experience is to be like the Allens, to somehow make myself worthy of everything they've given me, or better yet and more impossible still—to become one of them. To be a little junior Donna, smiling at the squirrels chasing each other in the yard, wanting nothing more from her day than to bake a pie and sit at the table with those she loves. There's a peacefulness to her, a contented silence, and I would like some of that silence for myself.

"You're that girl the pastor took in, right?" asks one guy when we're introduced. "Didn't your brother die or something?"

Or something. Like dying is so similar to other outcomes it's difficult to tease them apart.

I swallow hard. "Yeah." *He died or something.*

Danny's discomfort is worse than the reminder. I'm not sure if it's because he feels sorry for me, or if he's simply embarrassed by the connection. When a teenager from Haverford dies, it's usually because he's brought it on himself.

We wander outside, where Luke's seated by the firepit with a beer in one hand and a girl in his lap, though we've been here ten minutes at most. Unlike me, he's already been welcomed into the fold—because playing college ball carries weight that being someone's girlfriend does not.

"Juliet?" asks the girl beside me. She's adorable but appears, in no way, to fit in with this crowd. Her blond hair is cut in a neat bob. She's without a spray tan, false lashes, or makeup. "I'm Libby. My family just moved here, but I just wanted to say I heard you sing in church last week and you've got a beautiful voice. I feel closer to God just listening to you."

It's the kind of sentiment I've never felt even once, so foreign to me I'd assume she was bullshitting if her eyes didn't shine with sincerity.

She tells me she just finished her freshman year of college. I can't believe she's two years older than me, but I suppose that's because she's innocent and well-intentioned, and I'm neither of those things.

"Join the choir," I urge when she mentions she loves to sing. "I need someone else up there who isn't a thousand years old."

She laughs and then holds a hand over her mouth as if she's guilty she did it.

If I were a better person, I'd let Danny go. I'd let him leave me to fall in love with some sweet, pure girl who feels guilty when she laughs at a catty remark, who feels close to God at *any* point, ever. But I'm not a better person, and I'm not letting him go.

"Hey, Maggie!" a guy shouts to the girl exiting the darkened pool house, still buttoning her shorts. "You sure weren't in there long. Take me next time."

She laughs. "I like meals, not snacks."

Danny has been adamantly *"hands off"* seeing as I'm underage and my experiences prior to him were mostly unwilling—making the best of a bad situation. But there's a dazed, stuporous satisfaction on Maggie's face, the kind I've seen in other girls before. I want to know what that's like. And I want to know what it's like not to feel sick about it afterward.

I look away and catch Luke watching me, as if he can see through me, as if he knows exactly what I want. And for a moment, there's a weird energy between us, a heaviness to the air.

"This isn't really our scene," Danny says quietly, glancing from Maggie to the guy lighting up a joint to his right. "You want to head out?"

I nod, though the truth is that everything about this is my scene. In a world without the Allens, I'd be an entirely different girl.

Luke throws Danny the keys to the Jeep as we rise. "Don't wait up."

The girl in his lap is already sliding her hand into his waistband, and it makes something burn in my stomach. The rest of the world—girls like her and Maggie—get the things they want. They get to drink and dance and...experiment. Why can't I?

"Goodness is its own reward," Pastor Dan often says. But right now, it doesn't feel all that rewarding.

We climb into the Jeep, and Danny starts the engine before carefully pulling out. I wonder what Luke will do next. Will he kiss that girl as if she matters, or will he kiss her the way Justin kissed me, mostly to keep her quiet so she can't refuse?

"You're quiet," Danny says.

I turn toward him. "He doesn't seem like someone you'd be friends with."

Danny shrugs. "I might not approve of everything he does,

but he's a good guy, and he's had a hard life. Like, unimaginably hard. He's been homeless since he was sixteen...I guess his stepfather was beating his mom and they kicked him out when he tried to stop it. Can you imagine...homeless at sixteen?"

I laugh quietly. "Well...yeah. I left home at fifteen."

"You left by *choice*," he corrects, and my teeth grind. I wouldn't say I had much of a fucking choice, given that I moved out after my stepbrother dislocated my shoulder. Danny is almost willful, at times, in his re-envisioning of my past.

"He doesn't seem to like me much."

Danny shakes his head. "He's just a quiet guy. It's not about you."

I want to explain there's something hard in Luke's face when he looks at me, something that isn't there when he looks at everyone else, but I'll sound crazy if I keep arguing this. I just choose to hope, instead, that he decides to leave once the weekend is through.

WHEN WE WAKE on Saturday to go to the beach, there's a heavy breeze, and I deeply regret taking the day off, which I only did because I thought it would just be me and Danny. Late May in Northern California is hit or miss anyway. It can be balmy in the shade, or so breezy even the sunlight can't quite keep you warm. Today will be the latter, and with Luke acting like I poisoned the town well, the small appeal this trip held is completely nullified.

Danny and Luke come downstairs just as we finish pulling breakfast together. Luke's eyes are barely open, but I still spy that ever-present disdain in them when I look his way.

"Do you have your suit on, hon?" Danny asks me. "We're taking off the second we're done eating."

I can't. I can't spend the whole damn day with a guy who

hates me for being pathetic and needy and sucking up to the people who've taken me in. I can't.

"It's pretty cold out," I hedge. "And the wind is gonna kick the sand everywhere."

"It'll warm up," Danny says. "You've got to come. I haven't seen you in months."

That's how Danny gets his way—by being the one person who wants me around. I studiously avoid Luke's gaze as I agree.

They eat while I scrub the pans, and I've just sat down at last when Danny asks his mom if there's any more juice.

"I'll get it," I say, rising again and walking out to the fridge in the garage. When I return, Luke's eyes meet mine and he raises a brow. As if to say, *"I know exactly what you're doing."*

I raise mine right back: *Fuck you, Luke.* There's nothing wrong with the fact that I do my best to be helpful around here. To pull my weight. Maybe I'm doing it to convince them I'm not a bad person, or maybe I'm doing it to convince myself. Either way, it's none of his concern.

I walk outside to Luke's beat-up, ancient Jeep after breakfast, shivering in my hoodie, with a book and towel pressed to my chest. Luke looks at me, eyes beginning at my ankles and climbing up.

"Where's her board?" he asks.

Danny laughs and wraps an arm around me. "Juliet doesn't surf." He tried to teach me once, last summer, and it didn't go well. "Believe me, it's safer for everyone if she stays on the beach and looks pretty."

A muscle flickers in Luke's cheek, silent objection either to my failure to surf or the fact that Danny thinks I'm pretty. "Maybe you should take her in the truck. If she's already cold she'll freeze once we're on the road without the top on."

"You'll be fine, right?" Danny urges, giving my hip a gentle squeeze. "We're only going ten minutes down the road."

I nod. If Danny drives, his parents will have to share a car, and every inconvenience they suffer will, essentially, be all my fault. I try to avoid being at fault as often as I can.

I wedge myself into a tiny corner of the back seat, where the boards bang against my shoulder and the breeze from the open windows makes it impossible to follow much of the conversation.

My phone chimes with an incoming text. When I discover it's from my friend Hailey, I slide a little lower in my seat. I already know anything she's saying to me won't be fit for other eyes.

HAILEY:

SO...How was it?

She was certain last night would be *the* night. I was pretty sure it wouldn't be, and I was correct.

Uneventful. I told you it would be. He's just being careful, I think. It's kind of sweet.

Shane Harris is sweet, too, but I guarantee that wouldn't stop HIM if you get tired of the situation.

Would I have said, "*Yes*" to Shane's repeated offers if I wasn't with Danny? Maybe, but I *am* with Danny, and I'm living with his parents, so there's no point in asking myself the question.

The Jeep swerves onto the shoulder of the road when we reach Kirkpatrick. I'm shivering as I climb from the back, and Luke's eyes roll as I wrap my towel around myself for warmth.

I follow them to the beach and sit, tucking my knees inside my sweatshirt while they strip off their shirts and pull on wetsuits. The breeze carries the scent of sunscreen and sea grass and wild flowers, and though it's still chilly, I close my eyes and breathe deep, lifting my face to the sky. There are times out here, when the sun is shining and the breeze is gentle, that I almost believe I can be made whole again.

When my eyes open, Danny is already marching toward the water like some firm and capable soldier, but Luke is not.

He's still, watching me, but turns away when my eyes open, following Danny without a word.

He carries the board under one arm easily, as if he's carrying nothing at all. His height makes him look almost lean, when clothed, but he has the broad shoulders of a swimmer, and there's a gracefulness to him, one you wouldn't associate with football but you wouldn't exactly associate with ballet either. It's more like he's a tiger in human form, possessing a kind of sleek athleticism even when he's doing something as simple as walking to the shore.

They paddle out and get in the line-up while I bury my feet in the cool sand to shield them from the wind. It'll warm up soon enough, but I still wish I hadn't come.

Danny takes the first wave he can, the same sort of wave he always takes—moderate and predictable. He attempts to cut up into it but wipes out.

I wait for Luke to drop into the next one, but he doesn't. He lets wave after wave pass him by. Danny claims he's really good —he grew up surfing before his family moved away in high school—but I wonder if he's intimidated, having only surfed in San Diego. It's selfish of me, but I *hope* he's intimidated.

I hope he hates this and never, ever comes back.

Just as I think it, though, he sits up straight, peering into the distance, every muscle tense. Once again, he reminds me of a tiger, but this time it's one who's just spotted prey. The wave in the distance begins to thicken and swell. Luke flattens on his stomach and paddles hard, his broad shoulders in continuous motion as a wall of water forms behind him.

It's not a beginner wave—it's the kind of wave that could fuck you up if you didn't know what you were doing. And even though I don't like him and don't want him here, I hold my breath, braced for disaster.

He's upright suddenly, as if by magic. While Danny is methodical when he pops up, carefully planting one foot and then the other from the knees, Luke has somehow propelled his long body into the air in one seamless motion, landing effortlessly, his footing assured. It happens so fast I can barely process it, so fast that I wonder if I imagined it.

I thought his height would hurt him, but it isn't a factor at all. The wave is a monster, bumpy and ferocious. But he could be standing barefoot on the kitchen floor—that's how stable he looks.

He carves up into the wall of water, does an effortless aerial, and then carves again, letting his hand graze the wave, trying to slow his speed as he enters the barrel to make it last as long as possible. He looks like one of the pros: the guys training to surf Mavericks when the winter swell comes in. And even from a distance, I see now why he would be willing to drive eight hours north and endure staying in a pastor's house for better surf. He's *happy*. I've seen him smile, I've heard him laugh, but there's something different in him as he soars across the water, something deeply focused and complete.

Luke shoots through the end of the barrel at last, his board flying into the air as it glides back up over the crest of the wave's tail. Guys in the lineup cheer—guys who normally show approval with a chin nod, a quiet, "*Nice*". He's simply *that* good. He jumps down and is prone again, paddling, his joy replaced by something else, something better. Intensity. As if nothing matters in the world but doing it again.

Danny isn't like that. He doesn't want *more*. He's happy with exactly what he already has. I wish I was a little more like Danny in that regard. I'm trying.

When they finally return to the shore, two hours later, they are sandy and salty, beyond exhausted, but it's a different kind of exhaustion than the kind I feel after a shift at the diner. It's giddy and ecstatic. Despite their size, they remind me of little boys.

"Babe, did you see that?" Danny asks, exultant at finally pulling off a small aerial. "I think I finally get what I was doing wrong before."

"Surfing badly?" jokes Luke. "Is that what you were doing wrong?" And then he laughs—the sound low and husky and so unquestionably male that I feel a spark streak through me, snapping almost painfully inside my gut.

Danny kicks him and laughs, collapsing beside me in the sand. "Asshole."

Luke closes his eyes and turns his face toward the sun. "I never want to surf in San Diego again."

"So, I guess that means I've convinced you to stay for the summer?" Danny asks.

Luke glances at me before he looks away. "Yeah. I guess you did."

But his happiness has ebbed a bit. And I suspect what he is unhappy about is me.

3

NOW

Most people talk about going home with fondness. But for me, even the good memories of home are now tinged with pain, with a reminder of what I've lost. That's one reason I've waited seven years to come back, but not the most important one.

The freeway skirts around Haverford, which looks just as shitty as it ever did. Cash would laugh his ass off if he was here now. He'd bring up my *"white trash roots"* again, after a couple of drinks. He'd never stop bringing it up, most likely.

Donna pats my shoulder as her gaze follows mine. "I check on her occasionally," she says of my mother. "Not much has changed."

Meaning my mother is still a woman who will take her husband's side in any argument. A woman who hates me, though she has no problem asking me for money, time and again.

I pay it simply to buy her silence.

We continue on to Rhodes, exiting the freeway to a two-lane road that heads toward the coast, where the houses are polite and uniform with neatly trimmed lawns and mailboxes that no one has taken a bat to, as different from where I grew up as they could possibly be.

When we finally stop in front of Donna's yellow clapboard house, my stomach lurches. The new addition out back is so large that it dwarfs the main house, making it look minuscule and quaint by contrast, but I still remember how fine and brightly lit it seemed the night I first came here, symbolizing everything Danny had that I did not: parents who loved him and a place where he'd be safe. He had everything, back then.

They shouldn't have let me in the front door.

"Wow," I whisper as I climb from the car. "It's...like a different place."

Donna's fingers link with mine and she squeezes my hand. "Entirely thanks to you kids."

All we did was write checks. The real work occurs a few weeks from now when Danny's House officially opens.

Lots of places—some good, some terrible—offer emergency and long-term foster care, but Danny's House will have a highly trained staff with psychologists, lawyers, and educational consultants on retainer. When Donna first suggested the idea, it seemed too ambitious to ever come to fruition. It's why I agreed I'd come for the opening if she ever pulled it off—because I never thought I'd actually have to.

I didn't realize she'd extracted the same promise from Luke.

Stepping into the foyer is like stepping into the past—I half expect Danny to come ambling out of the kitchen, his skin glowing from a day spent in the water, his hair still damp—but the rest of the house has changed. The family room is enlarged, the dining room now seats thirty, and the kitchen has doubled in size.

Donna proudly shows me the massive, new, walk-in pantry, already stocked with snacks.

"Are you hungry?" she asks.

I shake my head.

Luke snorts. "Gonna be an interesting three weeks for you. No Patron, no lobster."

The excesses of my lifestyle sound ridiculous off his lips, especially given where he and I both came from, and they aren't even *my* excesses. I didn't create that tour rider, and I'm not the one who released it to the press, but I've been paying the price for it ever since.

"That was my manager, not me," I say wearily. "You really think I'm going to eat *lobster* before a show?"

He glances at me, the look deadly. "How would I have any idea what you do before a show?"

Touché, Luke. I guess you wouldn't.

Donna glances at us, quickly covering her worry with a forced smile. "I'm going to put you and Luke in the addition. We've got two kids arriving early, so this way when they get here, they can sleep in the main house and you won't have to move. Is that all right?"

"Of course," I say, my eyes flickering to Luke and away just as fast. He doesn't want to be anywhere near me. I don't want to be anywhere near him. This visit is just getting better and better.

Donna steers us toward the addition, opening a door to her left. There's a bed, a nightstand, and nothing else. The walls are bare, but the window looks out into the spacious backyard. We had to tear down the house behind Donna's to make it possible.

It'll be a good place for kids. A good place for anyone coming from a home like mine. I blink back tears and swallow hard, willing myself to hold it together. One good thing might emerge from this whole fucking mess, but I'll never stop wishing it just hadn't happened in the first place.

"It's not much, I know," she says.

"You know how I was raised," I tell her with a small smile. "As long as I've got a bed, I'm fine."

She wraps an arm around my shoulders. "I've seen the kind

of places you stay now. I imagine you've gotten used to much better."

She isn't wrong. I've become the kind of person who complains when turndown service hasn't been completed by the time I get to my room, who is put out when a suite isn't available. But at the same time, I'm still waiting to lose it all, and there is never a night when I climb into bed without half anticipating I'll be jerked out of it—my stepfather's hand wrapped tight around my ankle, yanking me to the floor to punish me for some infraction, or Justin, demanding I come outside so my brother won't wake. Maybe that's why I don't object all that much when Cash is rough with me—because I've lived through worse.

Or maybe it's just that I know I deserve it.

"It's perfect," I tell her, my mouth slipping into a smile. "I'll just have my assistant forward some six-hundred thread count sheets for the bed."

I was joking, but Luke rolls his eyes as he heads off to his room, and resentment bursts in my chest. I know I have absolutely earned his hatred, every bit of it, but does he really think I turned into *that* person so fast?

Sure he does. He'd assumed I was that person by the time I left seven years ago.

"I'll let you get settled while I start work on dinner. Bathroom's down the hall if you want to shower." Donna throws her arms around me, and the familiarity of the action makes my chest ache. "It's so good to have you home, Juliet."

I hug her tightly, fighting the urge to cry. I'd like to tell her it's good to be here, too, but with me, Luke, and all these memories under one roof...there's just no way to make it sound true.

The memories. I don't know how the hell to make them stop creeping forward, but I'd better figure it out. I need every last one of them tucked back where they're safe. Where she—and Luke—can't reach them.

4

THEN

JUNE 2013

Donna's in her element with the boys here. She enlists me to help her cook and clean and dote on them because she genuinely can't imagine I'd want to do anything else.

In some ways it's as if I came to her as a mound of unformed clay, and she's chosen to shape me into this thing she always wanted: a sweet, choir-singing daughter—a thoughtful and nurturing wife for her son. I didn't really have any plans for this ball of clay. I don't know why there's this occasional impulse to snatch myself back.

I straggle into the house after a double shift to find the boys are already back from surfing.

Donna smiles at me when I enter as if I'm the most beloved princess of a fairy tale, while Luke simply glares. He's already figured out that I'm the Big Bad Wolf.

"Can you start the rice for me, hon?" she asks.

I nod, going to the sink to wash my hands, wishing I could just sit for a moment. I'm always achy after a double, but today this girl from Danny's high school tripped me, so it's worse than normal. Every time I swallow, I can feel where my chin hit the chair as I fell, and as always, even when I'm not looking in Luke's direction, I know his withering gaze is on me, saying, "*You're not fooling me, Juliet.*"

Yet I can't hate him. Not entirely. There's something lean and underfed about Luke at mealtime, despite his size, that hurts my heart. He eats fast, the way you would if you were starving, the way you would if you'd spent a *lot* of time starving. And he might be; Donna isn't making nearly enough food, and he's a lot bigger than Danny and the pastor. He's also far more active. Danny's got a desk job at the church this summer, but Luke's working construction. And in addition to surfing with Danny all afternoon, he's getting up at dawn to surf before work as well. He must need way more food than he's getting, and when I reach the table after everyone else and discover he's already cleared his plate, there's this twist in my heart I can't ignore.

He leaves the table hungry every night. I'm not sure how Donna hasn't noticed.

"Oh, sweetheart," she says, watching me pour the rice into a serving bowl, "you made twice as much as we needed."

"Sorry," I reply as if I did it by accident.

I'm the last one to sit, and when I do, Luke's eyes darken as he studies my face. "What happened to your chin?"

I flush as everyone turns to look at me. "I tripped at work," I say quietly.

I'm not sure why he had to call attention to it or why his nostrils are flaring as if I just lied. Which I did, but what possible evil motive could I even have? Does he think I'm working as a dominatrix on the side? That I'm selling meth on the way home? When would I even have the fucking time? He's plowing through the extra rice I made like a champ, though. I've forgiven him long before I'm through telling myself I'm mad.

"No iced tea?" asks Pastor Dan.

"You want caffeine this late?" Donna frets. She manages him sometimes like he's her father, not her husband, especially since his visit to the cardiologist last winter.

"I've got to go back to the church for a counseling session," he reminds her. "I need to perk up."

She glances at me with an apologetic smile. "Juliet, honey, do you mind grabbing it?"

"Can you get the Tabasco while you're up too?" Danny asks as I swing my legs over the bench.

It isn't a big deal, but Luke's nostrils flare once more. The Allens have always made me feel like I can still become a better person, but Luke's silent, constant disdain says something else entirely. *"Juliet, you fucking fake. This isn't you at all."*

And I know it's not. But is it so wrong that I want to change? That I still think I can become better than I am?

"You're a saint," Donna tells me when I carry it over.

I sit and Luke's hard gaze meets mine. "Oops." He holds up the milk. "Looks like it's empty."

There's a challenge in his eyes. *Go ahead, Juliet. Be a good girl and hop up again. We're all half done and you haven't eaten a bite, but let's watch you play your part.*

A crack forms in my shell when he's around, and I can already feel the old, bad version of me slipping through it. "You've got two legs," I reply.

A glint flickers in his eye. "Not very saintly of you, Juliet."

"Neither is the way you wandered off with that blonde last night."

"Juliet," Donna gently scolds.

Luke has won this round. He wanted to prove I'm an asshole and he did. By the end of the summer, they won't want me anywhere near them. I grip the table, preparing to rise for the third time, suddenly near tears.

"Don't," Luke growls, standing up. "I've got it."

The air hangs heavy between me and Luke for the rest of

dinner, but the Allens don't even seem to notice. They are baby fish, being circled by two Great Whites. They won't know what's happened until Luke and I have devoured them all.

WE'VE STARTED HANGING out at the beach most nights with a group of surfers—Caleb, Beck, and Harrison—rich college kids who simply want to sit around a bonfire with a beer in hand and a girl beside them while they talk about surfing. Sometimes Libby comes—she's joined the choir too—but, otherwise, I stick out like a sore thumb.

Maybe it's that I'm not rich. Maybe it's that I'm not in college, but it's also that I don't dress like the other girls do, don't act like they do.

I'm not sitting in Danny's lap. I'm not making jokes about blow jobs or teasing someone about the *long, hard* night ahead. These girls are out here in little more than bikinis while I'm dressed like an Allen—nothing fitted, nothing cropped.

And I'm tired of it. I'm tired of staying covered up all the time, as if I've got something to be ashamed of, tired of the way things with Danny never progress.

I pull off my hoodie. I'm wearing a tank top and cut-offs, more than most of the girls here, but I feel conspicuous anyway.

Danny's in a heated discussion with the guy beside him about where the biggest waves are and doesn't even notice, but Luke's teeth grind as he looks away. The girl in his lap barely even has her nipples covered, but me and my *tank top* are an issue.

If Danny notices I've removed the hoodie, he shows no sign of it. For the next hour, though, Luke's jaw grinds and he looks at anything but me until suddenly he's on his feet, tugging the girl in his lap off into the darkness.

When Danny and I leave to get ice cream, he suggests I put the hoodie back on. "Just in case we see anyone we know," he adds.

So he *did* notice, and the only effect is that he's apparently...embarrassed?

I get mint chip with sprinkles, and he—fittingly—gets vanilla. A couple passes us as we return to the truck, pushing a sleeping baby in a stroller.

"I can't wait to have kids," says Danny. "This is a good place to raise them."

I love that he thinks about what would make his kids happy. I love that he thinks about the future. From what I've heard, my dad didn't think too much about the future, and he sure as shit didn't care about making his kids happy. He'd taken off before I hit my first birthday.

But the future is a long time away. I'm still in high school, and I've barely lived yet. I want to know what it's like to sit on someone's lap with a beer in hand. I want to know what it's like to be pulled into the darkness, willingly.

I want good memories to replace all the bad ones Justin left behind.

When Danny pulls into the driveway and I see that all the lights are out inside, I slide toward him and climb into his lap. "Kiss me."

He blinks, guiltily looking around before leaning down to give me a small, soft kiss. I can tell he's about to pull away, so I kiss him harder, my mouth open, my tongue seeking his.

He's been careful with me for so long but he doesn't need to be. I lean closer, pressing myself against him until I feel him harden. It thrills me, as if we've finally climbed aboard a train I've been waiting on for a very long time. But no sooner has it started than he grabs my hips and pushes me away.

"Come on, hon," he says, gentle and yet frustrated.

I sigh. "Danny, I turn eighteen this year."

"It doesn't matter how old you are...you're not that kind of girl."

"What *kind* of girl?"

"You know, the kind of girl who does that. Who has sex before marriage."

He wants to wait for *marriage*? It seems like the kind of thing he should have told me before now.

But I guess the fact that I *didn't* wait for marriage is the kind of thing I should have told him before now too.

And even if I wish my first time hadn't gone the way it did, I want the things that girl with Luke is getting right now. I want to walk into a room, mid-party, with that satisfied, secretive look Maggie had on her face. I don't even know what I want, really. I just want *more*. More than what I have now, which is so wrong, when I already have so much.

Danny walks me to my bedroom door, kissing me good-night in that way of his—making me feel like a treasured object, something fine and fragile that must be handled with care. Yes, occasionally I wish he'd kiss me like Ryan Gosling kisses Rachel McAdams in the *The Notebook*: full-on, hot, desperate. But there's something to be said for Danny's way too.

I just can't quite remember what it was as I look at Luke's empty room.

LUKE SOMEHOW ESCAPED GOING to church his first week here, but the jig is up by the end of the second. I'm already sitting with the choir when he walks in behind Danny, bleary-eyed on the two hours of sleep he got, looking like he's preparing for battle: hands in his pockets, shoulders hunched over while he stares at the floor. The only sign of life on his face comes when he realizes Danny has positioned them directly across from me. He starts looking around, hoping for an available seat elsewhere, but there isn't one, so his jaw locks and remains that way through the entire service, whether it's the pastor speaking, prayers being offered, or me doing my solo.

"That was lovely, Juliet," the pastor says as I take my seat. He turns to the crowd and starts talking about his time as a missionary in Nicaragua, an experience which provided him endless stories of human suffering—and his own goodness. I'd believe in his goodness slightly more if he wasn't always milking the misery of others to prove it.

"But we don't have to look to the third world for people in need, because they are all around us," he says. I stiffen. "Yes, they *are* all around us. They come in the form of a man who sits out on the corner begging for change, a woman who can't afford formula for her baby, a girl who stays in the school library because she's scared to go home."

My eyes lower to the floor, and my face burns as the church's collective gaze slides to me. They all know who this one is about. I'm used to it by now—the pastor's thinly veiled references to me in his sermons are par for the course at this point—but I wish Danny hadn't told his dad about the library thing and I wish Luke wasn't hearing it too. Maybe it isn't even his disdain that upsets me—it's simply the way it reminds me of all the ugly things I am, and that I'm unlikely—no matter how hard I fake it, no matter how hard I try—to be rid of them for good.

At the end of the service, I remain near the pastor and Donna, enduring the comments people make, the reminders posed as compliments.

"You sang so beautifully today, Juliet," says the church secretary. "You've really blossomed since the Allens took you in."

I force a smile, though I wouldn't say I've *blossomed*. The only difference between me now versus two years ago is that I have significantly fewer bruises. The price of being poor, I guess, is that there is always someone better off who will get the credit for your accomplishments.

Mrs. Wilson is the next to compliment me. "Juliet, what a lovely job you did." There's pity in her smile.

Luke, beside me, laughs as she walks away. "Prance, little show pony, prance."

I don't have to ask what he means because I already know: the pastor doesn't want me to sing because I've got a decent voice. He wants me to sing to remind everyone that he was the one who dragged me out of the dirt.

"Go fuck yourself," I reply under my breath.

His eyes lighten and his mouth twitches. "There she is," he says, only for me to hear. "I knew she was in there somewhere."

I take a long shower, rinsing off the day of travel. Luke's in the backyard, starting the lawnmower. His face, in profile, is a work of art—the fading sun marking the curve of his cheekbones, his sharp jaw, his straight nose. I step closer to the window, drawn to him. He tugs out a weed and when his bicep pulses there's a throb between my legs to match it. He glances up, as if he knows I'm watching, and I hustle off to the kitchen in shorts and bare feet, damp hair streaming down my back.

Donna's assembling ingredients on the counter but stops and smiles when she sees me. "There's my girl. You look just like you did when you first came to us."

I can't imagine that's true. I'm decades older on the inside. I arrived here at fifteen feeling dirty and used up, naively hoping I could be made clean again. I know better now.

"Sit," I tell her. I made chili often enough growing up here that I recognize the ingredients. "I've got this."

"You can help, but I'm not dead yet. I can still make a meal for two of my favorite people."

My smile falters. We still haven't discussed everything— whether she's gotten a second opinion, or what her plans are for this place once she's gone. I can't bring myself to ask any of it.

"I don't imagine you cook for yourself much these days," she says as I start chopping the onion. "You still haven't bought a place, have you?"

I shake my head. "I've been traveling so much it didn't really seem worth it. I'll get something eventually."

She runs a hand over my head, smoothing back my hair. "Juliet, you're running yourself too hard. Maybe it's time to take a little break?"

Dating Cash led to a surge in popularity—or perhaps just infamy—and I've got to ride the wave for as long as it lasts...if I'm even capable of continuing. I'm too young to say I've already burned out, but I feel like a dried-up husk most of the time now, and I don't know how much longer I can pretend I'm not.

"I'm fine. But you're not *really* going to make me work around here, are you?" I give her my sweetest, most pleading smile and she laughs.

"I really am. I have a list a mile long of things that need to be done to the addition before the first children arrive." This makes little sense since she has plenty of money to hire help if she needs it, but she barrels on before I can ask. "I just want it to feel permanent. It never was for you, was it? All that time you lived here and you never put a single thing on the walls."

My palm rests atop the onion and my knife stills. It wasn't her fault—it would've given the pastor one more thing to dislike me for.

"I was just happy to have a room," I tell her, but I'm not sure she believes me. I'm not sure if I believe it either. There was a time when I wanted to put things on the wall, a time when I still cared.

Dinner's nearly ready when Luke walks in, freshly showered, his t-shirt just damp enough to mold perfectly to that chest of his, well-honed from days spent surfing.

He was the loveliest thing I'd ever laid eyes on ten years ago, making my heart beat a million miles an hour if I allowed myself to look too long. He's even lovelier now. And my heart—the one I assumed was no longer capable of much—is beating just the way it did.

It can't.

He smirks. "I figured opening a room service menu was the height of your culinary ability these days."

"Your food isn't going to spit on itself. I thought I'd help it along."

Donna sighs. "I didn't think it was possible, but the two of you are fighting even more now than you did when you were younger."

My gaze catches Luke's, and for just a second it's all there again—that age-old tension between us and the reason it existed. God, I hated the way my world seemed to flip upside down anytime he walked in the room. I fought with him simply to hide it. But that was years ago, and I was someone else. So why am I still picking fights? Why is he? My hand curls tight around the counter's edge, willing the questions away.

We take our seats and mumble grace along with Donna, her voice the only one at the table that is confident and certain. I tried so hard to become an Allen, but it was in moments like this I felt the impossibility of it, because they were always so grateful in their prayers, while I was simply pissed off about the things I didn't have. Even now, blessed with the life a thousand girls in LA would kill for—money, fame, a hot boyfriend—I'm still not grateful. I'm still a little pissed.

"Look at the two of you, all grown up and doing so well," Donna says, passing me the salad and smiling more proudly than any mother possibly could. "Juliet, did you hear Luke took second in Hawaii this winter?" She turns to him. "What was that one called again?"

Pipeline Masters.

Luke hesitates. He has no desire to brag about his accomplishments to anyone. Me, least of all. "Pipeline."

"What a month that was. You in this big surf competition and Juliet in a magazine." She turns to me. "I can't tell you how silly I felt buying that magazine at the grocery store. I wish they'd let you wear more clothes for those things."

Yeah, you and me both. I bet no one ever asked Slash to pose naked with his legs wrapped around a guitar.

Luke's lip curls. "The lack of clothes is the only reason anyone but you bought it."

Asshole.

But then Luke digs into his chili, eating the same way he always did—hunched over and ravenous—and it opens this unfortunate wound inside me. Why won't it just close, that wound? What do I have to do to make it go away so that no one guesses it was ever there?

"You're eating like a savage," I tell him.

He raises a brow. "And you're *not* eating, like someone with a disorder."

I glance at my untouched food. I got out of the habit of meals while on tour. I don't like to go on stage full, and I guess all the cocaine didn't help either.

Donna, sensing tension, leans forward, reaching out to pick up a strand of my hair as I begin to eat. "I'm glad you stopped bleaching it," she says, "but you're so thin, hon. You're not with that boy anymore, are you?"

Luke stiffens and so do I. I wasn't that well known until I started dating Cash Sturgess, but man...the whole world knows about me now. Nothing like a little leaked footage of your boyfriend beating the shit out of you to garner publicity.

"It's complicated," I reply, because I can't bring myself to say, *"Yes, probably."* Cash is currently away at what they're calling rehab, though it's actually just some ayahuasca retreat in Peru, and my guess is that a month from now, he'll be "better" and I'll be back. Sometimes it's simply a relief to be with a guy who treats you like the piece of shit you already know you are. It's a relief not to have to pretend otherwise.

Luke's jaw clenches. "There shouldn't be anything complicated about it."

My eyes fall closed. This tiny hint that he cares, even if he's angry about it...God, it hurts. I ignore him while tucking this moment away, wrapping it carefully and placing it with all my favorite memories—every one of them of him. I'll unwrap it again when it's safe, when there aren't any witnesses.

When dinner concludes, Luke stands, gathering the plates and proceeding to the sink without a word.

"I think I'll go rest on the couch a bit," Donna says, "since it looks like you have this."

I watch her go, my stomach dropping. I wanted to believe she wasn't actually as sick as she said—perhaps exaggerating the situation to make sure I didn't no-show, which I might have —but the Donna I knew was tireless, always rushing off with a casserole for someone in need, or a bag of clothes to donate to Goodwill. This Donna needs to rest after a meal and walks slowly as she goes. She really is going to die.

Reluctantly, I follow Luke into the kitchen. He's standing at the sink, scrubbing a pan. Only Luke could make doing the dishes sexy. Only Luke could take an action as mundane as scrubbing a pan and make you realize how much more graceful you could be doing it than you ever realized.

"How much do you know about her cancer?" I ask, grabbing a dish towel and taking the pan to dry it.

He frowns. Being civil to me requires an effort he finds nearly impossible. "Not all that much. I looked it up online—

she's probably got a year at most and that's with chemo, which she's refusing."

No. *No*. There's got to be a way to throw money at this, to extend her life until a better treatment is available. "I'm sure they're doing studies. I'll have someone check into it. Stanford might—"

He grips the counter. "That's not what she wants. She doesn't want what we can buy for her. She doesn't want you to fucking fix this. She just wants you here."

"Sometimes people don't want what's good for them," I snap.

He turns to stare at me, his eyes narrowing. "You really think you need to tell *me* that?" Luke understands all too well about wanting what's not good for him.

I guess we both do.

We complete the rest of the dishes in silence before joining Donna in the family room. I take the seat on one side of her and Luke takes the other, sitting the way he does—his knees spread wide, arm resting along the back of the couch. He looks athletic, somehow, even at rest.

We watch one of those investigation shows where the lead character is always staring off meaningfully into the distance and saying something like, *"Looks like this case just got a lot more complicated."*

Donna whispers to us, telling us about each character as if they're real, as if they're friends. Seven years ago, she had an entirely different future planned out. One that involved growing old beside her husband, watching her son marry me, giving her lots of grandkids to run around at her feet. Now she sits here alone every night, and she's going to die.

She pats my knee at ten, and then Luke's. "I'm off to bed, and I'm sure you two have better things to do than sit here with an old woman."

She turns to head up the stairs, and I feel a fluttering panic in my chest at the idea of being down here alone with Luke. I jump to my feet, leaving him to stay behind and lock up.

In the safety of my darkened room, I listen for him as I sink into the mattress, slowly breathing in and out, memorizing the sounds he makes as he gets ready for bed: water running, the toilet flushing, the slap of his bare feet on the new hardwood floor.

His tread stops just outside my door, and my breath holds as if I'm praying for something. He walks away and I exhale.

I don't know if I'm deeply relieved or deeply disappointed because, somehow, it feels like both.

6

THEN

JUNE 2013

I haven't asked Donna for a single thing during the eighteen months I've spent under her roof, but one afternoon before the boys get home, when we've got a dinner guest coming and she's still only making enough food for four of us, not six, I can't stay silent.

"Luke's hungry," I tell her, my gaze focused hard on the potatoes I'm peeling as if what I'm saying doesn't matter.

"What's that?" she asks, distractedly, peering into a cookbook.

"Luke's hungry. He's a lot bigger than everyone else. He needs more food."

She glances up, blinking rapidly, slow to understand my meaning. "I'm sure he'd say something."

I don't know if I want to laugh or cry. *Of course he's not going to fucking say anything, Donna. He's your guest. What's he going to say?*

I straighten, setting the paring knife down to face her. "No. He wouldn't."

She studies me for a moment while I silently will her to see the situation as it is, not how she wishes it was.

She bites her lip. "I don't know how the pastor will feel about that. I'll need more money for the food budget."

I suspected as much. The church rents this house for them, but they don't have a lot beyond that. I see Donna sitting at the table every morning clipping coupons, fretting when a recipe calls for a half-teaspoon of some expensive ingredient. I should have been helping out all along, I guess.

"I'll start chipping in," I tell her. I'm saving so I can get my own place after graduation, but Luke's only here for the summer and I've got another year to go. It won't kill me.

She shakes her head. "Juliet, no. You work so hard. I don't want to do that to you."

I know she doesn't, but she's between a rock and a hard place. The pastor doesn't actually want me *or* Luke here. He's bearing us, nothing more, which is why he has me on my feet whenever he's coming home but begs me to relax anytime he's not around. If she mentions the issue to him, it could make things worse for all of us.

"Donna, it's fine. It's the only way."

She wants to argue. I know she does. Her mouth opens, then closes. "That's very kind of you," she says quietly.

Our guest, Mrs. Poffsteader's nephew, arrives a short time later with his shirt buttoned to the top and his thin brown hair neatly combed. Grady's in his last year of Bible school and will be able to work as a pastor once he's completed a one-year mentorship. He looks like a kid pretending to be an adult, and I can't imagine who the hell would spend an hour on Sunday listening to the thoughts of a twenty-two-year-old.

Especially *this* twenty-two-year-old.

The pastor shares some interminable story about indulgence, based on hearing a father tell his daughter she can't have ice cream, and Grady's eyes shine like he's sitting at the Dalai Lama's feet.

"What an amazing revelation," Grady says when he

concludes. "Your thoughts fascinate me. I can't wait to hear you preach."

When the pastor foists him off on us, suggesting we take Grady with us to the bonfire, I wonder if Grady's sucking up is too obvious, even for him.

"We'd love to have you along," Danny says politely, and my stomach sinks. It's bad enough spending a night being looked down on by Luke. I'm not spending the night being looked down on by *Grady* as well, especially not a night when the pastor and Donna will be gone and I could get the whole house to myself.

"I've got to stay home," I tell them. "I've got some summer reading to do."

I sound convincingly apologetic, but when I glance up, Luke's gaze is on mine with a hint of a smirk behind it. Somehow, he knows it's a lie. How? How does he know these things when my boyfriend of two years doesn't have a clue?

I clean up dinner alone and then go to the backyard with my brother's ancient guitar, the one thing my stepbrothers never managed to take from me.

I've got this new chord progression I can't get out of my head. I don't know where it would fit into a song, but I play it again and again, humming along. When I get too frustrated, I revert to "Homecoming", the one song I feel is truly completed.

Danny—the only person I've ever played it for—was unimpressed. *Why don't you try writing a happy song?* he'd asked. He praises me over the smallest of things: the way I fold shirts, and brownies I made from a mix. Hearing him say this song I wrote, created, and performed was *"sad"*, felt like his gentle way of telling me I should find a more realistic dream.

That was last winter, and I've barely played it since. But tonight, I'm listening to it, and I just think he was wrong. Yeah, it's a sad fucking song. But life can be sad too. There's just as much room for sad songs as happy ones in the world, isn't there?

I play it from start to finish without a hitch, pleasure that borders on euphoria rushing through my veins. It's not like I'm Taylor Swift or something, but it's just a good freaking song… the longing in the lyrics, the guitar, and even my voice. None of them are perfect on their own, but they come together in a way that just hits this sweet spot inside me, that makes me marvel a little at myself. *I did this. Me.*

The final notes die off at last, and it feels like all my joy—all my *everything*—goes with it.

Maybe this is why Luke doesn't trust me. Maybe when he peers into my soul, all he sees is empty space.

IF I THOUGHT I'd escaped Grady with my little lie about summer reading, I could not have been more wrong. Soon, he's dating Libby and with us nearly every night, though I can't imagine why he'd want to be when he doesn't drink or surf. He seems to resent everyone but Danny—but it's me he hates, and the feeling is mutual.

"Grady was suggesting we hang out someplace else tonight," Danny tells Luke over dinner. "He's tired of the beach."

Luke raises a brow, his thoughts clear: *then Grady doesn't need to come.*

For once, Luke and I agree on something.

Last night, Grady ridiculed me for using the word *misogynistic*. "*What big words you're using. Remind me what grade you're in again, Juliet?*" He smirked as he said it, with this gross little gleam of triumph in his eyes, so I countered by asking if Bible school even *has* grades, since it's not really college.

And Danny said, "*be nice.*" He didn't say a word to Grady but

I got scolded. So, on a night when the pastor and Donna will be out of the house, I'll be damned if I'm giving up a night to myself for any of them.

"I'm going to stay in and do some more of my work for school," I lie. He won't understand why I need time alone and he also doesn't understand why I've got a problem with Grady.

Luke's head jerks toward mine—he says nothing but I can almost feel it coming...the day when he will. The day when he starts saying, *"Use your head, Dan. Does what she's saying even make sense?"*

I wait until they're long gone before I go to the backyard with my guitar. I've been working out the new song in my head for the past two weeks and I think I might have it.

I try two variations and they're okay, but they're not quite right. Eventually, I give up and just play "Homecoming" again. It sounds, on the surface, like it's about a school dance gone wrong, but really it's about walking into your home and knowing you're no safer there than you are anywhere else. I wrote it about my mom's house, but I sometimes wonder if applies here too. Nearly two years into this arrangement, I still feel like I'm walking on eggshells, like I'm one mistake away from being out in the cold.

The last notes float away, and I'm about to start something else when I hear movement near the back door and freeze.

"That's good." Luke steps into the light, staring like he's seeing me for the first time. "That was really fucking good."

My heart rate spikes, anxiety pinging in my chest. "Why are you home?"

"Why are you lying to Danny about schoolwork?" His voice is soft enough to take the edge from his words. "You shouldn't have to hide this. You should perform."

"I sing at church." There's a hint of resignation in my voice. As if I'm still trying to convince myself it's enough.

His cheek sucks in as his jaw shifts. I picture tracing the

hollow with my index finger. "No, I mean alone, on stage some-where, and not just so the pastor can have everyone pat him on the back. I've never heard that song before. Who's it by?"

"I...uh, it's mine," I say, looking away. "I wrote it."

When I dare to glance up at him, his mouth is open. "Bullshit."

"Are you calling me a liar?" I snap.

His eyes lock with mine. "Are you claiming you *aren't* one?"

I say nothing. I lied about what I was doing tonight. I lie about being happy with the situation I'm in, and I've lied about way more than that. Whatever he doesn't know about me yet, whatever he suspects...it's probably right.

"That song is good," he says, reaching for the door. "But it's a little fucked up that you lied just to get a chance to play it. Don't you ever get tired of being treated like an indentured servant?"

I stiffen. "I'm not. Being part of the family means pitching in."

His eyes are flat. "Oh, yeah? How many times has *Danny* been asked to unload the dryer or help with dinner?"

I rise. "What exactly is your problem?"

He looks at me for a long moment, his eyes nearly black in the dim light. "You aren't cut out for this, Juliet."

I swallow hard and march toward the door. "I have no idea what you're talking about."

He steps backward to let me pass. "I think you do. And the longer this goes on, the more you're going to fuck him up when he loses you."

I round on him as my jaw drops. "He's never going to lose me."

His eyes fall, for a moment, to my mouth. "He's already lost you, believe me."

I stumble away. It's a ridiculous thing to say. And yet... there's some tiny voice in the back of my head wondering if he's right. Maybe I'm fake, maybe I'm here for the wrong reasons. Maybe I'm not pulling myself up to Danny's level, but instead dragging him down to mine.

Maybe this isn't something I can stick with for the long haul.

7

NOW

"I had the worst dream," I tell Luke.

He rolls toward me in the early morning light, smiling and sleepy, running a hand over the jaw he should've shaved yesterday. "Let's hear it."

I squeeze my eyes shut, trying to recall the details. My bad dreams never seem as terrifying in the light of day. "It was this whole thing," I tell him. "I don't even remember. I never left Rhodes, and I was going to marry Danny. It was like everything that could go wrong *did* go wrong."

Luke runs a hand over my head. "I've gotta tell you, I don't love waking up to discover you were dreaming about an ex."

But he smiles like a man who is not at all concerned, and why would he be? The sun rises and sets with him for me.

I press my lips to his neck and breathe him in. Even after a night of sleep, Luke always smells like he's fresh from the shower. "It's just weird how real it all seemed."

His hand slides over my hip and his breath quickens, his chest rising and falling as it presses to mine. His smile grows sly. "Did it seem as real as *this*?" It's the kind of question that leads to sex, that has no purpose *but* to lead to sex, but something inside me says, *"Make sure. Make sure it's real."*

I sit up and glance around me. The room is familiar, and yet it's not, so I walk toward the balcony and throw open the curtains.

That's when I see the cliff. Guys are jumping off it, trying to reach a wave far in the distance.

I snatch the curtains closed in a sudden panic. If Luke sees them jumping, he'll want to try it, too, and he'll never come back to me.

I turn, ready to beg him not to go out there, and realize where we are. This is the rundown house I visited during Pipeline Masters, where I watched him from the dunes, and then snuck away like a thief so he wouldn't know I was there.

We weren't together then. We aren't together now.

I wake with a start, in the dark, staring at the bare walls of an unfamiliar room.

The truth trickles in and drowns me—the nightmare came true, and the things I wanted most did not.

I fall face down on my pillow and weep, wishing I could find a way back to him, to the version of Luke who doesn't hate me. Who doesn't believe all the terrible things other people said about me wound up being right.

THERE ARE no blinds on my windows yet. I'd forgotten how fucking bright the sun could get this early.

I drag myself out of bed, rubbing the sleep from my eyes and bracing myself for another day of Luke's well-deserved hatred and Donna's undeserved adoration.

She's just starting breakfast when I enter the kitchen. "Good morning, beautiful girl," she says, pressing a kiss to my head. She should have had a whole village of children. I guess that's what she's creating with Danny's House...only she won't be alive to experience it for long.

I work on the eggs while she oversees the bacon, and Luke wanders in just as we finish, sleepy eyed and full lipped, running a hand through his messy hair. I see of sliver of abs as his shirt rises and think of that dream I had. His hand, possessive on my hip, his eyes so peaceful, so happy. Could it have been like that with us? I'll never know, and it's the not knowing that tortures me. For a half second my gaze lands on the cords of his neck, and I picture running my nose along the skin there, tasting it again. My stomach flips so hard I find myself pressing a hand to it, willing it to stop.

I don't eat breakfast, but I load my plate anyway and sit with them because this is what Donna wants: to pretend that the years haven't passed. To sit around a big breakfast as if Luke and Danny will be heading out to surf the moment we're done.

"Did I mention they finally tore down the diner?" Donna asks. "Put in some fancy place."

An ache hits before I can stop it, as if some phantom has slid inside my chest to grab my heart and give it a hard squeeze. My eyes meet Luke's, and just for a moment, before he looks away, I see a phantom in him too.

He turns to Donna. "You said you had a list of things for us to do?"

"The shrubs for the backyard were delivered yesterday," she says. "I think we need to get those planted first, and then I'll have the two of you finish the drywall in some of the back rooms."

Luke's raised brow implies I'm more likely to bring down the foundation of the house than I am to put up its walls, which is entirely accurate. And with the amount of money we provided, none of this is necessary. For two million, drywall should've been included.

"Donna," I begin, "that sounds like something for professionals. If you guys need more money I can—"

She puts down her spoon and meets my eye. "No. I don't need money. I need you to be involved. I need you to feel like this place is as much yours as it is mine or the children's."

I suppress a sigh. "I'm happy to be here, and I want to be able to spend time with you, but...why risk me putting a hammer through the drywall and ruining someone's room?"

"You need to get your hands dirty, Juliet. The way you live now isn't healthy for anyone. It separates you from your actual life. When was last time you did your own laundry? Or dishes?"

I press the bridge of my nose between my thumb and forefinger. It's just like Donna to believe that a little bit of good, honest work will turn me back into the eager teenager who first arrived in her home. And even if she's right, why does *Luke* need to be here? He's making money, sure, but no matter how much he makes, I guarantee he's living in some tiny place with no help whatsoever—his hands are plenty dirty.

Her gaze follows mine. "Yes, I know he does his own laundry. You've both made so much of yourselves over the past seven years, but I can't help but feel your lives have gotten off track somehow and I want to fix it before I'm gone."

There's so much pain and rage in Luke's gaze that I have to look away. *"She can't fix this,"* his face says, *"and she shouldn't have to."* Because I did this to him and I did this to myself. Every problem either of us has...it all started with me.

His jaw shifts before he glances at her, stoic as ever. "So, where do you want these shrubs?"

"I think along the back fence. Evenly spaced. And I'm making a list of things we need to buy for the addition, so if anything comes to mind, let me know. You guys can go pick it up later."

"Blinds," I say. "But maybe one of us could dig in the backyard while the other one shops? Just to save time?"

By which I mean *Luke* will dig and *I* will shop, of course.

"No," she says. "You need to do it together."

"Donna—" he starts.

She sets her fork down, staring at her lap. "There's a reason they disqualified you in Australia, and if you don't figure out what's eating you, I'm worried you won't survive the next competition."

My chest constricts. I've tried very, very hard not to think about what he does for a living. I've told myself that he is too big, too smart, too fierce to get hurt. But big and smart and fierce...none of these are a match for the ocean. And he was reckless in Australia—he took risks he shouldn't have and got in a fight in the line-up. It could have all ended very badly.

The idea of him dying causes a pain so sharp that I'd reach into my chest and rip it out if I could.

She looks at me. "And you let a man you're dating shove you out of an elevator so hard you hit the floor, and then you let him drag you out by your hair. Something has gone wrong, and whatever it is the two of you need, please find it here and figure it out together so I can go on to the next life certain you're okay."

My eyes close. I really wish she hadn't seen that video, and what she's hoping for...it's a lost cause. If I'm dating an asshole, a morning spent planting shrubs isn't going to fix me, and I can't imagine why she thinks it would. But if I've got to spend three weeks pretending to be a changed person, so be it.

I head out back once breakfast is cleaned up. Luke's already digging, the shirt clinging to his broad back and shoulders, his muscles delineated with each strike into the soil. He looks like he was made to do this, but that's the thing about Luke: he looks like he was made to do every damn thing he attempts.

He glances at me from head to toe before shaking his head.

"You can plant the bulbs." He nods at the boxes on the corner of the new flagstone patio.

It's a generous offer. I don't know why I'm so hell-bent on refusing it. I've never planted a tree in my life, and I assume none of the skills I've acquired over the past couple of years will be helpful. I'm good at singing, diverting reporters when they ask about what appears to be an abusive relationship, and flirting with other guys to regain Cash's wavering attention. These are skills with limited application.

"You realize I work out almost every day," I say. "I'm just as capable of digging as you."

He hands me the shovel. "Go ahead then. Show me how fit you are."

Well played, Juliet. Now you're doing the digging, and no matter how hard it is, you can't admit you're not up to the job.

For the next thirty minutes I slam the shovel into the ground, making only a fraction of the progress he did. My arms are shaking and my hands are blistered, and when his shadow finally looms over me, he takes the shovel without a word. It was like him to be a dick about it when I suggested I could shovel, but this is like him too: letting me off the hook when I probably don't deserve it. Taking pity on me when he could simply sit back and relish yet another of my failures.

"I had it," I mutter. We both know I didn't.

"Those foster kids would have grandchildren by the time you were done."

Stop being kind, Luke. Stop protecting me.

It's never gotten either of us anywhere.

8

THEN

JULY 2013

Before I met Danny, I dreamed of a different kind of life for myself. I hoped that maybe I could end up doing something I really love, that maybe I could *fly* rather than just *land*. That Luke liked my song has me hoping for it again. And wondering why I stopped thinking it was possible in the first place.

I'm not sure why I ignore all the negative shit he implied about me and Danny but listen to this. I just do. I hum that unfinished song under my breath when I work at the diner and when I help Donna with dinner. It's a puzzle I'm missing a piece to, but Luke's words have made it feel like finding that piece matters.

I hum it all day, every day—searching, searching. Wishing I could just get some time to myself to try to fix it, knowing it won't happen. Danny's got two friends from school visiting this week, and it's only made our days fuller. Every spare moment I'm not helping Donna, I'm being rushed off to some party I don't want to go to because one of them is meeting a girl.

They reach the house Saturday afternoon after a full day of surfing just as I'm biking in from a double shift at the diner.

They're upstairs while Donna and I get dinner on the table, and they're upstairs again while Donna and I clean up. It's a full half hour of scrubbing pans, loading the dishwasher, and sweeping the floor, while upstairs, the four boys laugh like naughty kids cutting class.

I silently fume, sick of...everything. Of fighting for a minute alone, of this weird tension between me and Luke.

I get upstairs just as Danny is exiting the bathroom, freshly showered. "Hurry, okay?" he pleads. "There's a party at the beach and Nev is freaking out about getting there."

I take a breath as I nod, inhaling my frustration. I wasn't even able to get a shower last night, with them hogging the hall bath, but now I have to rush. *I wouldn't have to hurry if you'd just help me. If I go away to school for nine months, will I, too, get the luxury of sitting on my ass all night and surfing all day?*

I'll never say it aloud. Danny wants to please his parents, and me, and his friends. It's not his fault that he's consistently failing at one of those things.

"I should probably finish my book for school," I tell him.

"Babe, come on," he says, crestfallen, and Luke's right over his shoulder, looking at me like I'm a fucking liar. "I haven't seen you all day."

My teeth grind as I agree to go. I love Danny, but I also *owe* Danny. It's sometimes hard for me to tell which fact is motivating me to give in to him when I do.

I rush into my bedroom, grab a towel and a change of clothes, and walk out to discover someone else has beaten me into the bathroom and the shower is running once more.

I slam my palm to the door. "Are you *kidding* me?"

The door opens suddenly, and Luke stands there with a towel hanging low on his waist while the water continues to run.

He smirks. "Is there a problem?"

It's the smirk that sets me off. If Danny had heard what I

just said, he'd have been concerned. He'd have said, *"What's the matter? How can I fix this?"* But Luke thinks he's won something by making me lose my shit and...fuck it. I don't need to impress him. I don't care what he thinks anymore.

"You're using up all the hot water," I hiss. "And now it's running and you're not even in there! You guys have had the whole day to yourselves. Is it so much to ask that I just get five goddamn minutes to shower after an entire day at work?"

He runs a hand through his hair. "No. It isn't. But you're incapable of standing up for yourself, so I wouldn't bank on you ever getting it."

The truth of this hits me. How is anything about my life going to change given the way I am now? I feel a sob in my throat, but rage follows right on its heels and something in me just *snaps*. Why does Luke have to make everything so much fucking worse?

I act before I've even thought it through, shoving him with all my might. He barely budges, of course. It's like hitting a wall. But his hands wrap around my wrists to stop me, pinning them to his chest...and the towel he was holding falls. My gaze drops reflexively and I stare for a moment in shock. He's *hard*. And if I didn't understand why those girls fight over him at night before, I definitely do now.

"Is that what you wanted, Juliet?" He makes no move to pick up the towel. "Go ahead, if you want to look so bad."

I shrug off his grip, horrified, and recognize for the first time what he seems to have already known: I want something I'm not supposed to want.

I stumble backward, blinking away tears. "Fuck you, Luke."

I expect him to gloat. But instead, his shoulders sag and there's something bleak and pained in his eyes. As if he isn't enjoying this at all. As if, perhaps, he's hated this summer as much as I have.

I want to rage at him for what just happened, for what's *been* happening, but there's this ache in my chest for both of us that I can't begin to understand. I turn and walk straight to my room, slamming the door behind me.

Absolutely nothing makes sense anymore.

After finally getting my—cold—shower, I ride with Danny to the beach, never mentioning what happened with Luke.

Danny's friends are already there, gathered around one of several small fires. I do my best to ignore Luke, his gaze on me darker than ever. It feels like the end of everything, and it's all his fault, so I don't know why I'm still thinking about the feel of his bare chest beneath my hands and everything I saw when the towel fell.

Danny's roommates produce a case of cheap beer. The more they drink, the more they seem to focus on...me and Danny. "Daniel Allen," says Nev. "You're a good man. You know why? Because if I had little Juliet living in my home, I guarantee I wouldn't let any of you assholes come visit."

Danny laughs. Luke does not. The girl he's with, Rain, is tiny and cute, and the more he ignores her, the more she tries to get his attention. So does her friend Summer, sitting beside them.

I wonder which of the two he'll wander off with tonight. For a moment, I let myself picture being the one he chooses. Is he gentle? Is he rough? A little of both?

I think he'd be a little of both.

"I don't know how you guys ever make it out of bed," Nev continues.

Danny laughs again, but it's cut off by the sound of Luke's voice, low, with an edge to it. "Watch it, Nev," he warns, though I'm not sure what he's objecting to.

The part I personally object to is Danny. The way he's laughing and going along with it, not correcting them. If waiting for marriage matters so much to him, *fine*, but he should be willing to say it aloud. I refuse to pretend we're sleeping together just so his friends will think he's cool.

Caleb pulls out a guitar and starts to play a really crappy version of "Sweet Home Alabama".

"Let Juliet play," Luke says when it ends, his voice ringing with authority. I gawk at him, and his gaze meets mine, unrepentant, issuing a challenge. "I heard her the other night. She's good."

I can't believe he's ratting me out like this, not just in front of Danny but in front of *everyone*.

Caleb holds the guitar out and I take it unwillingly, my stomach in knots, but there's something reassuring about the feel of it, too, as I settle the guitar in my lap. As if it's shielding me, though it's really doing the opposite.

"Play the song I heard," Luke says. "The one about coming home."

I glare at him. "That's not ready."

"It was absolutely fucking ready," says Luke. "But if you don't want to play it, just play something else."

I glance from him to Danny, who gives me a tepid smile and a small nod. I get the feeling he'd rather I *didn't* play, and it's this, more than anything else, that has me settling in and attempting a few chords to get a sense for how the guitar has been tuned. Luke shouldn't have called me out, but I also shouldn't feel bad about *wanting* to do this either.

I start with an acoustic version of "Umbrella". I have every intention of stopping when the song concludes, but I just can't. I know, now, what it is I see on Luke's face when he surfs. It's not happiness. I'm better than happy. I'm fucking *full*.

This is my wave. This is me figuring out where to put my voice next to a chord, finding one sweet spot and then the next. The song ends but I don't want to stop. I've slid down the face of the wave and now I want to enter the barrel. I want to drag my hand along the wall to slow myself and make this last. The transition is uneven, bumpy, and I have a moment of wondering if I should ditch out, but I keep going. I morph into "Wild Horses" by the Stones. It was always a wistful song, but it sounds even more so tonight. I channel every ounce of the longing inside me and even *I'm* surprised by it—by how much I want from the world, how much I mourn that I won't be getting it.

The song ends and for a moment I can't even hear anyone breathing. I wait with my stomach in knots, unsure if I've succeeded or if I've shown myself and ruined everything.

"Holy shit," whispers Caleb. "You play like *that* and you *sing* like that and you sat there listening to me fuck around on the guitar without saying a word?"

"That was amazing," says Rain. She's so genuine I find her slightly less easy to hate.

"Dude, you should be in Hollywood," says Beck. It's three more words than I've ever heard him say.

Luke just leans back, arms folded across his chest, eyes on me as if he can't bring himself to look away. And I look back at him, for just a moment too long.

Maybe, just maybe, he was trying to help me.

My heart starts drumming in my chest, my lungs expanding...and I force myself to look away.

Whatever door I just opened needs to be shut again, and locked up tight. *Luke was not trying to help me. He wasn't.*

And I wouldn't be thinking or feeling any of the insane things I am if Danny and I were just...more. If he wasn't treating me like a little kid, if we had a relationship *half* as adult as the ones Luke has with girls he barely knows.

I wait until Danny and I are alone by the fire, after every single one of his friends has wandered off to hook up with someone or chase after a girl at another one of the bonfires.

I reach for his hand. "Danny," I whisper, staring at the sand at our feet, "I don't actually want to wait for marriage."

He looks around us as if even the discussion of this topic is forbidden, though we're the only ones here. "I thought you agreed with me," he says. "I thought you wanted it to be special."

"It can probably be special whether we're married or not." In the distance a girl laughs, and I wonder if it's the girl Luke is with right now. If his hand is sliding from her back to her ass. If she's letting her body curve against his to remind him she's female and willing, just in case he forgot.

"I think you're spending too much time around Luke," he concludes.

And even though he's got it all wrong...he's also right. I'm definitely spending too much time around Luke.

9

NOW

That afternoon, we have our first meeting with the board of Danny's House.

Donna arranged it at the last minute so we could meet everyone, but of all the things she wants me to be a part of —the interviews, the opening ceremony, the fundraising gala— it's this stupid meeting I dread most. Even after all these years, I can't shake those early experiences of the mean old ladies in the diner, sitting there talking about how Danny could do better and it would all come to no good.

The shittiest part is that they were a hundred percent right.

I move toward the room but come to an awkward halt when I see Libby at the table. I'm not sure what kind of reception I'll get.

She sees me and rises with a shy, tentative smile. She's as cute as she ever was...and extremely pregnant. "Juliet," she says, throwing her arms around me. "It's so good to see you."

I swallow. It's good to see her but sickening at the same time. She's one more person I treated terribly. "I'm so sorry I fell out of touch."

By which I mean, *I'm sorry I missed your wedding, I'm sorry I*

never returned your calls or emails or texts. I'm sorry I left town
without a word and acted like you didn't matter.

She waves her hand. "Your life is so crazy! I can't imagine how you do it all. I've been watching, though. I'm so proud of you."

It's typical of Libby to be kind like this. I wouldn't be, in her shoes.

I glance down at her stomach. "Looks like your life's about to get crazy too."

She smiles, thrilled and embarrassed at once. "It took a while," she says. "But we're nearly there."

She and Grady have been married for over six years, and I suspect, based on things Donna has said, that Libby was hoping for a child most of that time. I can just imagine what it must have been like for her, with Mrs. Poffsteader patting her on the shoulder every fucking Sunday, consoling her and acting like she was at fault, simultaneously. I wonder where those old crones go to breakfast now that the diner is gone, where they can clutch their Bibles while they shit-talk everyone and fail to tip.

The room quiets, which means it's time to take our seats. Libby grasps my hand. "Can we get lunch one day before you go? I know you're busy, but if you can fit me in, I'd love to catch up."

"That would be great," I tell her. And I mean it. I would love to have lunch with Libby, but I'm absolutely not going to do it. I'll make an excuse of some kind or throw myself in front of a bus if necessary. Almost any interaction I have in this town could turn out to be a mistake, but spending time with Libby? It's almost guaranteed to be.

A small, tidy woman steps to the front of the room, offering all of us a forced smile. "As most of you know," she begins, "I'm Hilary Peters, the new executive director." There's something smug about her, and now that I've given up on trying to be an Allen, I'm not going to restrain the urge to judge her for it.

"Let me start by welcoming everyone. Especially our celebrity guests, Luke Taylor and Juliet Cantrell." Is it my imagination or is there a hint of sarcasm in her voice when she says the word *celebrity*? I sneak a peek at Luke to see if he's bothered by her, but his face is blank. He's always been far better than I am at hiding what he feels. Hilary has everyone go around the room to introduce themselves, and then starts handing something out. "We've got a lot going on in the coming month, which is the reason I called this meeting."

You didn't call this meeting. Donna called this meeting. I was there when she fucking emailed you.

I look at the agenda she's passed around. It's mostly a list of interviews, the bulk of them set up by my publicist, with the groundbreaking ceremony and the gala at the end.

"Now, for the interviews, Luke and Juliet, I thought it would be nice if both of you could really lean in to the whole identity as foster children. You know, talk about where you were before the Allens took you in and where you would have ended up without them."

This time, when I glance at Luke, he's already looking at me. I've carefully culled most of the truth from my past and so has he. We don't need it coming up here.

I push the paper away from me. "I was more than happy to secure these interviews for Danny's House, but the fact that I was a foster kid here—and Luke wasn't one, by the way—was never mentioned as part of the strategy."

Her smile turns patronizing. "There's a world of difference between having a celebrity get an interview for something and having a celebrity personalize the experience so that readers understand how meaningful it is. Surely you understand the difference?"

Oh, you fucking bitch.

"I understand the difference. However, discussing that is a personal decision, one I'll make in my own good time."

"Listen, Juliet," she says with a tight smile. "I understand that it might be uncomfortable for you, but it would mean a lot to the—"

"She said *no*," Luke growls.

Hilary blinks rapidly. Apparently, Luke's *"No"* carries weight mine did not. I guess I shouldn't be surprised by that. When has anyone ever respected what I thought about anything?

"Juliet has already done enough for this place. She doesn't need to do more. And as she mentioned, I wasn't a foster child. I just stayed here over the summer during college."

"Well, you did have a difficult adolescence, didn't you?" she asks. "You could lean in to that, perhaps, and—"

"How about I decide what I want to say and Juliet decides what she wants to say?" he asks. "We're the only reason you're getting this publicity in the first place."

She frowns, glancing at the board members closest to her with a look that says, *"I told you they'd be a problem."*

"Okay, let's table that for now. Libby, can you tell us a little bit about how the plans for the gala are coming along?"

Libby smiles. She has the same sort of inner sweetness Donna has, the sort that just seems to ooze from her whether she intends it to or not. If she'd asked me, I might have gone along with the interview suggestion. If she asked me, I'd probably agree to almost anything, which is why I'm best off staying away from her.

She details the plans for the gala, which I mostly tune out. There will be a lot of people I'd rather not see there—and one person in particular resenting the attention I'm getting, perhaps hoping to undermine me. The whole thing is risky, and I can't let myself forget it.

Hilary cuts Libby off halfway through to start talking about the opening ceremony.

"We'll have Donna begin," Hilary says, "and then the pastor will say a prayer, I'll speak, and then I thought it would be nice if Juliet could sing 'Amazing Grace', since it was Danny's favorite hymn."

I stare at her. There is absolutely no way I will be able to get through that song *there*. I'm stunned she thinks I could.

"No one mentioned that I was expected to perform."

The whole room's gaze is on me, shouting, *"Stop being a troublemaker, Juliet."*

"I assumed you wouldn't mind," Hilary says, her smile sharp. I remember women like her among the dozens of social workers I dealt with as a kid. She's the sort who didn't get into this field because she cares—she got into it because she enjoys feeling superior.

"Given the situation, given how emotional the ceremony might be, I'm not sure I could get through that."

"You're a professional, aren't you?" she asks. "I'm sure you can figure it out."

"She said *no*," Luke says for the second time. "And I would suggest you stop trying to walk over her, or you'll discover how much *less* we can cooperate than we already are."

I stare at him in shock. It's not the first time Luke has defended me.

But I hope I'm the only one who notices he's still doing it.

10

THEN

JULY 2013

It's later than normal, just after dusk, as I bike home along the coastal road after work. Stacy had childcare issues and I couldn't leave until she got in, but none of that matters right now—the air is balmy, the sky is striped in hues of peach and purple, and I've got a few minutes to myself.

I hum "Homecoming" as I pedal. Is it any good? Danny would have come up with a better adjective than *"sad"* if that was the case, but Luke finally pushed me into playing it for everyone the other night, and they *applauded* when it was done. *"And here I thought Luke was going to be the most famous of us all,"* Caleb said afterward.

I feel something inside me being freed a little more each day. I'm wondering, once again, if I can make a living with my voice. Right now, all I'm destined to become is Danny's wife. I'm not sure it's enough.

My brain spins with the possibilities: could I afford to live in LA? How would I support myself? How do you even go about getting discovered?

I'm so lost in my own thoughts that I don't hear the catcalls until the car is nearly beside me.

Before I've even looked over to understand what's happening, an arm is reaching out of a window to grab my shirt, which is wrenched so hard that the buttons pop open and the bike is pulled off balance, wobbling uncontrollably. My heart slams against my ribs, and I jerk away in desperation. He loses his grip on me, and I go flying onto the shoulder of the road. A shocking, bruising pain shoots along my side from the impact, and gravel cuts into my skin, head to toe, the bike pedal slicing into my calf.

I'm stunned for a second, but when I see the car's brake lights ahead, adrenaline shunts everything—pain, shock, outrage—to the back of my mind. Because those brake lights mean they aren't driving off.

They're coming back for me.

I didn't want to deal with these guys on a bike, so I sure as hell don't want to deal with them while *prone*. I scramble to my feet. Every inch of skin screams in pain but I ignore it, stumbling desperately toward the dense trees across the road. I slide from view just as they back over my bike and stop the car.

I don't know if I should run or stay motionless, but my ankle is swelling and I'm not sure how fast I'll be able to move anyway. I reach for my phone, hands shaking as two guys get out of the car, scanning the woods for a moment with grins on their faces as if the whole thing is *funny*. I crouch lower, making myself as small as possible, too scared to even call the police—they won't get here in time to help me, and the sound of the keypad might give my location away.

Another car approaches. The guys glance at each other, and I hold my breath, my heart hammering, until they get back in the car. It's only when they drive off that the adrenaline leaves me and I collapse to the ground, suddenly shaking with cold though it's a warm day. My impulse is to curl into a ball and stay until it all feels better, but I've been injured often enough in the past to know that the longer I wait to move, the harder it will become.

I force myself to stand on shaky legs. My bike is fucked, and I'd probably be too scared to get it anyway, so I start to walk, hugging the woods just in case they come back.

I suspect my ankle is sprained, but I just keep moving forward, holding my shirt together, because I know how this goes. If you stop to notice the pain, it'll drag you under. And when the tears finally begin to slip down my face, it still isn't because of the pain. It's simply that no matter how old I get, no matter how safe I think I am, I doubt there will ever come a day when I'm not hit from behind by something, when I'm not limping off toward safety, wondering if I'm somehow at fault.

By the time I get home, the boys are back from surfing. It would be easier if they weren't. Danny believes anything, but Luke won't be so easy to convince.

I limp up the front steps. *Get your shit together, Juliet. You can't go in there and make a big deal of this.*

"Juliet?" calls Donna as I open the front door. "That you?"

I take a deep breath. "Hi!" I call. "I'll be there in a second! I just need to change."

My voice wavers with something that isn't normally there, something bright and false.

"Hurry for me, hon," Donna calls back. "I'm in the middle of making this pie and the chicken needs to turn."

You're late is what she means, and I take in a shuddering breath.

Is this worth it? Is *anything* worth it? Today at the diner a woman told her son that if he didn't study harder, he'd wind up waiting tables just like me. Charlie called me a moron. Two gross old men asked me how much extra for a little sugar after their meal, and when I told them sugar was right there on the table they said, *"That's not the kind of sugar we're talking about."*

What's on the other side of all this? What about any of this makes it worthwhile? Nothing. But how the hell would I ever make it in LA when I can't even exist safely *here*?

The sob I was holding in swells, choking me as I reply.

"Okay," I call before swallowing, my voice too high and thin. "Just one sec."

I have only taken one limping step toward the stairs before Luke marches out of the kitchen, staring at me with rapidly darkening eyes. I grip my shirt tighter, and his gaze follows the motion.

"What the fuck happened?"

"Nothing," I whisper, wiping my face on my shoulder. *Pull it together. Pull it together.* "I fell."

He is frozen in place. "Don't fucking lie to me. What happened?"

Donna peeks into the hallway, her eyes going wide as she wipes her hands on a dishtowel. "My goodness, hon, you've got gravel stuck to—" Her eyes fall to the blouse I'm holding together. "Oh, honey."

Danny crosses the room and places his hands on my arms.

I suck in air at the contact. "My arm," I whisper.

"Sorry! Sorry," he says, releasing me. "What happened?"

I glance from him to Luke. I want to lie about this, but I guess the ripped shirt gives it away, and Luke always seems to know when I'm lying anyhow. "Some guys tried to pull me off my bike on the way home. I'm fine."

"You're not fucking fine," growls Luke. "You're limping, you're scraped from head to toe, and they ripped your goddamned shirt."

Donna winces at the language he's using but doesn't say anything. "Do we need to call the police, sweetie?"

I shake my head quickly. "No. It wasn't a big deal."

"The hell it wasn't," Luke says.

Maybe he's right, but the police aren't going to do anything. They'll probably assume I'm at fault, and who knows...maybe I was. Maybe I should have changed into different clothes before I biked home. Maybe I shouldn't have been singing. Maybe I shouldn't have been biking in the first place.

"I'm fine. I am. I had to leave the bike. I think the frame was bent."

"The boys will go get it," says Donna, placing a hand on my good elbow. "And I'll help you get cleaned up."

Donna leads me toward the stairs and Luke just stands there, watching me go, fighting some impulse I don't understand before he finally stomps away.

Donna has to get tweezers to pluck the gravel and glass from my skin. I bite my lip, bracing my thighs and digging my nails into my palm to distract from the pain.

"That's the worst of it," she says at last and I release a long, relieved exhale. She turns on the shower for me but hesitates when she reaches the door to leave.

"If...it was worse than you implied downstairs, you can tell me," she says. "No one else has to know."

My eyes well. She thinks I was raped, and she's willing not to tell Danny if that's the case. I believe her too. "It really wasn't worse. They barely even stopped the car."

She looks at me for a long moment, uncertain. She probably thinks that if it was as simple as it sounds, I shouldn't be so upset. And maybe she's right. Maybe it's just that I haven't always been this lucky, and the memory has stained me. I can't seem to wash it off.

Danny and Luke are both in the kitchen when I get downstairs. Luke rises and Danny, watching him, follows suit. I thought the scrapes looked better once I was out of the shower, but Luke's face says something else entirely.

"Hey, hon." Danny gingerly reaches out an arm to touch my good side. "Feeling better?"

"Good as new," I tell him.

I look over to where Donna is working, trying to figure out what she needs.

"Don't," Luke growls.

"I can just—"

"Juliet," he says, and his voice is commanding in a way I've never heard it, "*sit*."

"Yes, hon," Donna urges, "of course. Get off your feet."

I limp toward the table and Luke walks around to my side.

"Change places with me," he demands. Because from his seat, on the far side of the table, it would be difficult for me to jump up and down throughout dinner.

I open my mouth to argue, and his eyes darken so dangerously that I do as I'm told.

"What was the car like?" he asks.

I glance up. Even if the Allens believe the world is fair, I know the truth and I suspect Luke does too. People lie. People will save themselves first, always. I could know the make, the model, the license plate. I could ID a mole on the guy's inner right thigh and have his skin under my nails and he'd still say it was an accident or a misunderstanding and everyone would believe him.

"It doesn't matter. Even if I knew who they were, they'd deny everything and say I fell off my bike on my own."

"I know that," he says. "I just want you to tell me what you saw."

"It was a silver car. Small. I have no idea what make. Surf-boards on the roof."

"Did you see any of them?"

I close my eyes. "I only remember the one who grabbed me." Another stain in my memory. His eyes were so...cold. He saw me bleeding, he saw my ruined bike and ripped shirt and he was still laughing. "He had a pierced eyebrow. A tattoo on his knuckles. That's all I remember."

The garage door opens, signaling the pastor's arrival. Donna frowns. "We should stop talking about this."

Luke's head jerks toward her. "Why's that?"

She blinks in surprise at his tone, then swallows. "Because I think Juliet would prefer this story remain...between us."

It takes all of us a long second to understand what she *hasn't* said: that if we tell the pastor, he'll work it into a sermon. He might even wait a few months, but then give just enough detail that no one doubts it was me. *"A young girl, biking home from her job at the diner,"* he will say, and the whole congregation will shift toward me, remembering those weeks when I was bruised.

Most likely, they'll think I brought it on myself, and I don't know why I hate them for it when I'm thinking it too. Whether it's logical or not, it still feels that if I was a better person, it wouldn't have happened at all.

If I was the kind of girl the Allens think I am, would my father have left? Would my brother have died? Would I need to work at a diner to save money so that I'm not homeless once I finish high school?

If I was that other, better girl, would Justin still have done what he did? Would those guys have tried to grab me?

I can't escape the feeling I somehow brought it all on myself.

"What state?" Luke asks. "What state were the tags?"

I shake my head. The answer isn't going to help. "California," I reply quietly as the door opens.

The pastor looks at me, sitting on the far side of the table. I'm not even sure it's the scrapes that catch his attention so much as it is the fact that I'm in the wrong place and not being helpful. "What's this?"

"Juliet took a little spill on her bike," Donna says quickly.

Luke's nostrils flare in silent argument.

"You fell?" the pastor asks me. "Were you wearing a helmet?"

I shake my head. *Trust the pastor to find a way to make it my fault.*

The pastor frowns at Donna, looking at the mess on the counter. "You shouldn't have to do this all on your own."

He's not saying the boys should have helped. He's saying, *"Falling off a bike is no excuse."*

I brace myself to stand but Luke climbs to his feet instead. "I can help," he says.

But the look he shoots at the pastor's back is lethal.

THE DAMAGE to my bike is deemed irreparable. I have enough saved for a new one, but I'm just not ready—there is never a moment when I'm outside now, even when I'm just walking nearby, that I don't feel that rush of wind at my back, the whisper of warning that something's coming for me. So I take the bus and it's twice as long, and the pastor is slightly cool to me on those nights I haven't helped Donna, as if it's a choice I made on purpose.

Luke's been going out without us since it happened, but when I get home from work a week later, he's weirdly insistent that I come out.

"There's a big party on the beach tonight," he says. "We all need to go. I'll drive us."

I frown. There are frequently huge parties on the beach, and Luke's never cared about going before, so I don't know why this one matters. And he always drives separately since his evenings end very differently than mine and Danny's do.

"Sure, whatever," Danny agrees cheerfully, never questioning why Luke is changing the plan.

I get the feeling he ought to have questioned it.

When we arrive a few hours later, we find hundreds of kids. It's a party that will definitely get broken up by the cops.

"Are we even going to know anyone here?" I ask.

"Yeah," Luke replies, distracted. "Some of the guys from the line-up mentioned it."

We move through the crowd. I assume we're here for a girl Luke's meeting, as if he doesn't have enough girls down at Kirkpatrick, but he's watching me more than he is the people around us. We've wandered aimlessly for ten minutes before I tug Danny's hand toward the south end of the party, where music is blasting. He won't want to dance, but I do, and I'm sick of just following Luke around so he can fuck someone new.

Danny tugs back. "Come on, Juliet," he pleads.

That snapping thing inside me unfurls. "Come on...for *what*?" I lash out. "So we can wander through this big crowd of strangers for no reason? So Luke can find some girl he's after? So I can sit around listening to you guys talk about college and surfing all night?"

His jaw falls open. "What the hell, babe?"

I shake off his hand. Why is it asking so much to do one thing I want? I've followed along meekly the whole goddamn summer and the little I've asked for—a romantic night out, a relationship that feels more adult than the ones I had when I was twelve—has been denied. And it's been denied with so little pushback from me that he's dumbfounded when it happens.

I turn toward the music. I don't even *want* to dance anymore, but if I don't go, I know I'll wind up apologizing and I just fucking refuse.

I plunge into the crowd of people dancing and close my eyes, trying to pretend we didn't just argue, trying to pretend Danny's not out there making excuses to Luke as if I've done something wrong.

It's *bad* Juliet taking over, asserting herself in ways I'll regret and apologize for later, but it works for a minute or two. I forget. And then the song ends and it's Luke I see first, standing just outside the circle. His gaze paralyzes me.

He's probably pissed, but he doesn't look pissed. His eyes are feverish and feral. Possessive.

It's not the way he looks at those other girls. It's *more*.

"Juliet," says Danny, moving in from my right, and Luke's face goes blank again. "Can we go now?"

His voice is gentle, as if I'm a wayward child who escaped at the mall, one he loves though she tries his patience. How do I get angry with him for that? How do I *not* get angry with him for that? My shoulders sag in defeat. I let him take my hand and pull me away, back to continue this mysterious mission Luke's on.

We walk and walk, until we're well past the party. Luke stares down stragglers on the beach, and even Danny is frustrated. "Bro, who are we looking for, anyway?" he asks.

Luke frowns, glancing briefly at me then away. "Never mind. Let's just go."

It feels like we're a mile from the Jeep at this point. We start to walk back through the crowd, and then I come to a stumbling halt.

I recognize the eyes first. Their coldness. The details I actually remembered—the tattooed knuckles, the pierced eyebrow...those come a second later. I freeze, and Danny hasn't even noticed but Luke has. His gaze jerks from me to the guy.

"Is that him?" Luke asks, close to my ear. His hand rests at the small of my back. "The guy who grabbed you?"

I have no reason to be terrified. Outside of the car, he's just a guy of normal height and normal weight. Bigger than me, but no match for Luke or Danny. I'm frozen anyway. I make a noise of assent, nodding...and Luke takes off after him at a sprint.

The guy's eyes widen and he starts running, but he's no

match for a college athlete. Luke tackles him, and they've barely landed before Luke's fist is driving into his face. It's as if something has unleashed inside him, something terrifying, something he's barely held onto.

That's why we're here, at this huge party. To find this guy. And Luke's been looking for him since it happened.

My mouth opens but no sound emerges. Danny, beside me, seems frozen too. It's only when the guy's friends dive at Luke that we both wake up. Danny runs forward, grabbing one of them and holding him back while I dive to the ground, snatching a beer bottle, the only weapon I can find.

By the time I reach them, though, Luke's shaken off the guy Danny isn't holding and is hitting him—his fist plunging into the guy's stomach, then his face, then his stomach again.

I'm almost glad I hear sirens in the distance because Luke's going to kill someone if it continues. And he's already done plenty of damage, so I need to get him out of here, *fast,* before the cops arrive.

Danny shouts at Luke to stop, and Luke simply turns and swings, hitting the guy Danny's holding dead in the face with a blow that makes his knees give way.

"Jesus Christ, Luke, stop!" Danny yells.

Luke turns to the bloody kid on the ground, the one who grabbed me. "If you even breathe in her vicinity again, I'll fucking kill you and I won't think twice. I'll beat you until you can't fight back, then I'll hold you under water until you've taken your last breath. That's a promise."

The drone of the police walkie-talkies parts the crowd, but Luke remains where he is, rigid and unmoving—lip and knuckles bleeding—as if he doesn't care about getting arrested.

"Run," I hiss. "Go! You threw the first punch. That makes it assault."

His face is carved in stone.

"If you do something, you own it," he says without inflection or fear. He throws Danny the keys to the Jeep. "Go ahead. Get her out of here."

Danny looks between us, torn. He doesn't want to get in trouble, but he also knows Luke might need our help. When his gaze turns back to me, I shake my head.

If Luke won't run, I'm not running either. I won't abandon him.

"I have no idea what the hell I'm going to tell my dad," Danny says bitterly as the cops push through at last.

"Tell him I took care of something you should have been a little more concerned about," Luke snaps.

There's no time for Danny to respond, though I'm not sure what he could have said. It never felt like Danny wasn't upset enough on my behalf. I'm questioning it now, though.

Luke and two of the kids he hit are taken in the back of a squad car. "That was fucked up," says Danny as we follow them. "I don't know what he was thinking. We could lose our scholarships over something like this. You understand that, right? If I'd gotten involved, I could have lost my scholarship. He *still* might. And you don't solve violence with violence."

He slides his fingers through mine as he waits for my answer.

"Yeah," I reply without conviction. "I get it."

But the old Juliet, *bad* Juliet, is smiling wide, feeling like the world is being set right again.

WHEN WE GET to the station, Luke has already been led away to be photographed and fingerprinted. I wonder if he needs a lawyer, and I already know he's screwed if that's the case. None of us have that kind of money.

Danny is taken to give a statement, and a few minutes later

a cop appears, looking at me as if I'm the guilty one, as if I'm the one who started this.

"You're up," he says.

I follow him to his desk, where I tell him about the guy who pulled me off my bike, embellishing the story just a bit in case it doesn't sound bad enough on its own. I don't know why I feel compelled to lie. Maybe it's just that, so many times, the truth wasn't enough. Even now it isn't.

"Why didn't you file a report when it happened?" he asks.

"What good would that have done?" I retort. If I'd filed a report, they'd have found a way to blame me. Some condescending bullshit about not biking along the coastal road, about being more careful, how I should have worn a helmet. So I didn't file, and they're using that to make me look guilty too.

"Well, for starters, it would make me more inclined to believe the story you're telling me now."

So...file a report simply to provide a defense in case shit goes down later—does he realize what fucked-up logic that is?

"I didn't file because I figured you'd turn it around and make it sound like it was my fault, kind of like you are right now."

"Look, I'm not saying you're at fault, but your boyfriend charged at a guy who's half his size, with no provocation—"

"Luke's not my boyfriend. Danny—the one who just gave a statement—is."

He raises a brow. "So your boyfriend did nothing and his *friend* started the fight?"

It sounds bad. It looks bad. If the incident with the bike was as awful as I've made it sound...you'd think my boyfriend would be out for blood. And he wasn't.

"Danny's dad's a pastor. He's...not like that."

"Fine," he says, as if he doesn't believe me again. "Well, then, *Luke* charged at this guy with no provocation and apparently threatened to hold him under water until he stopped breathing, so you suddenly crying rape is—"

"I never did 'cry rape'," I say between my teeth. *Crying rape.* No one accuses someone of 'crying assault' or 'crying robbery'. Nope, just rape. Just shit that happens to defenseless teen girls and not as much to men with a little power. "Like I said, he pulled me off my bike and tore my shirt, and if you don't believe me, Mrs. Allen can tell you herself about how she had to pull gravel and glass out of my face with tweezers." I point to the remaining scrapes down my left side and to the faint bruising on my cheekbone.

He sighs. "So do you want to press charges against this kid? The one who grabbed you?"

"I won't if he won't," I reply.

He doesn't like this answer. He taps his pen against the desk repeatedly, staring me down. "You know, your boyfriend... Danny? He's in the clear. Every witness stated he wasn't involved, and the other kid, Luke...he sounds like a pretty violent guy. He already has a record and it's not the first time he's done this. He's no one who deserves to be protected."

Yes, he is.

I shrug. "I just want this over with."

Danny is eager to leave but I refuse, so we sit in the lobby until Luke is released. He walks down the hall, slowing in surprise when he realizes we waited. He's like me—fully expecting to be abandoned, every fucking time. "Thanks," he says.

"Of course," Danny replies. "You're family."

But it was me Luke looked at when he said it.

ONLY A WEEK LATER, the guys are leaving for football camp. As long as the summer felt at times, the end has come too fast.

We walk them to the car, and Danny presses his lips to my forehead. "I'll call you when I get to school," he says.

Luke shakes the pastor's hand and hugs Donna before he turns to me.

I study his face: the dark eyes, the full lips, the unshaved jaw. It takes a second to realize what I'm doing.

I'm trying to find a way to hold onto him because I don't know if he'll ever be back, and he's looking at me in exactly the same way. I suspect he's done it before—I was just too busy assuming his reasons were nefarious to see it clearly.

"See ya, Juliet," he says quietly.

"Bye, Luke," I whisper, and it's only then, of the whole morning, that I burst into tears.

11

NOW

The reporter from *The New York Times* suggests meeting at the house, but I can't imagine answering her questions with Luke somewhere in the background, listening. I also don't need this reporter saying, *"Wait a minute...you and Luke Taylor are both sleeping here?"* The tabloids would love to make that into something it's not.

"Let's go to the new place in town instead," I counter. "I'll text you the name."

What was once the diner is now The Tavern, with hunting lodge décor and a menu featuring artisanal cheeses and osso buco.

Every head in the restaurant turns when I enter, but none of them are familiar. They're simply watching me the way I get watched everywhere now, and as much as I dislike it, that's better than heads turning because they remember who I once was.

I'm led to the reporter. She's older and a little dowdy, unlikely to be a fan. If I'm lucky, this means she'll focus on Danny's House and the good work it'll do. If I'm unlucky, this means she'll look at everything carefully, attempting to turn over stones best left unturned.

We make small talk until the waitress appears, asking for our drink orders. The reporter gestures for me to go first and it feels like a test: *Is Juliet Cantrell a heavy drinker? The kind of princess who demands a plate of sliced lemons for her diet soda?* I order a glass of pinot and she says she'll have the same. I guess if it was a test, I passed.

While we wait for our wine, she proceeds with her first few questions. Most of this is information anyone could have told her, which means she's throwing softballs. Reporters are always friendly at first—I doubt it'll last.

She asks what I'm doing to help with the opening just as the wine arrives. I take a polite sip and tell her about planting trees and realizing I'm not as fit as I thought, how I'm hoping Donna isn't *really* planning to make me hang drywall. I don't mention Luke's name once.

"Now, it's my understanding that Donna initially wanted to open something like Danny's House in Nicaragua, but there was some controversy about it?"

I hitch a shoulder. "It was a long time ago but yeah, the church agreed to her proposal and someone objected. Someone will *always* object, even when you're trying to help."

"You sound deeply tired of public opinion."

I force a smile. "Nope. Just tired of assholes who'd want to keep a woman from opening an orphanage in a foreign country."

"You lived with the Allens for most of high school, yes?"

I freeze. There is no mention of me living with the Allens anywhere in the press I have done up to this point. As far as the world knows, I was simply a mediocre student who sang in a church choir and sent out home recordings until she found someone willing to give her a shot.

"Who told you that?" I ask. "Was it Hilary? Because I told her that wasn't something I wanted to discuss."

Her head tilts, and I feel like I'm being analyzed, not interviewed. "I heard it from several people, actually. I got here a few days ago to do some background."

Fuck. Rhodes is a small town, and if she's discussed Danny's House with pretty much anyone, they might have mentioned it. I was just hoping they'd forgotten, and it was a really stupid thing to hope for.

"I understand your reluctance," she continues, "but I mean...look at you now. Think about how inspiring your story would be to kids in foster care."

My nails tap against my wine glass. "No offense, but I'm not sure a whole lot of kids in foster care read *The New York Times*."

She shrugs. "True. But—"

"Next question."

She sits up a little straighter, agitated, and clicks her pen unnecessarily as she looks over her notes. There's something wary in her eyes when she glances up again, and I brace myself for questions about Cash.

"I've heard various theories suggested about Danny's death," she begins.

I stiffen. It's not about Cash—it's worse.

"Some people think what he did was too out of character to have been an accident. It sounds like he had a lot to live for and was in a good place. What do you think?"

My teeth grind. "He was really excited for the future. That's all I want to say about it. And I'm not having anything to do with this if you're planning some deep dive into what happened to him and implying it was suicide. That would kill his mother, and she's already suffered enough."

She gives a quiet laugh. "Juliet, you realize I do need to write about *something*. And if you're here to draw attention to

Danny's House, there's no better way to do that than by discussing your experience there. Your story could draw the kind of attention and funding that sees this program replicated around the country."

Bitch. It was her strategy all along: get me to talk about my past by suggesting she'll talk about Danny's death if I don't.

But would it be the end of the world, admitting I left home at fifteen? It will ultimately help Danny's House, and the stuff with Luke...that's so far in the past. There's got to be a point at which all my paranoia is unnecessary.

It's Danny's legacy, and Donna's too. Don't they deserve to have it be *big*? Don't they deserve some credit for how they helped me?

I take a careful sip of my wine and blot my lips. "If this article's purpose is to attract positive attention to the charity, I guess you wouldn't want to *sour* the whole thing by suggesting Danny's death was anything but an accident."

She gives me a diplomatic smile. "You don't need to worry about that. I'm sure the facts will speak for themselves."

Yeah, nice try, lady.

I push my wine aside and lean forward with both palms flat on the table. "I'll discuss living with the Allens if you can assure me you won't imply Danny's death was suicide. Donna just... doesn't need that right now."

She hesitates again, which tells me she had indeed intended to do just that, but she nods. "Agreed. So...tell me a little bit about why you had to leave home."

I wonder how much I should say. Just because I've agreed to discuss this doesn't mean she needs the *entire* truth. So I start with a simpler answer and even that feels like too much.

"I never felt safe, not once, until I moved into the Allens' house," I begin.

I don't mention it was *Luke* who truly made me feel safe,

however. As far as I'm concerned, publicly, he no longer matters.

I wonder how long you have to lie to the world before you believe something yourself.

12

THEN

AUGUST 2013

The remainder of August, leading up to the start of school, is painfully quiet. I work more hours to take my mind off the fact that the boys are gone, but I feel their absence every minute of the day. Sometimes, when I'm passing Danny's room, I stop and peer in, hungry for something: a scent, a memory. As if I can stand here long enough to carry myself back in time.

There's nothing, of course. The sheets on the twin beds have been changed, the laundry is gone, the floor is swept.

Our dinners are simpler, and quieter. The pastor and Donna talk, and I sit in silence with nothing to add. It's hard to contribute when all I'm allowed to say is what they want to hear. I can't tell them I dread school and dread work and that I have this strange, constant ache in my chest that just won't go away.

The one thing I gain in Danny's absence is time. I don't play guitar when the pastor is home—he is bothered when he sees me being "unproductive"—but when he's gone, I practice, and those moments fill me in a way nothing else seems to. Donna always manages to give me a quick hug afterward, to tell me how pretty it was. It's her way of letting me know she approves.

But aside from that, I'm empty—so empty—and it wasn't like this last year. Yes, I was often tired, and I wished my life was a little more exciting—but it wasn't *this*. Those few months with the boys here have changed everything, and not for the better. I no longer fit in anywhere. Not here, and not at school, where everyone but me is talking about college.

I've done the math: all those long hours I spent last summer cleaning up ketchup-covered tables, being hit on and conde-scended to...they don't even amount to enough to cover a single semester. And I know I could get loans, but then what? The only thing I'm really interested in is singing, and how's a degree going to help me there?

I let most of the rites of passage slip by, simply because of the cost. I had to replace the bike—getting to the high school in Haverford requires three different buses without it—but I don't feel safe biking at night and can't afford Uber, which means no football games or parties. I spend Senior Skip Day working. Shane Harris asks me to Homecoming *"just as friends"* but a dress would cost money I shouldn't be spending, and I can't imagine explaining to the pastor and Donna that I'm going to a dance with someone else.

Hailey's the only one who still texts, and even she has stopped asking me to hang out because she's tired of my excuses.

The highlight of my week, the only highlight, is watching Danny's games on TV every Saturday.

"I can't tell them apart," says Donna. "I'm not sure I'd even recognize Danny if they ever let him play. Which one is Luke again?"

"He's the wide receiver," says the pastor.

I know exactly which one Luke is. Even in a helmet and

pads, no one else on the field combines his height and agility. He's as graceful and powerful there as he is in the water.

When he runs, it's a thing of beauty. When he leaps in the air, his large hands plucking a football high above him without a moment's hesitation, I marvel at what the human body is capable of. The pastor has never said a single word on Sunday that makes me believe in God, but watching these games makes me think there must be something greater out there, something miraculous. Because what else could possibly explain Luke?

"You sure you don't want to go to Homecoming?" Danny asks during our next phone call. "If this guy said it was just as friends, I really don't mind."

"He doesn't want to be her friend," growls Luke, closer to the phone than I first realized. Something lights up inside me at the sound of his voice. "Pull your head out of your ass, Dan."

Danny laughs. "You're too cynical, Luke."

"And you're too fucking trusting," Luke replies.

Luke's right. Danny's too fucking trusting.

When San Diego plays San Jose State in November, Donna, the pastor, and I all attend. The pastor wanted to save money by driving out on the day of the game, but for once, Donna prevailed and we left the night before. It's our only real chance to get time with Danny since he'll be busy before the game and will leave immediately afterward.

The pastor didn't feel it was appropriate for me to stay in the same room as him and Donna but agreed to let me pay for an adjoining room. Donna swallowed down her disagreement... she'd pushed him to let us come a night early and she's worried he'll just abandon the whole plan if she continues to fight.

I'm not sure how she wound up in this position—with so

little power, begging to ever get her way about anything—but I know I don't want that for myself. I wonder if there's a way to attain Donna's kindness and contentment with life without giving myself away entirely.

The team has already arrived by the time we check into the hotel. We meet Danny in the lobby to take him to dinner. "Thank you for coming," he says against my ear as he hugs me. "You have no idea how good it is to see you."

The pastor takes us to a restaurant in town. Donna asks about Luke, and I listen without saying a single word. "I wish he'd come with us to dinner tonight," Donna says, and Danny looks from her to his father.

"I told Danny this should only be family," the pastor says.

I catch the briefest flash of anger in her eyes before she gives her husband a small but firm smile. "Luke *is* a part of the family."

Good for you, Donna.

The pastor's mouth opens to argue, but something in her face silences him. Maybe he's starting to realize he doesn't hold all the cards, that there's nothing to stop her from leaving him now that Danny's out of the house and I'm nearly out too.

After dinner, we return to the hotel. Danny and I tell his parents goodnight and take a cab to some sorority party on campus. My stomach is tied in knots on the way—I don't know how the team got invited, but it certainly seems like the kind of thing Luke would be attending.

I follow Danny into a stunning house that is crammed with people, most of whom already appear to be drunk. The lights are bright, the music loud. Couples are pressed to walls, atop each other on chairs, ignoring the splendor—the high ceilings, the built-in bookshelves and ornate moldings, the hardwood floor a guy scuffs carelessly as he drags a chair across it.

I wonder if the girls who live here—on someone else's dime, with no supervision—can even *grasp* how free they are, how lucky they are. They don't have to help make dinner. They don't have to clean. They probably don't even fucking work. No one's going to ask them why they're late, no one's going to make them feel guilty about drinking a beer on a Saturday night or taking their boyfriends upstairs.

"Out back!" someone yells to Danny, and we go through the French doors leading to the terrace.

Outside, there are kids everywhere in folding chairs, couples entangled with no shame whatsoever.

Someone calls Danny's name from the darkest part of the yard, and we follow the sound blindly, eventually stumbling on a group of guys in a circle, Luke among them and already with a girl, of course. He gives me the smallest nod in greeting, nothing more, as if I don't matter, as if he'd forgotten me. I'm not sure why I care.

We sit and I listen to them talk about some incident at dinner with the coach, and a bunch of football stuff I don't understand. They ask Danny if the pastor is going to let him sleep in my room, then they tease Luke about spending more time in the water than in class. "If you were half as interested in football as surfing," one of them says, "we'd be winning this season."

Luke doesn't look at me once the entire time, and I'm not sure how I ever convinced myself there was something between us that shouldn't have been there. Maybe I just got so accustomed to hostility from him that I mistook its absence for care.

There's a couple pressed to the bathroom door when I go inside, the guy's hand in the girl's skirt. I ask if I can get by and they don't stop what they're doing, but simply scoot over a foot. They aren't ashamed of what they want—that's the part that strikes me most.

When I reach Danny again, he's alone, waiting for me. I wonder if his friends are trying to give him some privacy. This part of the yard is entirely dark, so we'd have it.

"You ready to head home?" he asks.

No. *Enough*. I'm tired of acting like we are ten years old.

I swing my legs over his lap to straddle him, the way I've seen girls do to Luke.

"Juliet," he whispers, suddenly tense. "This isn't a good idea." He places his hands on my hips as if he intends to push me away. I ignore him. I want more. I *need* more.

I can't keep being this girl who holds hands and doesn't drink or dance and who only gets one moment to be who she is —that solo in church, singing something I didn't choose and don't even like. I need more. This discontentment, this dissatisfaction with him, is a barrier I can just break through if he'll help me do it. There has to be a way I can remain with him and also...*like* my life.

I kiss him.

"Juliet," he argues, but I feel him pressed between my legs, hard, and all the blood in my body seems to flow to that exact spot. I shift against him and stifle a groan. The walls at the Allens' house are thin and the rooms are close together. Even in the dead of night, I'm too scared to touch any part of myself.

"You should probably get off my lap," he says. Despite the dim light, I can tell he's flushing, unable to meet my eye.

I place my hands on either side of his face. "I think that's a natural reaction to having a girl in your lap."

I kiss him again and he responds, giving in at last. I move against him again, nerve endings snapping to life, forgetting anyone could walk up on us and not especially caring.

He gasps, suddenly, grasping my hips. "Stop!" he yells, pushing me off him.

I hit the ground hard, my back absorbing most of the fall, and blink up at him, stunned. I can't believe he shoved me. I want to think it was an accident but...he yelled at me. So it wasn't, really.

I sit up gingerly, wincing at the pain in my back, while the noise of the party continues around us, unabated.

"I don't understand what just happened," I whisper.

His shoulders sag and he doesn't meet my gaze. "I...came."

"From *that*?"

"Yes," he says, his voice sharper than I'm used to. "You were moving all over the place and then the kissing and...what did you think was going to happen? I told you to get off my lap."

I can't think of a time when he's been mad at me before. But his anger sparks my own. "What's the big deal, Danny? You think you're not getting into heaven because you came *by accident*?"

He rises. "It wasn't an accident! We made bad choices and this was the result."

He storms off toward the house and I remain where I landed—sitting on my ass in this dark corner of a backyard, hours from home, and feeling guiltier by the second.

I took something he didn't want to give. Am I any different than Justin, cornering me, acting like all my objections were some coy game I was playing?

Tears slip down my face. I don't know why I always want to do the bad thing, why I can't just be happy with my easy, safe life and my wonderful boyfriend.

I'm ashamed of myself, and I'm angry at the same time. Why is it that all the people inside get to drink and grope each other and whatever else they do? Why am I the only one who has to choose between good and evil, when the rest of the world gets a little of both?

I'm too upset to stay here or to go inside to look for him, not that he seems to want me looking for him anyway. I just want to return to the safety of my room, a quiet place where I can rest my head and figure out how to fix this.

I slip through the darkness to the gate on the side of the yard. The hotel is less than five miles away. God knows if I can stand on my feet at the diner for ten hours a day, I can walk five miles in flip-flops.

The neighborhood turns rough a few blocks from campus. I'm out in the open. Vulnerable. Easy prey. I pass a group of men on the darkened main road and their faces gleam with that ugly kind of interest, which I know more about than I should. It terrifies me, so I break into a run because what else am I going to do? I can't walk back into that party with my tear-streaked face, begging someone to help me find Danny.

My flip-flops start to curl beneath my feet, so I slip them off and carry them, heedless of the gravel digging into my soles. It hurts, but I was already hurting, and fear is currently my dominant emotion.

The air is colder, and the sweat against my skin makes it worse. My teeth chatter, and a car's headlights loom behind me, but the car slows rather than passing.

I think of the incident last summer and run faster, slipping down a side street and then an alley, realizing fully what a terrible idea it was to take off on my own the way I did.

I shouldn't have run away from Danny; I should have listened, and yet it feels like something inside me will die if I continue to live this way. He wants what's best for me and he's usually right. Perhaps this thing in me *should* die, but the very thought of it makes me want to lie down in the street and give up. Without that small, hopeful flutter in my heart—the desire for things I can't picture or name—I wouldn't be able to go on.

"You aren't cut out for this." Isn't that what Luke said?

Except what option do I have? I can't hurt Danny.

Footsteps pound the pavement behind me, and then hands grab my shoulders, tight as a vise.

"Juliet," Luke snarls.

I gasp as he turns me toward him, his eyes wide and incredulous.

"What were you thinking?" he hisses. "It's not safe out here at night. Jesus. You could have been raped."

My shoulders sag. I tried to do something tonight to change my life. I let Danny see who I really am, and then I ran away, and it was all for nothing. I look like a fool, and now I'm being returned to him like a beaten dog, head hanging low.

"Come on." He places his hand at the small of my back, guiding me down the street to an unfamiliar car before opening the door. I fold myself inside in defeat.

He pulls off his sweatshirt and tosses it into my lap. "Put it on. You're shivering."

I do as I'm told, wondering just how bad this situation must be for Danny to send someone else after me. "Why are you here?"

He starts the car. "Danny was going to come after you and I convinced him to let me come instead so you wouldn't feel like you'd been captured."

I look out the window. "I'm not sure I see the difference." He's returning me to Danny as if I'm an escaped prisoner. He's returning me and it doesn't matter, does it? I'd have returned myself in any case.

"I'm not here to drag you back to him, Juliet. I'm just making sure you get to the hotel okay."

"Why are you even bothering?"

He's silent for a moment. "Anything that matters to Danny matters to me," he finally says.

I don't know why his answer hurts. Did I believe, for a moment, that he might have any other reason? I hate this piece of me that wanted there to be one.

We pull in front of the hotel, and I start to take off his sweatshirt, but he stops me.

"Keep it. I'll watch to make sure you get in safely, but I've got to return this girl's car."

I try to laugh but make a choked sound instead. "God. I've

never seen someone so desperate to get rid of another person." My eyes well as I reach for the door.

He winces. "I'm not trying to get rid of you."

I round on him. "Of course you are. It's not even *surprising*." Tears clog my throat but I no longer care. "Why do you hate me so much, Luke? What did I do?"

That muscle in his cheek contracts. His eyes squeeze shut, and when they open, they land on me in a way they never have before, as if I'm made of glass and a thousand times more valuable. He's showing me, at last, something he's hidden so well for months.

He swallows. "I don't hate you."

For a fraction of a second, the truth rests between us.

He doesn't hate me. He has never hated me. And I've never hated him.

I grab the door handle, practically snapping it in my haste as I scramble out of the car. "Thank you...thanks...I, uh, I really appreciate you coming to get me."

I think he says my name but the door is already shutting and that's probably for the best. I'm scared he might say something he can't take back, and I might too.

I go inside and shower, trying to rinse it all away. The incident with Danny, yes, but most of all the things I learned tonight: about Luke, and about myself. By the time I'm done and clad in pajamas, there's a text from Danny saying he's waiting outside my room and that he'll stay there all night if he has to.

I open the door, and he pulls me against his chest. It's easy, now, to throw myself into his arms and apologize, over and over. Because I am someone who thinks terrible things, and wants terrible things, and I could never, ever deserve Danny, not in a million years. "I'm so sorry. I'm so, so sorry."

"No," he says, "*I'm* sorry."

I blink up at him. "What? Why would *you* be sorry?"

"Luke yelled at me after you left," he admits. "He didn't even know what happened, but he said I was an asshole for walking inside without you and that I treat you like you're my kid sister. I don't mean to, you know that, right? I'm just trying so hard not to be tempted by the wrong things."

I nod. I *do* know. He wants me to be safe, and he wants us to do what he believes is the right thing. I just don't happen to agree with him. I want Donna's contentment with life, her innate goodness...I'm just not sure blindly adopting the pastor's values is the only way to get it.

"You're everything to me," he whispers. "More than my parents, more than the entire town. I'd give up everything for you."

I think of the time Luke said that one day Danny would lose me, and that the longer this went on, the more I'd fuck him up when it happened.

I made a decision when I was fifteen...to be with him, to become part of his family. It felt like a life raft. Now it feels like I might've been slowly drowning this whole time instead...and taking Danny with me.

13

NOW

Luke hangs the drywall without my help, which is probably for the best, and I am tasked with priming it. We're not working together like Donna wants, but I don't know why the hell Donna thinks that would matter anyway.

She's asleep on the couch when we finish for the day. I can't help but wonder if *life* is what made her sick. My losses have been minimal compared to hers, but even I often think it would be easier not to wake in the morning.

I go to the kitchen to figure out dinner. I find a package of thin-sliced steaks, the kind Donna used to batter and fry for Danny. I'm not sure if it was a favorite of his. It's becoming harder and harder to remember the specifics. Only our last moments together are ironed into my brain, and they're the ones I'd like to forget.

"What's wrong?" Luke asks.

I didn't even realize he'd walked into the kitchen.

I can't tell him I was thinking about Danny, that I was thinking about how much I've *forgotten* about Danny. "Nothing. I'm going to start dinner since Donna's asleep."

I brace for the derision that's coming, for the implication that I am now too fancy and useless to make real food. Instead, he gets out a pan and then hunts for the oil.

I wonder what Luke does when he's not here. I truly have no idea what his life is like—does he cook for himself? Does he have a girlfriend somewhere making him meals?

My guess is Luke is never without companionship for long, but I can't bring myself to dwell on it.

He opens a bottle of olive oil and frowns as he sniffs it. "This is garbage."

I hide a smile. You don't often find a man Luke's size in a kitchen, mumbling about the quality of the olive oil. "Do you do a lot of cooking?"

His mouth presses into a tight line. "Do me a favor, Juliet, and don't pretend you care."

It cuts me to the bone and I look away. *Thanks for the reminder, Luke.* I don't say another word to him, and that's probably for the best.

Donna enters just as we're finishing up. "Look at the two of you working together."

Luke and I aren't even beside each other, but we step apart anyway. Old habits die hard, I guess.

"Take a seat," I tell her. "It's ready."

We carry everything to the table, and Donna frowns, watching Luke load his plate.

"You were right," she says, turning to me, "when you told me I wasn't feeding him enough. And there I was, insisting he'd tell us if that was the case."

God, Donna. Please don't do this here. Don't unravel all this in front of him.

Luke freezes, his fork in midair.

"Looking back on it, I can't believe how blind I was," she continues. "Obviously you were hungry. You were so much bigger than Danny. I can't imagine why Juliet had to be the one to tell me. It's shocking sometimes, when you look back on what you did or didn't do, and the things you should've known. It seems so obvious now."

It feels like she's talking about something much bigger, but she can't be. If Donna truly knew about the things that were obvious, the things she should've known, she wouldn't allow either of us under her roof.

Luke slowly lowers his fork, his gaze flickering to me. "I don't know what you're talking about. There's always been plenty of food."

She holds the napkin to her lips, her shoulders sagging. "No. There wasn't. When you first got here, you'd finish everything on your plate halfway through dinner. I told myself maybe it was just the way you were raised, but it wasn't that. You were so hungry. And Juliet...she kept pretending she *wasn't* hungry so she could put half her food back for you. Pretending she'd messed up and made too much of whatever I'd tasked her with."

He glances at me again, searching my face for the truth. I look down, refusing to let him find it.

"And when all that didn't work," Donna continues, "she told me I wasn't feeding you enough. She never asked for a single thing of me aside from the things she asked for you."

He stares at me as he replies to her. "I don't know what this is about, but I don't remember ever going hungry."

"You don't remember being hungry," she whispers, "because Juliet started giving me money for you out of what she earned at the diner."

No. No, no, no. This is nothing he ever needed to learn. Especially not now. *God.*

"What?" Luke freezes, his voice empty, barely audible.

Donna's head hangs. "I should never have accepted it. I just didn't know what else to do." Tears well in her eyes as she looks at me. "You worked so hard, and put up with so much, and I still took your money."

I feel Luke's stare and ignore it, reaching across the table for her hand. "Donna, it was fine. You didn't have a choice anyway. Let's be honest, the pastor didn't want me here and he probably didn't want Luke here either. You were constantly worried that one small thing would be the straw that broke the camel's back. What else could you have done?"

Luke shoves his plate away. "I don't understand. Juliet was giving you money...to *feed* me? That makes no sense. I offered to pay room and board when I arrived here, and you refused."

"The pastor didn't want your money," she whispers. "It was a pride thing. He was embarrassed to have you think he couldn't afford you here."

"But he was okay with taking *Juliet's* money?" He runs a hand through his hair, gripping hard. "I made way more than she did and needed it less."

She exhales heavily. "I didn't tell him. I spent so much time being scared of his reaction over such small things. I hate that. And I hate that I resent him for them now when he can't even defend himself."

Luke turns to me, his eyes dark as night. "How long did that go on for?"

I push my chair from the table. Any appetite I had is gone, and I need to get the hell out of this room. "I don't even remember. It really wasn't a big deal."

"How. Long?"

Goose bumps crawl along my arms.

"She did it for both of the summers you were with us," Donna replies. "Two full summers."

He winces. "So even when I was being awful to you. Even then you were *paying* for me to be here."

He wants an answer beyond a simple *"yes"* or *"no."* Because, really, he's asking a different question entirely: *How could you care about me that much, and then do what you did?*

He can spend his entire life waiting for the answer. I'm never telling him a thing.

He stands outside my door that night for a very long time.

14

THEN

DECEMBER 2013

Danny arrives home for winter break on my last day of second quarter.

We only go to one Westside party and nothing at the beach at all, which I'm fine with. There are also no dates, but I guess there never were, aside from when Danny and I first met. The shit I've seen on TV is laughable anyway. How many high school students are actually enjoying candlelit meals in fancy restaurants or riding in limos like they do on *Gossip Girl*? None that I know.

With Luke gone, though, everything is better. I'm not the third wheel. I don't feel fake and conspicuous when I help Donna around the house, and I'm capable of at least *trying* to see the world the way she does, finding comfort in the small joys: a crisp winter night, a roaring fire, the smell of the Christmas tree. The Allens are content people by nature, and I am not, but if I could even manage to get halfway to where they are, that would be enough. Life is easier when you're not wanting more than you have every minute of the day.

The diner closes early on Christmas Eve, so I spend the afternoon helping Donna with supper. We eat in the dining room rather than the kitchen, which Donna and I have set with candles and holly. Christmas music plays softly and the whole house smells like pine.

This is a good life. There's a spark of something in my heart, a taste of that contentment Donna and Danny find so easily. I silently pray as we start eating, that I can help build that spark into a fire. That I can convince myself it's all enough.

The pastor talks about the work he'd like Danny to do next summer, his role expanded now from what it was. I didn't think of pastoring as a profession you passed down to your son, but the pastor sure seems to be doing his best. Danny would be good at it, too, certainly better than the pastor, but I'm not sure I could ever be Donna—I'd school those bitches who come into the diner so fast if I had half her authority.

"So will Luke be coming home with you next summer?" Donna asks.

I stop chewing, waiting to hear his answer.

"I don't know," Danny replies. "The construction firm he was with last summer offered him a bonus to come back, but now he's talking about staying in San Diego."

Donna's brow furrows. "Well, that makes no sense at all. Did he meet a girl?"

Danny laughs. "There isn't a day that goes by when Luke isn't meeting a girl. I don't think that's it."

Suddenly, nothing about tonight brings me contentment. The pie crust sticks to my tongue, the air smells sickly sweet, the music is overly sentimental.

It's last summer all over again. I'm trying so hard to be like the Allens, but somehow, Luke manages to ruin everything for me, even when he's not fucking here.

～

OVER DINNER on Danny's last night home, the pastor revisits his thoughts on indulgence. He suggests we all look at 2014 as the year of restraint, the year we don't give into our whims. I wonder if Danny told him what happened at the sorority house.

And it seems like an easy thing for the pastor to say. He's an older guy in moderately poor health. He doesn't drink or smoke and I'm not sure other vices call to him. I'd like to see what he'd do, though, if Donna followed him to the letter and didn't offer dessert every night.

"I like what my father said tonight," Danny says later as we walk through the neighborhood, hand in hand, enjoying our last moments alone before he leaves. I brace myself for another of his mini lectures on how we need to behave—there've been several since he got home—and I feel that wedge between us as if it's palpable.

Is Danny at fault for it because he's insisting on doing things his way? Am I at fault because I've kept so much to myself? Even Luke knows things about me that Danny does not.

"I need to tell you something," I whisper.

He squeezes my hand, encouraging me to continue.

"Last summer, I told you I had to read for school but I would sometimes...play guitar instead."

He frowns. "Why'd you lie?"

"Because I thought if I told you the truth, you'd try to convince me to come out with you guys. It felt like every minute of my day was taken."

His mouth presses tight, his jaw locks. My reasons don't justify the lie, I guess. Or maybe he just doesn't like the implied criticism—that my days were too full, that he tends to push me to do things I don't want to do.

His nod is slow and reluctant. "I appreciate you telling me. But from now on, I just want the truth, okay?"

My breath holds. I hadn't planned to tell him everything, but maybe this is the issue—that I'm worried he won't like who I am if he knows it all.

I slowly exhale. "The thing that happened this fall—"

"I know it's hard, watching everyone else get something you'd like for yourself. I mean, it's hard for me too. But that's what will make it so special when—"

"Danny," I say, cutting him off because I can't listen to another word of this, "I'm not a virgin."

We're nearly back to the house. He comes to a dead stop, staring at me, his face blank with shock.

"*What?*" he asks with a small, nervous laugh.

He wants it to be a joke. He *assumes* it's a joke. That makes me feel worse.

"You never asked me, so it's not like I've been lying to you about it," I whisper. "You just assumed, and I let you assume it because I was worried you'd judge me."

Even in the dim light, I don't miss the way his shock is quickly turning to disgust. "With *who*?" he asks. "I thought I was your first boyfriend."

I wince. "You were. You are. It doesn't matter."

"I don't understand. You were fifteen when we met. How could you have already done that?"

I could probably strip a lot of the judgment from his voice if I told him the truth, but that would just make things worse.

"It's complicated."

His eyes flash. "You should have told me. That was a gift I was saving for you, and I thought you were saving it for me too."

"Danny, I'm not the outlier here. You are. I'm fine we're not having sex if that's something you value, and yes, I should have told you, but it's bullshit for you to act like I'm intentionally depriving you of something."

He slaps both hands to his face in frustration. "Well forgive me for not handling it perfectly, Juliet. I've just discovered you've been lying to me the entire time we've been together and, yes, I'm mad. It feels like you've stolen something that was supposed to be mine."

Fuck this. *He's* mad? Fuck this. "Yeah? Well, it was stolen from me, too, Danny. I'm not thrilled with it either."

He pales. "You were raped?"

My eyes fall closed. I don't know. I don't know if I can call it rape. It wasn't like something you see in a TV movie. I wasn't grabbed by a guy in a face mask and dragged into the woods. I don't know what to call it.

"Sometimes you go along with things because you know fighting back is useless. I was smaller than he was, and I knew he wasn't going to stop so I just—" I shrug. I gave in. That's all there was to it. I'd like to claim now that I'd fight, but I probably wouldn't. I've seen how that works out too.

After a moment, he reaches for my hand. "So it was just the one time?"

"No," I reply, my teeth grinding. He still thinks he's the one who deserves to be consoled, reassured. He wants to believe that I'm *gently* used, at most.

"More than once doesn't sound like rape to me," he says, releasing my hand once more.

I grit my teeth. "I never said it was."

"You couldn't have been all that unwilling if it kept happening. Did you even try to stay out of the guy's path?"

My shoulders sag. This would be so much easier if I actually believed I was innocent, if defending myself didn't feel like a lie. If you say, *"No"* to someone, again and again, but you sometimes *responded* to what he did, can you still claim you weren't at fault? I don't know. "You know nothing about it," I whisper.

"Then tell me who it was!" he shouts. "Tell me how you possibly couldn't have avoided this guy."

It feels like the end of everything. This is a closely guarded secret, the thing I hate about myself most. I'm not sure I trust Danny with it, but I'm not sure I trust anyone with it.

"Because it was Justin."

He goes completely rigid.

"Your *stepbrother*?" His mouth falls open, his voice cracking with disgust. His reaction is exactly why I never tried to tell people after that first failed attempt. When your own mother, the person who's known you longer than anyone else, suggests you're a liar or brought it on yourself, you know better than to continue looking for a sympathetic ear.

I nod and he stares at me. "Isn't he...isn't he, like, in his late twenties? That's not even legal."

A miserable laugh bubbles inside me. "Neither is forcing someone to have sex with you after she says, '*No*', Danny."

"Why didn't you tell someone?" he demands. "Why didn't you tell, like, your mom, or a counselor or someone?"

My eyes sting. I knew this part would come.

"I did tell my mom, and she accused me of making it up. And I didn't tell anyone else because I figured I'd get blamed for it, just like you're blaming me now."

I wait for him to deny he's doing it. He doesn't.

"Was it going on when—" He stops, flinching. "Was it going on when we were dating?"

He's asking if I was cheating on him. Was there more I could have done to stop it? Maybe. I can't claim to have exhausted every resource...I expected the worst of anyone who might have helped me, and I still do. But the possibility will always exist that I could have stopped it if I'd just done things differently. I'll never know for sure.

"I didn't want it," I whisper. "He was trying to pull me out of the house and I was doing my best not to go when he dislocated my shoulder. I did my best."

I have to swallow to avoid a crack in my voice. I'm not going to beg for his pity. I don't want to *trick* him into feigning forgiveness he doesn't feel.

He stares at me for one long moment. His mouth opens to speak, but then closes again. He shakes his head and walks inside alone. By the time I follow him, he's already gone to his room.

I stare at his closed door, feeling emptied by shock—both that I told him, and that it went so badly. I thought he might be the one person who'd be able to see past the ugliness of it all. The one person who'd pull me against him and say, *"Oh, Juliet, I'm so sorry that happened."*

If even Danny can't forgive me for it, who the hell ever will?

DANNY LEAVES for school the next morning, telling me he'll call. "I know we need to talk," he says. "I'm just not ready."

But he doesn't call. For three nights, there's no word from him and even Donna's pondering aloud at the silence.

It breaks my heart, but I'm angry at the same time. He's taken the thing I most hate about myself and he's made me feel like it's even worse than I thought. All that kindness he aspires to seems to have disappeared the moment it was put to the test.

And what will happen to me if he ends things? If the Allens kick me out, where do I go? I won't be old enough to rent a place until April, and I doubt what I've earned at the diner this summer will be enough to get me through the entire school year anyway. For Danny, it's simply the end of a relationship. For me, though, it would be the end of everything.

Four days after he left, I'm at work when I notice a Jeep, just like Luke's, across the road. It can't be him, but my gaze jerks toward it as it drives away. I know it was wishful thinking. I want someone to hold me right now, someone who will tell me it's going to work out, that it wasn't my fault. But that person wouldn't be Luke anyway.

Danny calls that night, at last. "I'm sorry," he says. "I'm really, really sorry."

I'm so relieved that I burst into tears, but I'm furious at the same time. He left me wondering for days whether or not we were over; he left me believing he was disgusted by me.

"I know it was wrong," he says. "I just needed to wrap my head around it, is all. I ended up having too much to drink last night, and Luke said—"

My jaw falls open. Of all the possible outcomes, it never occurred to me he might share my worst secret with someone else. Especially *that* someone else. "You told *Luke*?"

"I didn't mean to, hon. Like I said...I was drinking, and you know I never drink, and the whole thing spilled out."

I squeeze my eyes shut. It was bad enough that Danny knew, but having Luke know...it's just too much. "You shouldn't have told him," I whisper.

"Believe me, I know. I've got a black eye to show for it."

"*What?*"

"He punched me and then he yelled a whole lot of stuff. I was pissed at the time but after he left, I realized he was right— you'd have been fifteen or younger and probably had nowhere else to go. I handled it really badly. I'm so sorry."

"You left me hanging all week, Danny," I whisper. "I didn't know if we were even staying together."

"Of course we were. I was just focusing too much on..." He trails off, and my stomach drops.

"Focusing too much on what?"

He sighs. "That you, you know, you seem to...*want* that. Sex. Like the thing last fall."

My chest tightens. He was thinking that I was a slut, that I brought it on myself. "Wow, Danny."

"I know, I'm sorry. Look, I'm just not used to that. I grew up hearing one thing from my father and it always surprised me when you wanted more. But when you told me what you did, I just pictured...I don't know. I pictured you being the same way with him." His voice breaks. "Please forgive me. Please."

A churlish part of me doesn't want to. But how can I blame Danny for thinking something I've wondered about myself?

"Luke isn't going to...tell anyone, right? Like he's not going to report it?"

"He won't report it. He's the one who told me you probably didn't report it in the first place because then everyone would know."

Thank God. I can just see the reaction at church if they all heard I'd slept with my much older stepbrother. A whole lot of them, perhaps even most of them, would quietly blame me.

"Okay. Just...make sure he doesn't tell anyone else. Please. Just because he isn't reporting it doesn't mean someone else won't."

He sighs heavily. "I haven't seen him since the fight, but yeah, when he gets home, I'll tell him."

I still.

"He's been gone since yesterday? Is that normal?"

"No," he says, "but he was really mad."

I consider telling Danny what I thought I saw earlier, but there are tons of Jeeps like Luke's, and I'd sound crazy even suggesting Luke drove eight hours north for *me*.

Then again, when I think of his reaction to the bike thing last summer...maybe it wouldn't sound crazy at all.

I'M WOKEN JUST before daylight by someone knocking on the front door. The pastor and Donna are already there with two policemen by the time I get downstairs.

The pastor turns to me, his eyes dark and unhappy. "Your

stepbrother is in the hospital." He folds his arms. "He thinks Danny and Luke are behind it."

I frown. "That's impossible."

"We told them that," he says. "They're eight hours away. But someone matching Luke's description was at the scene, and his Jeep was seen in town earlier."

I swallow hard. *God, Luke, what did you do?*

Except I already know. He defended me.

And more importantly, he *believed* in me. He didn't suggest I was to blame. He didn't demand to know what part I'd played and why I hadn't tried harder to save myself.

He just went straight to the source, Justin, and made him pay for what he did.

"I spoke to both of them last night," I reply, bold in my terror. "At their apartment."

"Are you sure about that?" one of the cops asks.

Donna looks at me for a long moment. "I answered the call," she adds. "I spoke to both of them before she did."

She lied—for me or for Luke, or both of us. She lied.

I excuse myself to get ready for school. The second the cops leave, I take off without a word to anyone and call Luke as soon as I'm out the door. I've never called him before, and only have his number from texts Danny sent us both. My heart beats hard as I wait for him to answer.

He picks up on the fifth ring, voice groggy and hoarse.

"Juliet?"

"The police came to the pastor's house a few minutes ago, looking for you. I told them I spoke to you last night. If they show up there, you've got to tell them you were home. I'll get Danny to back the story up."

He's quiet for a moment. "I stand by what I did, and I'd do it again. I'm not lying about it."

I squeeze my eyes shut in frustration. It's the same bullshit as the fight on the beach all over again...Luke defending me, in his own way, but refusing to defend himself.

"Luke, please. You're going to allow a child molester to be the victim here while you go to jail for aggravated assault?"

"I am not going to slink away like I did something wrong."

"If you won't do it for yourself, then do it for me and Donna. We both just lied to the police on your behalf. And if this whole thing comes out, everyone will know what happened. Do you know what that'll be like for me, sitting in front of the whole church every Sunday with the pastor talking about a girl who was molested? God, he's told half the stories already. Everyone there has heard about my dislocated shoulder and how I was scared to go home."

He sighs. "Jules, it wouldn't matter anyway. I'm sure I was caught on camera somewhere between here and there. I wasn't in class yesterday either."

"Just try," I beg. "Please."

After a moment, he sighs again. "I'll do my best. And I'm sorry. I wasn't trying to turn this into a thing that would come back to bite you in the ass."

"Luke..." I begin, and my voice breaks, "don't apologize. I love what you did. I love it so much."

I hang up before I burst into tears, because I need to keep my shit together for the next part of this, and I really pray it goes the way I plan.

It takes three buses and a short bike ride to get to the hospital. At the front desk, I ask for Justin Mead, choking a little as I say I'm his sister. They tell me they're running tests, but I'll be notified when he gets to the room. I wait for two hours before I'm led back. I'll get in trouble for being this late to school but I can't worry about that now.

Justin's alone, thank God, and asleep. His entire head is bandaged. I wouldn't even recognize him if I didn't see his name on the hospital ID bracelet. The cops said Luke fractured his eye socket, among other things.

"Justin, wake up," I say, shoving his shoulder.

He groans. Beneath the bandage, one bleary eye turns toward me. "You did this, you fucking bitch."

"I *wish* I'd done this," I snarl. And it's true. I've spent so much time feeling culpable, and in a way, I still do, but Luke's reaction tells me...that maybe it really wasn't my fault. "By the way, do you know the penalty for statutory rape if the victim was under sixteen? Four years. But that's just for *one count* of statutory rape. How many counts would they bring against you, I wonder?"

"You lying bitch. That wasn't rape and you can't prove a thing."

"Really? What would you call it when a really young girl says 'No' and you do it anyway? What would you call it when she says 'No' and you dislocate her shoulder trying to force her? I have witnesses, by the way. I told Hailey when it was happening and the Allens too."

The last bit is a lie, but he won't know that.

"Hailey's a bigger whore than you are." He tries to laugh but it comes out as a cough. "No one's gonna believe her either."

I shrug. "Maybe not." I hold up my phone. "But I bet they believe you admitting to it all right here."

He scowls, but his mouth stops running. He knows he's screwed at this point.

"What do you want then?" he finally asks.

I hand him his cell phone. "Call the cops. Tell them you fucked up. Tell them you were hallucinating. Tell them it couldn't possibly be Danny or his roommate because they're eight hours south. Tell them you owe some guys money and it was probably them."

He waves off the phone. "I'll call later."

"You think I'd trust you after all the shit you did? Call them, *now*."

I don't leave his room until I've heard him thoroughly recant his statement to two different officers, and then I hustle out of the hospital, hoping that if I make it to school by lunch, they won't tell the pastor. I'm thirty yards from my bike when I see my mother walking up with a woman in her late twenties— Justin's girlfriend, I assume.

I'm her only remaining child and I haven't seen her in a year, but I know this will go badly. I've been a thorn in her side since I was small—the burden that sent her first husband running for the hills, and then the teenager her second husband enjoyed looking at too much. *"Good riddance"* was all she said when I told her I was moving out.

I glance around me, hoping to flee, but her gaze catches on me and she starts walking faster in my direction.

I guess this is happening.

"What are *you* doing here?" she demands. "You've already killed my son and now you've got the nerve to show up after you nearly killed my stepson too?"

"I wasn't responsible for what happened to either of them."

My voice doesn't exactly ring with conviction, though, because I sort of agree with her. I'm the reason Justin's in the hospital, and I'm probably the reason my brother is dead.

"You're poisonous," she hisses. "You came out of my *womb* poisonous. I better not see you around here again."

The woman beside her, a woman who's never even met me before, nods vigorously. "And keep your boyfriend away from Justin."

"Ah, you must be the girlfriend?" I ask sweetly. "Surprising. You're about fifteen years older than he likes."

My mother's hand comes at me so fast I can't even prepare for it.

My left ear rings, my left cheek burns, and for a moment I'm simply stunned. You'd think a lifetime of being slapped in the face would have had me on guard already, but I've gotten soft over these two years with the Allens. I'd almost forgotten there are people like my mom who think giving birth to you means they can hit you whenever and wherever they want.

My hand itches to swing back at her, to give her a taste of her own medicine, but she's still my legal guardian and I've got another few months until I'm eighteen, which she could make difficult if she so chose.

So, I hold my temper, but take one long step until I'm in her face. "I'm keeping count, *Amy*," I reply, because I will never call her *mom* again, "and every time you hit me, I'm going to remember. And when the time comes, I'm going to fucking pay you back for every one of those slaps you love to dole out." I walk past her, ramming into her shoulder so hard that she stumbles into Justin's girlfriend.

"You fucking bitch!" she screams from behind me, and passersby turn to stare. "I should have aborted you!"

I keep walking to my bike as if I haven't heard her. I unlock it, holding myself stiff, and it's only once I've biked around the corner that I climb back off and crumple to the ground.

That *sticks and stones* saying is bullshit. Words are the worst kind of pain because they're the kind that never fucking leave. It doesn't matter what I claim to the world: the things my mother has said, the things Justin has said—I carry all those words like a stain, and I already know it'll never wash away.

I seethe—at all of them and at everything that's happened —but when my tears finally dry, I feel the start of something else, something quiet and hopeful. Because as terrible as it all is, it's also beautiful.

Someone finally took my side. Someone knows what happened and took my side.

It allows for the possibility that I can be stained and *poisonous* but, someday, be loved in spite of it. It almost feels like I already am.

15

NOW

With the drywall up, Luke starts helping me prime the walls.

We work in different rooms and barely see each other, but when we do, I can sense him trying to understand. He has a thousand legitimate reasons to hate me, but now there's one small reason not to, and he can't make those competing truths line up. I wish he'd just stop trying.

When we run out of primer, Donna asks us to go get some together. She's been in the dining room sorting photos all day, and I open my mouth to suggest we don't both need to go, or that perhaps *she* could go and I could work on the photos...but the look on her face silences me. She still believes the two of us can cure each other even though Luke and I barely speak and are rarely civil when we do, and I doubt I can convince her otherwise.

We drive to the hardware store in town, saying nothing to each other for most of the trip, but just as we park, he turns to me. "How much of what you made at the diner went to feeding me?"

I force a laugh as I open my door. "Believe me, I no longer need the money if you're feeling like you need to pay me back."

His hand lands on my forearm. "Why didn't you tell me?"

I shrug him off, climbing from the car. "You're making a big deal out of nothing. You looked like you were starving to death. No matter how evil you think I am, I'm not a fan of watching starvation in progress."

"Then take a look in the mirror," he mutters from behind.

Ha fucking ha, Luke.

I sigh in relief when we enter the quiet hardware store, taking in the empty aisles. Other than the guy at the register, no one even seems to know me. Luke gets the primer and I get more drop cloths. He insists on paying though I probably earn more than he does.

We're loading it all in the trunk when the click of a camera hits my ear. Some dumb kid has his iPhone raised, and he hasn't even had time to lower his arm before Luke's closed the distance and is towering over him.

"Delete it," Luke snaps.

"You can't make me delete that," the kid replies. "We're in a public place. It's legal."

I've got to give him credit...it takes balls or a rich father to stand there spouting off about your rights when a guy Luke's size looms over you.

"I don't give a shit whether it was legal or not. I'm not *letting you* take a picture without her permission. Delete it."

The kid tries to move the phone to his pocket, but Luke is faster. He snatches it away and walks into the street, slinging it into a storm drain. "Problem solved."

The kid mutters under his breath as Luke returns to the car.

"You didn't need to do that," I say quietly.

His shoulders sag, as if disappointed in himself. He can't stop defending me, even now.

For everyone's sake, though, I really wish he would.

THAT NIGHT, after dinner, Donna pulls us to the dining room table. "Look at these photos I found. I don't know if you even remember, but the local paper did a story about the surfers at Long Point and gave me hard copies."

In the first photo—the one they published—I stand between Danny and Luke, all three of us in swimsuits, the breeze blowing our hair. Danny is smiling at the camera, and I'm looking at Luke. I know exactly how I felt in that moment: that I couldn't *not* to look at him, *not* step a little closer. I would capitalize on the moments when no one was watching, then inhale him in large, desperate gulps.

It's how I still feel. When I see his arm reach for something, it's a struggle not to reach out, too, not to let my fingers trace the veins in his hand, in his forearm. When he takes a seat, it's a struggle not to press my lips to the top of his head and see if his hair still smells like salt and that shampoo he always used. When he walks into a room, I'm fighting not to walk straight to him, as if magnetized, and let my head rest against his chest.

I'm fighting every bit as hard as I did then to hide what I feel. I just didn't realize until this moment that I used to be so... bad at it. I wonder if I still am.

Luke slides out a photo from beneath the top one, and goose bumps crawl along my arms. Danny and I are smiling at the camera, and Luke is looking at me—exactly the way I was looking at him.

Jesus, does Donna really not see it? Did Danny not see it? It's so fucking obvious what existed there. If they'd just figured it out, this whole disaster could have been avoided. I'd simply be Danny's teenage girlfriend, the one no one keeps track of anymore, the one he was well rid of.

And Luke and I...I don't know. I don't know what we could

have been. All those *could-have-beens*—for Danny, for me, for Luke—they threaten to crush me, over and over again.

"I think I'll go to bed," I whisper, and Donna pats my hand, giving me credit for the wrong kind of sadness.

I manage to brush my teeth and strip off my clothes before the tears start. In the darkness I weep and wonder how it is that after all this time, nothing has changed. I'm still crying over the wrong guy. I'm still feeling like I will die without him.

I'm woken by my door as it opens. The wood floor creaks loudly beneath Luke's feet as he approaches in nothing but a pair of pajama pants. I suck in air at the sight of him—at his well-honed muscles, broad shoulders, and the way his pants hang off narrow hips.

Our eyes meet and my heart hammers, but I can't look away.

It was never like this with Danny, a burning in my veins. I feel stretched thin waiting for something I can't allow to happen, and the burning continues, grows, making me feverish and blind with it. By the time he finally reaches the bed, I am so strung out, so needy, that I'm past saying no. Incapable of it.

His nostrils flare as he takes me in, as if he hates me or himself for what's about to happen.

I don't care if you hate me, Luke. Just don't stop. Don't walk away.

He climbs onto the bed, caging me in—a forearm planted on each side of my head. And then his mouth lowers, hard on mine, as if no time has passed at all. His kiss is all heat, his tongue seeking, his hand threading through my hair.

He smells just like he always did, that combination of skin and soap and sand that was always his alone. I breathe deep, wishing I could save this forever, wanting everything to slow and also to move faster before one of us is stricken by our consciences.

Luke lifts himself just enough to pull away the sheet that

separates us. His erection presses to my abdomen, his hard chest bearing down. His hand slides beneath my camisole, spreads itself wide over my bare skin, climbing upward, cupping one breast, squeezing and pinching my nipple, forcing a small cry from my throat.

He pulls the camisole down to expose me, and his mouth follows, tugging and sucking while I arch against him, silently begging for more but unwilling to ask for it.

I don't need to ask; he knows me better than I know myself.

He reaches down and removes my shorts, grazing a single finger between my legs then slipping it inside. A rough exhale pushes past his lips at the feel of me, wet and tight, gripping him.

I shove his shorts down just low enough for him to spring free, and then he is against me, rubbing against my damp heat. I say nothing, just meet his gaze, and that's enough. He knew the answer would be yes. It was *yes* from the moment he walked in the diner ten years ago, long before I realized it, and nothing has changed.

He thrusts inside me and groans. *"Jules."*

It's been so long since he called me that.

Pulling out, he then pushes back in, each thrust rougher and harder than the one before it, with his hands palming my ass, spreading me wide to take more of him.

God, I've missed this. His weight, his smell, the fullness of him inside me, the way it's nearly too much. My hands go to his hair, dig into his back. I claw at him, arching to get closer, urging him to move faster. There's no one to stop us but we might just stop ourselves. We *should* be stopping ourselves.

He complies, giving me everything, stifling his grunts against my neck, our bodies slick with sweat. I gasp hard as it clicks inside me, as my muscles clamp down on him and heat shoots through me.

"I'm—" is all I manage before I come so hard, so unexpectedly, that it makes the rest of the world go silent. I'm blind, deaf, mute, only vaguely aware of those few sharp thrusts he makes as he follows me, sinking his teeth into my shoulder as he comes.

His weight sags as he collapses, crushing me beneath him, and I relish it. I want this, I want the smothering wholeness of him. I want to stay like this forever.

Luke rolls to the side and pulls me into him, pressing my face to his chest and wrapping his arms around me. It's all I've wanted for years and years, and this could have been us if I hadn't fucked everything up. But I did, and none of it can be fixed now. I'm going to have to say goodbye to him all over again in a few weeks.

I thought it might kill me before. Now, I'm not sure how it possibly *couldn't* kill me.

Tears slip down my face and my shoulders shake. "I think you should leave now," I whisper.

He freezes, and there's a flash of pain—pain I've seen in the past—before his expression turns absolutely flat.

After climbing from the bed, he leaves without a word.

I hurt him. It's probably for the best.

16

THEN

MAY 2014

My final months of school feel especially anticlimactic. Hailey isn't going away to college either—the only school she applied to was in LA, to be near her boyfriend, and she didn't get in—but everyone else is. They come to class in their college sweatshirts. Girls compare bedspreads they've picked for their dorm rooms and share rumors about what's to come, and it's as if everyone around me has an engine they've just started, but when I turn the key in mine, it simply clicks once, then dies.

I have failed to launch. Eighteen seems too young to be deemed a failure, but no one even asks what I've got planned. They already expected little from me, or nothing at all.

I've taken vocational tests online, and every single career choice sounds more dismal than the one before it. I like music, but I don't want to be a music teacher. *Symphony fundraising* was another, but I can't imagine enjoying either fundraising *or* the symphony. Even the tests themselves are grasping at straws, saying, *"This girl isn't qualified for anything...just make some shit up."* I'm hoping I'll have enough saved by August to get a room somewhere, but that's the extent of my plans.

"Not everyone goes to college," Danny soothes when we talk. "Maybe you're just meant to be a wife and a mom."

The low rumble of Luke's voice hits my ear like a gift. "She isn't."

"There's nothing wrong with being a wife and mom," Danny argues.

"No, but that isn't what she fucking wants from life. That's just what you want from *her*."

"That's not true," Danny replies before he clicks the door shut behind him.

I wonder if it's the last time I'll hear Luke's voice until next fall, but only a few days later, Donna is all smiles when I walk into the house. "I've got good news," she says. "Luke's coming for the summer."

The pastor is frowning, poking a tongue in his cheek. *Only good news to one of them, then.*

"That's great," I reply. My voice is muted, my smile forced, but it's not because I share the pastor's lack of enthusiasm. It's because inside me a spark has blazed into a wildfire. I'm ecstatic, ebullient, joyful; my heart races and I can't reveal so much as a hint of it without revealing it all.

I wonder what changed Luke's mind.

I SKIP MY GRADUATION. It wouldn't feel like much of a celebration to me anyway, but mostly I'm worried my stepbrothers will show up and cause trouble.

On the night the guys are due back, I bike home from the diner. They surfed somewhere to the south on the way up, and they're still in the garage pulling their stuff from Luke's Jeep when I pedal inside, soaked to the bone from the rain that started halfway home. I prop my bike against the garage wall, looking like a drowned rat, and my gaze goes past Danny and straight to Luke. It's an effort not to take in huge sips of him—his dark hair wet, pushed off his face but for a single errant strand, his eyes gleaming in the evening light.

Danny hugs me gingerly since I'm wet. "I'd have picked you up if you'd texted me."

"That's okay," I tell him, wiping off my arms with a paper towel. "I had to bring the bike home anyway."

Luke frowns. A year ago, I'd have assumed he resented Danny's care or the mere idea of being forced to come get me. Now, I'm not sure what I think.

Over dinner, the boys talk about school, though Danny has more to say than Luke. The only time Luke really comes alive is when they discuss surfing. He went somewhere near Cabo for spring break, chasing another big wave. He also entered several competitions this spring and won each of them. It's clear school is an afterthought for him at this point.

"You need to enter Santa Cruz this summer," says Danny.

"There's no way," Luke replies, his shoulders sagging as he stabs his fork into his pork chop. "My board is garbage, and it's a much more competitive field."

"Luke, I hope you're paying a fraction of attention to the actual reason you're *in* San Diego," the pastor intones. "You can't make a living off playing in the water."

"Kelly Slater makes three million a year," I say before I can stop myself.

Everyone looks at me in surprise. Even *I'm* surprised. I never, ever, argue in this house.

The pastor's mouth tightens. "I assume he's a surfer, Juliet, but you've only proven my point: he's the exception, not the rule, and I've never even heard of him."

For a fraction of a second, Luke's gaze meets mine. An entire unspoken conversation occurs between us, one in which Luke tells me not to bother arguing on his behalf, and I tell him I refuse to let the pastor crap all over his dreams. We're silently bickering again, just like last summer, except this time we're looking out for each other. We're defending each other against *them*.

We'd be far better off if things would just go back to the way they were.

That night we go to the beach and meet the same crew we hung out with last year—Harrison, Caleb, Beck, their assorted girlfriends and two other guys, Liam and Ryan.

Libby and Grady come too. It's good to have Libby back from school but I can't say the same of Grady—now that he's graduated and is about to begin his internship with the pastor, he's even more uptight and judgmental than he was. I still don't understand why he even wants to be out here, listening to them talk about surfing.

Danny tells everyone he's certain he'll start this year because the first-string quarterback just graduated. They are kind in response, politely enthusiastic, but Luke is the one they want to discuss.

"Forget about football," says Harrison. "Forget about college too. You need to start entering the bigger competitions. Like the WSL stuff. That'll get you sponsors."

Luke shrugs. "It's too expensive. The guys who enter the best WSL meets each have four good boards and are spending about fifty grand a year on travel. I don't have fifty grand to spend on something I *hope* might work out. I don't even have fifty grand for something I *know* will work out."

Except...there is nothing he would love more than to surf professionally. And what could be better than having a career you love so much you'd do it for free?

"Start a GoFundMe campaign," I suggest quietly.

"I'm not sure Luke's desire to *surf* counts as a charitable donation, Juliet," Grady says with a derisive laugh, but no one laughs with him.

"There are lots of Go Fund Me's that aren't for charity,"

argues Caleb.

Grady rolls his eyes. "He's not making fifty grand that way."

I glare at him. "He might at least get enough to buy the surf-boards and pay some entry fees. It would be a start. I suppose your suggestion would be that he just *prays* for the money?"

"Juliet!" Danny scolds softly.

Luke's gaze holds mine, the fire reflecting in his eyes. He raises a brow. *"You won't stand up for yourself but you'll stand up for me,"* that look says.

"Yes," I reply silently. *"Get used to it."*

I SING ON SUNDAY MORNING, but the second the service is over, Donna and I hightail it back to the house to get ready for a visit from Aaron Tomlinson, the head of the state church council. She tells the boys to go surfing so they stay out of our hair, and I struggle not to be irritated that I'm the only one who has to help.

Mr. Tomlinson arrives early in the evening, right after the boys get home—a pale man with chubby hands and a fake smile, driving a Ford Taurus that's seen better days. He seems just as impressed with himself, however, as Donna and the pastor are with him.

Over dinner, he grills the pastor about his plans for the church and the services he offers the community. He grills Donna about how she spends her day and ponders whether she might be able to carve out more time to run a church women's club if she spent less time on the garden.

I want to choke the guy with my bare hands long before he turns to me.

"And what about you, Juliet? The Allens gave you an amazing opportunity, removing you from your home the way they did. Surely you don't plan to squander it."

My cheeks heat. I didn't realize, until this moment, that Mr. Tomlinson knew about my past. I thought I was here as Danny's *girlfriend*, not as some bad-girl-made-good. Donna winces, staring at her plate, but it's Luke I notice most. His eyes are narrowed and he's gripping his fork so tight it's putting Donna's flatware at risk

"I'm taking classes at the community college this fall," I finally reply.

"Yes, dear," he says, "but what is your *plan*? Surely you don't intend to continue depending on the pastor's charity for the rest of your life?"

Luke's hand lands on the table so heavily we all jump. Everyone dismisses it, as if it was an accident, but I suspect—based on that locked jaw of his—it was not.

"We love having Juliet here," Donna says, her voice ringing with sincerity. "If it were up to me, she would stay forever."

"But what about the mission you talked about opening in Central America?" he asks. "You've talked about that plan for a decade."

I look up from my plate. I knew Donna had vaguely discussed the possibility of one day opening a mission somewhere. I didn't know it was a certainty.

Donna gives him a diplomatic smile, accompanied by a small shrug. "We're still young. There's time for all that later. Besides, we wouldn't want to go until Danny was out of school. It's going to take all of us to make this work."

My mouth falls open as I look from her to Danny. She thinks he'd go with them? Is that what he thinks too?

It's the oddest thing, but the idea of them leaving doesn't fill me with fear—it fills me with light. If the Allens are leaving, then I could leave...*them*. That plan, the one that's been percolating in the back of my head for months, suddenly becomes a possibility. I'm not even sure I knew it was percolating there, until this moment.

I've been claiming to anyone who will listen that I've got no clue what I want to do with my life. Maybe I had a clue after all...I just couldn't see how to make room for it.

Mr. Tomlinson returns to me, unaware or perhaps just ambivalent about the chaos he has brought to the table. "That, my dear, is why you need some kind of long-range plan. You need to create a goal for yourself beyond *community college*."

It's impossible to miss the slight disdain in his voice, as if he already knows I won't be making anything of myself, as if he already knows that I'm never going to get this degree—one he clearly considers worthless anyhow.

"I've been thinking about moving to LA," I reply. It feels like a lie—it's not as if I *seriously* thought about it. It was a dream, not so different from my dreams of attending Hogwarts when I was small. But maybe the only difference between a dream and a plan is how committed you are to making it happen. "Once I save enough money, I mean. What I'd really like to do is sing."

Luke's gaze meets mine. His eyes blaze with something...hopeful?

"But, Juliet, you don't have to go all the way to LA to do that," Donna says, a hint of desperation in her voice. "You can stay right here. Get a degree in music and teach at the high school."

I picture it: me in a beige skirt and cheap flats, leading a bunch of apathetic teens through scales and tepid acapella versions of pop songs.

"*That* is an excellent idea," says Mr. Tomlinson.

They think LA is a childish dream, one that will leave me homeless, playing guitar on a street corner and begging for change.

"She doesn't want to teach," Luke says between his teeth. "She wants to sing." He stares at his plate, but it feels like his anger is directed at Donna, the last person who deserves it.

"They're right," I say quietly, because I can't stand to hear

Donna criticized, even subtly. "LA is probably a pipe dream. I need a back-up plan."

Donna smiles and reaches out to cover my hand with hers, rewarding me for saying the right thing. It's a little pat on the head, and like the child I am, I relish it.

Except...Luke was right. And if I were braver, if I were brave like him, I would have told them all the truth.

Later that night, after Tomlinson is gone and the kitchen is clean, Danny and I sit on the front porch, alone for the first time all day. "Did you realize your mom assumes you'll move to Central America with them?" I ask.

He shrugs. I guess that's a *yes*. "I mean, it's not like I'm gonna play pro ball. It might be okay, you know? My mom wants to open a school there too. It'll take a while, but eventually...I could teach business and you could teach music. We wouldn't have a lot of money, but I don't guess we'd need it, either. Everything's cheap down there, and we could probably grow a lot of our own food."

I stare at him. The life he's describing is plucked straight from a children's cartoon, the kind where coconuts fall from the sky when you're hungry and bananas rain down by the barrel. Kids in some third-world village aren't going to want to take fucking *business* classes or learn how to play "Jingle Bells" on a guitar.

"Danny...I'm not sure I want to teach. I think I want to perform. Like, create my own stuff."

"You know how many people want that and fail?" he asks. "There are lots of ways you can perform without moving to LA, but the odds of you going there and it all working out are probably worse than your odds of winning the lottery."

I don't argue with him because he's right. But I also know Luke would say that if I want to play the lottery, I should fucking play the lottery, because it's my life, not Danny's.

"I JUST SEATED YOU," says Stacy. "He asked for your section."

My head jerks toward the tables in the corner, to where Luke is sitting by himself, his hair still damp from a morning in the water.

He's studying the menu, and something about the sight of him there, so big and alone, does a weird thing to my heart. It's a tiny pinch of emptiness, but I sense an abyss somewhere beyond it, somewhere I don't want to look.

I'd assume he was in my section by accident if I hadn't been told otherwise.

His gaze lands on me as I approach, in that way it always does, as if I'm something deadly he can't allow out of his sight. Not a single muscle in his face moves otherwise. No smile, no hint of anything. Just those eyes of his, always watching.

"Hey," I say, swallowing my nerves. I lean my hip against the table, the only hint that he isn't a regular customer. I want to thank him for taking up for me the other night, and I want to apologize for what I said in response. It's just all locked up in my throat.

He looks back at the menu. "What's good?"

This is so weird. *Why are you here, Luke? Why are you in my section when you mostly seem to wish I was elsewhere?* I don't voice my questions, mostly because there's some strange part of me that doesn't want him to leave. That wants the next twenty or thirty minutes to just gaze at him, big shoulders hunched over as he wolfs down a solitary meal.

"All of it if you like meat and potatoes," I reply. "None of it if you hope to live past fifty." I give him a nervous grin.

He doesn't offer one back, but instead continues to stare at the menu. "The number four, please."

"Coffee?"

He shakes his head. "Water's fine."

I suspect he'd like coffee and is trying to save money. I suspect he'd like a whole extra meal. He was in the water for hours this morning. If he was my friend, I could ask him. But he's not my friend and he's made that clear.

I take his menu and put in his order. Every time I glance over, he's watching me, and he looks so hungry and alone that I finally can't stand it. I swipe him a Danish and bring it over with coffee and juice.

"I didn't order this," he says.

"You look hungry," I reply, already scurrying away. "It's on the house."

He says nothing as I refill his coffee, his juice, and deliver his meal. He just watches me and doesn't say a word until I drop the bill on his table.

He pulls out his wallet. "Don't listen to Donna. You don't want to fucking teach."

He rises from the booth without another word and walks away to pay at the register before his big frame edges through the door like GI Joe in a miniature dollhouse.

The restaurant feels emptier without him in it. I reach down to grab his plate. He's left a tip under it equal to the size of his bill. I put it in my other pocket, away from the rest of my money, as if it's special.

IT WOULD HAVE BEEN easy enough to casually bring up Luke's visit to Danny—*Luke got seated in my section this morning*. It would have been easy enough for Luke to bring it up too— *Stopped by your girlfriend's place of employment, this morning. The food there sucks*.

Yet neither of us do.

By the end of the week, I'm wondering if I read too much into it. I pull that twenty he left out of my dog-eared copy of

Wuthering Heights and stare at it as if I might find a hidden message in its folds.

Maybe the question I should be asking isn't if I read too much into it. It's *why* I read too much into it, and what was I hoping it meant? Better yet, I should be thinking about what he actually said: *Ignore Donna.* It's just...she makes it so hard. Her love, her investment in me, is like a warm coat you continue to wear indoors on a winter day. I can't bring myself to shrug it off, even when I know I'll just wind up colder in the long run. And every time I think about shrugging it off, she leans over and zips me up with her most loving smile.

"I've got some good news for you, Juliet," she says over dinner. "I spoke to Miss Engelman. She teaches at an elementary school down in Santa Cruz. She said she can set up an internship for you there next year, assisting the music teacher."

She beams at me as if she's given me a gift, which makes me feel like I've missed something important. "An internship? Is it...paid?"

She frowns. "Well, no, it's not paid. But if you're living here, you don't really need the job, do you? And Miss Engelman said there are actually scholarships for school employees. Once you've been there for a while you might be able to get them to cover some of your classes."

I know I'm supposed to be grateful, but all I hear is *I've arranged for you to work full-time, for free. You don't need anything of your own because we've got you covered.* It leaves me wanting to press my face deep into my plate and cry.

Across the table, Luke's gaze meets mine, and something clenches deep in my stomach. He's the only person in this house who'd think I was right to be upset. He may be the only person in this house, and maybe this state, who really gets me at all. And that should scare me, but it doesn't. It's just such a fucking relief to have someone understand.

17

NOW

I wake alone. The sun is pouring through the windows and the smell of coffee wafts toward me. I wonder, for just a moment, if last night was a dream. But there is an ache between my legs that is unmistakable.

God. How did that happen? What was I thinking?

But I *wasn't* thinking, and that's the problem. I just spread my legs for him like a fucking whore. He didn't even have to ask.

Donna sits at the table alone, reading the paper. "Well, good morning, sleepyhead," she says. "Luke is painting outside. Good day for it. Not too hot."

I pour my coffee, barely able to meet her eye. How could I have done that, last night, in her home? In Danny's home?

"I have an interview," I reply. "I've got to get cleaned up."

Get cleaned up and avoid Luke, both. I have no idea how I'm going to face him now.

"*New York Times* or something else?" she asks.

I give a small shake of my head. "Some dumb paper I've never heard of." *One of the ones Hilary set up*, I don't add. I don't like Hilary and I don't trust her motivations, nor do I trust her to run Danny's House when Donna's not around to monitor things...but who the hell am I to judge anyone's motivations? No matter how bad Hilary is, she isn't as bad as me.

"If you need anything in town, just give me a list," I tell her. Hopefully this will postpone another of her forced trips with Luke for a day or two.

She smiles at me over her coffee. "Great. Can you check on Luke before you go and make sure he doesn't need anything too?"

Dammit. I was hoping to avoid him. Given the way I told him to leave last night, maybe it goes without saying that what we did won't be happening again. But if I'm wrong about that, I'm not ready to deal with it now.

I walk out the back door and cut across the yard to find him painting the left wall of the garage. For a moment, I lose track of why I'm out here at all, watching the muscles flex in his back as he leans over the ladder, his arms tan and capable. I think of his weight on mine last night, the huff of his breath against my neck as he pushed inside me, the way his hands bruised my hips. I never, ever, want to forget.

When I jolt myself back to the present, I know I've been standing here too long. It's not like it matters—he's ignoring me, his specialty. Maybe nothing needs to be said. Maybe he just wanted to see if he could still get some and wasn't planning to try again anyway.

I clear my throat. "Donna wants to know if you need anything in town."

He sets the brush in the paint tray and turns. His eyes are completely lifeless, as if I'm inanimate, something that simply happens to be in his field of vision, something he won't even remember he saw.

"Nope." He turns away and starts painting again.

We're back to hating each other. Good. That's just as it should be.

~

I'm a little on edge as I head to today's interview. I moved the location to a run-down tiki hut out at the beach, ten miles south. It's not about keeping everyone in town from thinking the *wrong* thing about me but about keeping them from thinking of me at all.

If I could magically wipe their memories clear of me, I would.

There are miles and miles of untouched shore here, long beaches, the waves crashing in the distance. Surfers dot the water—black wetsuit-clad specks—the entire way. Of course it makes me think of Luke, but then...everything does. How could I have allowed last night to happen? Who could that have served? And why the hell would Luke even want me after everything that's passed?

I park and trudge through the sand to the mostly empty bar. The reporter is male, my age or younger, in khakis and a polo shirt and the only person here who isn't barefoot. His hand is clammy as it clasps mine in a polite greeting, and he can barely meet my eye. An interview like this is unheard of for a paper the size of his, and I suspect he's a nervous wreck, which is why I forgive him for dredging up the same old questions everyone seems to ask: *What's it like? What's next? What made you you?*

I offer him my standard one-two combo of partial truths and outright lies. But today, the lies I tell are more of a struggle. Luke has shaken something loose inside me. He's unlocked the safe place where I store my memories of the things that matter, and those memories are entirely of him: his smell of sand and salt and soap, his weight and that look in his eyes, always asking me to let him in and assuming there's something worth caring for inside me.

The kid fumbles with his notes. "I've read that you got

started singing in a church choir. It's a pretty unusual place to start, given the songs you sing now."

The hint of sarcasm in his voice sets my teeth on edge.

I raise a brow. "Was there a question in there?"

My publicist would scold me, but I didn't want to do this interview in the first place, so fuck it, and who gives a shit if *The Sunny Day Times* claims I was defensive? I'm so sick of the implication that I was once doing something *right* before and no longer am.

"Sorry," he says, glancing at his notes. "I was hoping you could give me a little insight into what led you from singing in a church choir to singing about, I don't know, cocaine and oral sex."

I smirk. "Well, I wouldn't have minded singing about cocaine and oral sex back then either, but the church wasn't really a fan of it."

He laughs. I expect him to move on but he doesn't. "So what got you started? What got you outside of the church to sing?"

If he actually did his research, he probably already knows the answer to this, or at least the answer that I have provided many times: that I sent out some recordings and about a year later, a producer finally replied.

But Luke has opened the box, and the truth—the beautiful and painful truth—is spilling like a stain inside me.

I didn't just send out some recordings. The reason any of this happened was because once upon a time, someone wanted to put me first. I can let that much be known, even if I never say his name.

"A boy gave me a microphone," I reply.

18

THEN

JUNE 2014

Two days after Donna tells me about the internship she's gotten me, the one that will have me staying with them for another year, Luke shows up in my section again. He shouldn't be here, and I shouldn't want to stay right by his side while he is.

I arrive at his table with coffee and juice and a bagel before he's said a word. They're all I can give him for free, and even the bagel might be a problem. I'll pay for it if Charlie notices.

He smells like sunscreen, and the saltwater drying in his hair gives it a little curl. There's something inside him that seems to glow after he's spent the morning surfing, something that makes me want to be near him even more than I already do.

"How were the waves?"

"Knee high and glassy." There's a tiny glint of humor in his eyes. He surfs at Long Point in the mornings when Danny isn't around, and Long Point has not had a *"knee high and glassy"* morning since the beginning of time. They're double overhead on their worst day, the water churned up and unpredictable thanks to competing breezes.

I smile. "Sure it was. I guess you're not hungry at all, then."

His eyes flicker from the menu to my face, his mouth almost twitching. "I could probably eat."

I laugh. Luke *"could probably eat"* if he'd just cleaned out a buffet. Luke *"could probably eat"* if he'd just finished fourths on Thanksgiving.

"Same as last time?" I ask.

For a fraction of a second our gaze locks. By referencing the fact that he's been in before, I've referenced that we've kept it a secret. I'm admitting I remember what he ordered, and I probably shouldn't remember.

Something softens in his face. "Yeah. Same as last time."

We haven't done anything wrong, but as I put in his order—two eggs over easy, bacon, sourdough—I know I should end this. I know I should return with a stack of pancakes and act as if his last visit meant nothing to me, that it didn't manage to imprint itself in any way and that the tip he left isn't still hiding dead in the center of *Wuthering Heights*. But I wouldn't do that to him, even if I wanted to. Luke is like me—he's alone in ways the people around us are not. The Allens might claim to love us, but they aren't family. They can turn against us without blinking an eye if we displease them. I want Luke to know that I see him, that I'm in his corner, that I won't turn against him no matter what happens after this.

When his food's ready, I set it in front of him like a gift. *I remember you were here. I remember every word you've ever said. I see you.*

"Do you get to eat?" His tone is devoid of inflection as if he's asking a question that doesn't matter at all, that doesn't matter enough to even be asked.

Is he asking if I'm free? If I can sit down with him now? I'm not sure.

I sigh. "Yeah, but only later, once it's slow."

"Don't take that internship."

Something sags inside me. "Donna went to a lot of trouble to make it happen. I feel like I have to."

His lip curls. "Exactly how much trouble did she go to for that internship you never implied in any way you wanted? She knows you don't want to teach. *She* wants you to teach. More to the point, she wants to make sure you stay nice and safe in her home, waiting for her son to come back and claim you."

"You're making her sound evil and she's not."

He runs a hand over his face. "I don't doubt she thinks she's got your best interests at heart. But she doesn't care what you want from your life. She's decided it for you, and she's guilted you into accepting it. She just told you to quit your fucking job, the one that might get you a little independence, and go work full-time for *free*, Juliet. Do you really think that's entirely altruistic, or do you think maybe a part of her is scared of what happens when you don't need them anymore? Because I am fucking sure that's a factor, no matter what she says to you or herself."

I swallow. "Donna isn't like that. And she's probably right. It turns out badly for most people."

"If everyone stopped trying to do shit other people had failed at, we'd still be cooking over fire and wishing wheels existed. Whatever. I got you something." He reaches to his right and hands me a small package. "It's a mic. It attaches to your phone."

I have no clue why he'd give me this or what I'd use it for. "Oh, uh...thanks." I sound more confused than grateful.

"I thought you could use it to record yourself singing. I looked it up. People have gotten discovered just by sending in their home recordings, and that mic is supposed to have better sound quality than the rest."

Five seconds ago, the package in my hand seemed weird and mostly meaningless. Now, it's as if he's handed me something priceless beyond measure. Not simply because he believes in me, in my ability to become something when no one else believes the same, but that he cares enough to show up here and insist on it.

I blink back tears. "I love it," I rasp. "Thank you."

"Don't thank me." He picks up his fork and stabs it into an egg yolk. "*Use* it."

I'm the one who sets up the GoFundMe for Luke. He tells me no one's going to donate but I'm hoping he's wrong. If we can just get him a few good boards—two decent shortboards and a board for big waves—that might be good enough. There's a pretty big contest in Santa Cruz this summer and everyone thinks he'd have a shot. Maybe he'll get some attention, get a sponsor or two, and build from there.

The pastor drones on at dinner about what Luke might do with a business degree—marketing, or car sales. He thinks *I* might qualify to work at a preschool later on, once I have this year of interning under my belt.

There's nothing wrong with what he suggests. It's just not what either of us wants. My gaze meets Luke's.

"*Just because they say it,*" his eyes tell me, "*doesn't mean we have to listen.*"

I smile in response. He's right.

19

NOW

I lie in bed waiting for the sound of his footfall against the wood, for the sigh of the mattress as his knee sinks into it. When he arrives, I'll tell him to leave. I will. Even if it's the last thing I want to do.

But I fall asleep waiting, and when the bed sighs and his weight is above me, I'm somehow unable to form the words I need to form. I want him to stop and I don't want him to stop, and it's only as my eyes fly open that I realize I'm alone.

I'm relieved and I'm empty, all at the same time.

For two days and two nights we avoid each other, and by the third night I'm *praying* for the sound of his feet. All night I dream of the floorboards creaking as he approaches, the rasp of his breath as he comes. I wake each day with my body on fire, the sheets twisted between my legs, devastated that he isn't coming back to me.

I'm angry at him for making me want him this way, and desperate for the sight of him anyhow.

Donna smiles when I walk into the kitchen. "He's surfing." I guess it's obvious I was looking for him. "You know our boy. He can't stay away from the water for long."

Tears sting as I turn away from her. I don't know how she can say those words after what happened to Danny. If I were her, I'd have moved as far from the ocean as possible, trying to forget, trying to pretend it doesn't exist. How can she drive down the coastal road without remembering? Because I can't.

"I think I'll take over painting the garage," I tell her.

"You sure, hon? I don't like you on that tall ladder."

I laugh. "But you didn't argue with Luke on that ladder, did you?"

She waves a hand at me. "He's Luke."

Because if that ladder fell, he'd grab onto a gutter and swing himself Tarzan-style to safety, or somehow ride the ladder as it descended and roll away at the last moment. He does things you wouldn't imagine were possible until you witnessed them yourself.

"I'll be fine," I tell her. "If you had to be a world-class athlete to climb a ladder, there'd be a lot of unpainted houses."

I go outside and gather supplies from the garage. I bang my shin simply by carrying the ladder, and the paint's so heavy that I have an angry red line across my palm by the time I've gotten it across the yard.

Then I climb, and all that cockiness with Donna dies a quick death.

It requires a surprising degree of coordination to climb a ladder while carrying a heavy can of paint in one hand and a brush and paint pan in the other. When I finally make it, sloppily pouring paint into the tray, I nearly dump the whole pan onto the ground and barely catch it. I begin with too much paint on the brush and as it drips down the wall, I sigh heavily. *Goddammit, Luke. Why do you make everything look so easy?*

It takes about twenty minutes to relax and find my rhythm, to decide I sort of enjoy the mindlessness of painting. The temperature outside is perfect—the sun warm on my arms, the breeze cool. I picture Luke out on the water right now, jogging his board forward to increase his speed as he cuts through the waves, making every trick look ridiculously easy to the dumb kids watching.

Thoughts of him are normally painful, but for some reason this one isn't. I picture him happy, and my mind allows itself to empty at last. I start humming and I know that it will eventually be a song about him—most of mine are—but it's been a while since I've felt so alive in the creation. It doesn't feel distant, for once.

The slam of the screen door knocks me from my reverie. I jolt, dropping the paint brush. The ladder rocks as I reach for it, the paint can above me wobbles, and suddenly I'm no longer on the ladder at all, but flying backward toward the ground.

Somehow, though, I land safely in Luke's arms, his body tight around mine as he absorbs the blow. I land on top of him, blinking in shock.

His breath is on my neck and my heart is pounding at twice its normal rate. I know it was an accident and yet it somehow feels like I wanted it to happen. Like my subconscious did it on purpose.

He runs a hand over my back. "You okay?"

"Yeah." I exhale shakily. "Thanks."

He releases me and I clumsily right myself and climb off him.

He pinches the bridge of his nose. "Jesus Christ, Juliet. You could have broken your back. Let me handle the climbing from now on." His chest rises and falls rapidly, like he just finished a sprint.

Luke, who's never scared, was scared for me.

I don't want it to affect me, but he's already shaken a little more of the past loose. Enough to be dangerous.

∼

THAT NIGHT his footsteps echo in the hall and falter outside my door. I silently will him to enter, to be the guilty party so I don't have to be. But his steps continue on, and a moment later his door shuts behind him.

I remain in place another five minutes, but when the decision is made, I stop thinking entirely. I can't get to him fast enough, outrunning the doubts that will come if I give them a chance.

I try his handle, wondering if he'll have locked it, but it turns easily in my hand.

He's on his back, with his arms folded beneath his head, his eyes heavy-lidded—but not with sleep—as if he was waiting for this.

He watches me approach, and when I get close enough, he moves fast, his hand coming from behind his head, reaching out to wrap around my waist as he pulls me on top of him. I feel his low groan as much as I hear it.

He slides his fingers through my hair, pulling my mouth to his.

He smells like soap and salt, his chest damp with sweat though the night is cool. His cock is a thick steel rod between us, ready long before this moment. Did he know I'd come, or has he just waited like this, night after night, the same way I've waited for him?

I run my tongue along his neck and reach for his boxers, pushing them down.

If this were different, if we were different, I'd slide down the bed and pull him into my mouth. I'd tease him and torture him until he was gasping, begging to come. But I can't. There's no time.

I slide my shorts to the side and work him inside me, biting my lip to stifle a gasp. I'm so full, for a moment, that it hurts to move. But it also hurts not to.

His hands grip my hips, pulling me up an inch and back.

Up two inches and back. He releases a small groan, desperate for more. "Jules. *Fuck*."

I brace my hands on his chest and begin to move, and his hands continue to grip my hips, slamming them against him, harder and harder, faster and faster.

We say nothing. I'd like to tell him how good it is, how it's never been like this with anyone else, but I don't.

I just dig my nails into his skin as I break, hoping this was enough to drive him out of my system so I can finally move on.

20

THEN

JULY 2014

He comes into the diner almost every morning now, and I wait for him. I wait for him like a child waiting on Santa. I wait like I've left my family behind to pan for gold in 1860 and he's my monthly letter from home.

I wait for him as if he means everything to me.

I have no idea what we're doing, but all that matters is the sight of him, ducking a little as he walks through the door, his eyes catching mine. There's a secret knowledge resting there. It feels good to be known, to be seen, to be believed in.

We have our routine. I bring him what I can for free, and also a Danish, which I pay for myself because Charlie caught me. I put in his order and ask how the waves were, and he lies and tells me there wasn't anything going on.

He walks in this morning, seeking me.

I grab a menu, not that he needs one, and start walking to a free table in my section. He follows.

I pour his coffee and his fingertips brush mine as he takes the cup. "You changed up that song you played last night. I like the new bridge."

I smile, suddenly shy. "Thanks."

I've stopped waiting for the house to empty to play my guitar. I have four songs now, songs I wrote mostly in my head before attempting them outside. I recorded them using the mic, too, though I haven't quite summoned the courage to send them out.

Danny seems slightly irked by the guitar playing, as if it's an embarrassing hobby he wishes I'd let go of. If he comes outside, it's mostly to see if I'm ready to leave. But Luke is out there often, and I only realize it when I hear the shuffle of feet as he goes back inside.

He isn't Donna, saying, *"Doesn't she sing like an angel?"* as if I'm a child who needs to be propped up because she has nothing else going for her. Luke's quiet words in the diner mean more than all the faint praise about my voice in church ever could. He understands how much the songs mean to me, songs Danny doesn't want to hear, and he's listening more carefully than anyone else ever has. He will never get a quiet pat on the back for who I've become. He just wants me to know I'm seen, that I'm worth watching.

I want him to know he's worth watching, too, but he's probably already figured that much out. I can barely look away when he enters the room.

~

IT'S RAINING when my shift ends. I walk outside to find Luke waiting in the Jeep. He tells me he just happened to be here.

"You didn't have to do this," I tell him. "I'm used to biking in the rain."

He hands me a towel from the back seat to dry my damp head. "You shouldn't have to get used to hard things, Jules."

Except he won't always be around. Whether I'm still in Rhodes or somewhere else, I'm going to have to fend for myself eventually.

He's silent as we start down the road, and then he glances at me. "My mom is like that." His voice is quieter than it was. "She was used to my dad being a drunk, and when she finally left, she married a guy who was worse, and I think it was mostly because he seemed so familiar. Another useless drunk."

"There's a pretty big difference between being someone who marries alcoholics and someone who's willing to bike home in the rain."

His mouth twitches. "I meant that she was used to hard things. I don't want you thinking it has to be like that too."

"Do you...still talk to them?" I bite my lip. "Sorry. You don't have to discuss it if you don't want."

"I'm an open book."

I laugh. "No one is less of an open book than you, Luke."

A smile flickers over his face. "For you, I'm an open book. And no, I don't still talk to them. But I have an older sister. I talk to her sometimes."

"I can't imagine you as anyone's little brother."

"Oh, believe me, I was. She still teases me about Mr. Maple, this stuffed animal I used to carry everywhere."

He's turned the heater on for me and the car is now cozy inside, the rhythmic back and forth of the wipers surprisingly soothing. "You named a stuffed animal Mr. Maple?"

His mouth twitches. "I'd spilled syrup on him."

I picture a little Luke, carrying a stuffed animal around by the ear in footie pajamas. I hate that the tiny version of him had to suffer.

"Do you miss them?"

He shrugs. "My mom, yeah, though I don't know why. You know what my last memory is of her? Her hunting under the couch for a tooth my stepfather knocked out. And then her taking his fucking side when I kicked his ass."

My heart aches. I know exactly how alone he must have felt because I lived it.

"I'm sorry," I whisper, letting my hand rest over the top of his for a moment before I pull it back. "Believe me, I know what it's like to have your mom take the wrong person's side."

He sighs. "Yeah, I figured. That's why you allowed yourself to wind up with the Allens."

We pull into the neighborhood—our ride is nearly over and I don't want it to be.

"How's the GoFundMe?" I ask, though I know. I check it every morning.

He slows as he turns onto the Allens' street. "Forty dollars. And most of that's from you."

"Not enough to buy four professional quality surfboards then?"

He grins. "They're like a grand apiece. So close, but not quite."

We pull into the driveway. He tips his chin toward the house. "Go inside so you don't get soaked. I'll get your bike."

"Then you'll get soaked."

"Better me than you." He frowns. "*I'm* not spending the next two hours cooking."

I hesitate and then smile, hoping it conveys everything I cannot say: *Thank you for taking my side, Luke. Thank you for putting me first. I wish I could do the same thing for you.*

And then it occurs to me that maybe I can.

THE GUYS we hang out with most nights are in a similar position to Luke and Danny: college kids, scraping by. Liam works construction like Luke does. Ryan works at a bar. But I suspect the prep school guys—Caleb, Harrison, and Beck—have loads of money. They *talk* like kids with money—they golf, they compare Park City to Telluride for skiing, they argue over whether Kauai or Maui is a better island—and Harrison drives a new BMW. It continually surprises me that I find them likable, but I do. They're kind to everyone, even Grady— ignoring him when he's being an uptight prick—and they cheer Luke on like a brother.

They could definitely afford to help Luke out, so once they're all gathered, I nervously, ostentatiously clear my throat. I'm glad Grady isn't present to hear me begging and admitting defeat.

"Luke needs new boards," I announce. "For the contest coming up."

Everyone blinks at me in surprise. I don't talk much, normally. "I thought you did a GoFundMe?" Caleb asks Luke.

"It wasn't successful," Luke replies, embarrassed. "Don't worry about it."

"You're making good money doing construction, right?" Beck asks. "You ought to be able to swing a decent shortboard, at least."

Luke gives a terse nod. "I have to use it to pay my living expenses during the school year. Seriously, it's cool. I'll be fine."

"No, you won't," I reply before I can stop myself. "You're at a disadvantage in every contest right now." I'm pushing too hard, but I don't give a shit; he needs those damn boards.

He glances at me, a look that asks me to let it go, and the other guys stare at us, perhaps surprised to see me lobbying on Luke's behalf when I mostly act like he doesn't exist.

I feel like an absolute idiot, but the next morning there's three grand from an anonymous donor in Luke's GoFundMe. And I'm pretty sure I'd suffer any amount of feeling like an idiot to see the look of pride on Luke's face a week later when he pulls the thousand-dollar Ghost he just bought out of the Jeep.

He runs a loving hand over the epoxy surface. "Isn't she beautiful?"

"So she's a *she*, huh?" I tease.

He grins. "The beautiful things always are."

We all go out to watch him surf on Saturday, and the difference in his performance is shocking. He's so much better than he was a year ago, and better still on the new board. He walks out of the water, grinning ear to ear, like a kid on Christmas morning with a toy that's wound up being even cooler than he ever imagined.

I'm the one he smiles at first as he walks out of the water. *"Your turn,"* that smile says. *"Send your recordings out."*

Maybe he's right. Maybe both of us can actually get out of here.

I'M ALONE in the backyard, trying to get a good recording of my new song, when Danny walks outside. He's had more free time this summer because he's getting in shape for football in the afternoons rather than surfing. I try not to be annoyed that he seems to think I should free up my time as well.

He takes a seat in the grass, listening, and there's nothing impatient in his demeanor, but I sense it anyway. Given he's never encouraged my music, it seems like a fair assumption. He's never even asked me about the microphone or why I'm recording.

He rises when the song concludes. "Is that new?"

"Yeah." I wonder if he hears, like I do, the note of challenge in my voice.

"It's pretty," he says mildly. "I just don't know why all your stuff is so depressing. You've got a decent life."

I think of Luke in the diner this morning, tanned and glowing, eyes crinkling at the corners as I approached his table, happy to see me. He said he'd been singing part of my new song in the line-up.

"Everyone heard me singing that line about snow," he'd said.

"They started calling me Father Christmas. I'm never gonna hear the end of it."

"I didn't know you could sing."

"I can't," he'd replied. *"That's half what I won't hear the end of."*

God, my heart felt so fucking full in that moment. So full I didn't know if it would spill over as laughter or tears.

Danny's words do the opposite. They make me empty. And that wants to spill over as tears too.

I sit up a little straighter. "Every life contains bad and good. It's just the kind of music I like."

He dismisses my explanation with an amiable shrug. Danny doesn't like to argue, but for the first time, I resent it—the way he's choosing to let this discussion go as if he's right and I'm wrong and *he's* being big about it. "Well, I'm home early. There are a few shows recorded. We ought to take advantage of it."

I'd like to refuse, but I can't, because this is his house, and I'm lucky to be here. It was implied simply in what he said, wasn't it? If he wants to spend time with me, I should drop anything I'm doing the minute he shows up.

Will there ever come a time when I'm allowed to have my own preferences? When I'm not going to be the *lucky* one? When I get to pick the show, or get to choose not to pick any show at all?

"Let me just get through one more song," I tell him. It's rebellion on the most minor scale, yet I see a flicker of irritation in his eyes before he kisses my head and tells me he'll be waiting inside.

I swallow hard as the door shuts behind him. I didn't actually have one more song in mind to play, and now everything I can think of is angry, written by others. I launch into an old, pissed-off Smashing Pumpkins song, and when it's done, I'm near tears. What the fuck am I doing? How can I possibly be mad at Danny when he's given me everything I have?

I set the guitar on the grass and bury my head in my hands, but it jerks up again at the sound of feet approaching. Luke steps into the light, freshly showered, glowing from a day spent outside.

"What's wrong?" he demands. His tone leaves no room for the vague denial I'd probably have offered.

"Danny told me my songs are depressing and that he doesn't get it because I've got a really good life."

It was more than that, but I can't put the rest into words. Or maybe I could but it would be too disloyal to the Allens to do so. To say, *"I'm tired of feeling like I'm in debt. I'm tired of feeling like I don't get a say."*

Luke steps closer. "He doesn't understand you. It's nothing against Danny. But his mind doesn't work the way yours does."

I rise, picking the guitar up with me. "What do you mean?"

His eyes fall to my lips, slow as a caress. "He doesn't want depth, Juliet, and he doesn't need it. Not everyone does. There are people who skim the surface their entire lives. But you're not one of them. That's why you write a bittersweet song that's full of fucking layers and he comes away with one word—*sad*, and Donna would use the same word. It doesn't mean they'd be right, and that's why you've got to stop listening to them."

"I owe them a lot, though. I can't just...not listen."

"Something can be good for you once. That doesn't mean it's always good for you. You can't let them hold you hostage."

"Hostage?" I repeat, embarrassed and irritated at once. "Do I look like a hostage?"

He steps so close that I can feel the heat of his skin, smell his shampoo and the lingering hint of sunscreen beneath it. "You look like something rare and wild," he whispers, pushing the hair back from my cheek. My breath catches at the feel of his fingers on my skin. "Something they locked up in a cage. And I think you were so relieved to find a safe place to land you didn't even realize it happened. I thought I could save you if I came here this summer, but even if someone opens the cage, you've got to be willing to fly away, too, Jules."

He swallows and steps away from me, looking down as if he's said too much.

And I'm pretty sure he did.

21

NOW

I wake in my own bed. I didn't stay for long last night, once it was done, and he didn't say a word as I crept away. Surely Luke of all people knows better than to expect anything of me, but when I walk into the kitchen, there's something in his gaze that wasn't there before.

There's something different inside me too. I know nothing is going to change—I can't *allow* anything to change—but I feel alive again, as if I've been dunked into ice water then brought into the sun. The blood that moved sluggishly through my veins a few weeks ago now seems to zip along, made young and sprightly and unreasonably hopeful.

Donna smiles at me from the table, waving me over to eat pancakes with them. "You're finally starting to look healthy again," she says. "I like seeing those roses in your cheeks."

My face heats, and I force myself not to look at Luke.

"I was just talking about the twins who are coming right after the opening ceremony." She loads three pancakes on my plate and then slides a folder to me. "They're the same age you were when you came."

I open the file, frowning at their pictures. "They look really young. You're sure they're fifteen?"

Her smile is a little sad. "Honey, fifteen *is* really young. You looked like that when you showed up at my door, I promise."

I raise a brow in silent disagreement. Mentally, I saw myself as an adult at fifteen, maybe because I'd lived through such hard things. I couldn't possibly have been as small and uncertain as the kids I see in these photos.

"You don't believe me," Donna says. She walks out of the kitchen, and Luke and I share a glance.

I worry that I've offended her. I worry that what Luke and I did last night has shifted the balance here, and we are—once again—misweighted, destined to crash what remains of the Allens into the ground.

But she returns with a photo. "Danny took that picture of you the night you met." Her smile flickers and her voice catches. She'll never stop being sad about him. She'll die sad for him. And that's entirely my fault.

It's a picture of me on stage at the county festival where he first saw me. I'm standing with two other girls after we'd performed an acapella version of some Taylor Swift song. I'm the smallest of the three of us, smiling like a little kid, apple-cheeked and wide-eyed. I wasn't a fucking adult, not by any stretch of the imagination.

Justin blamed me for what happened. He said I'd seduced him, that if I hadn't wanted it, I wouldn't have walked around the house in my pajamas, that I wouldn't have walked out of the bathroom after a shower with a towel wrapped around me. That I wouldn't have dressed the way I did for parties and worn so much makeup. And no matter what I said aloud, I believed him. Some part of me has thought all along that I must have been gross and wanton in ways other girls my age wouldn't have been.

But I was *little*. I was naïve. I had no one to turn to for guidance about anything. I've spent the past decade blaming the little girl in the photo for sometimes responding to what he did, for not pressing charges against him though I'd have been absolutely defenseless if I had. I've blamed myself for not telling more people, though the people I *did* tell accused me of lying. Even after he went to jail for manslaughter, after being arrested dozens of times for other shit, I blamed myself.

And I really, truly was not at fault. I see that now. But forgiving yourself for the past is a slippery slope. Because if I forgive myself for the way I handled what happened in high school, it'll become easier to forgive myself for everything else. One day, I'll look back at a photo of me at twenty and think she was a kid too. I might convince myself that the mess I created with Danny and Luke wasn't my fault, that I handled things poorly because I was so damn young.

And I might start thinking it's safe to come clean about what really happened. I glance across the table at Luke, his eyes on that photo of me, his jaw tight.

For his sake, I've got to hang on to my guilt. It's the only way to make sure he's safe.

22

THEN

JULY 2014

The night before Luke and Danny are due to leave for training camp, we head to the beach to celebrate Luke's win earlier in the day—a shortboard contest at Steamer Lane that finally got him the attention he deserves from potential sponsors. When we arrive, Luke's just getting out of the water and wearing nothing but a wet suit, peeled down and hanging off his waist. His body is a symphony, every muscle a separate instrument, coming together to make something so beautiful it hardly seems real. As he takes a seat, I have to look away.

"Someone should call the police," Grady says, on another of his rants, which are a regular occurrence. "It's disgusting."

He's carping about "the gays" again—the guys who hang at a beach nearby, minding their own business. I've never seen them do anything but ogle the surfers and listen to music, but Grady insists it's a hotbed of sexual depravity somehow. I wish Libby would tell him to stop, but she says nothing.

A joint is passed around. Danny demurs and I do, too, and from the other side of the fire, Luke lifts a beer bottle to his lips, watching me. *"Hostage,"* that look says. *"Ask yourself if this is really what you want."*

I already know the answer to that question. It isn't what I want, not anymore. I don't really have the money to leave now, but the bigger issue is I've assumed I'd end up with Danny for so long that it's hard to seriously consider another outcome. We've been together for nearly three years, a sixth of my life, and it's the only relationship I've ever been in. *Not* being with him, somehow, never occurred to me.

Ending this also seems so...ungrateful, after all they've done. *Thank you for sheltering me throughout high school. I no longer need you and am moving on with my life.* But do I repay my debt by weathering something that isn't serving any of us, or do I pay it by letting them hate me for walking away?

And for better or worse, the Allens are my family. The only family I have. There will be no one to spend holidays with if I leave. No one to worry if I'm home late, no one in the entire world who still cares.

"Luke will care," a voice says at the back of my head. But I dismiss it. Luke is off limits because I can't do that to Danny, and Luke is never going to come find me in LA.

Danny's telling anyone who will listen that he's definitely going to be starting quarterback this year and describing his workouts in grueling detail. Libby keeps trying to talk to me about a group she'd like to start at the church for teenagers, suggesting I can do it this coming year since I'm staying home.

I press my fingers to my temples. I don't want to be out here tonight. I don't know how I'll survive remaining in Rhodes at all without Luke. I'd love to tell Donna I don't want that internship, but she's freaking out about some upcoming surgery for the pastor to fix a blocked artery. It just doesn't seem like the right time.

I'm beginning to wonder if it ever will.

Grady picks up his rant where it left off. "I'm sure it's illegal," he says. "Public indecency, at least. Who even knows what they're doing down there?"

"Bro," Caleb finally groans. "Enough already."

"It's in the Bible," Grady counters. "Leviticus calls it a detestable sin, point blank."

"Maybe Leviticus was fighting his own impulses," says Ryan. "If not, he just didn't know what he was missing."

My eyes widen. I've never seen Ryan *without* a girl.

"So, you're saying you'd...do *that* with one of them?" Grady sputters in disbelief.

Ryan grins, holding his arms out expansively. "Have and will continue to. I love all God's children, of every gender, race, religion, or creed. I'd let any one of you suck my dick."

Everyone but Grady laughs.

"Then I feel very sorry for you," he says, "because you'll spend eternity in hell."

Ryan hitches a shoulder. "At least I'm making the most of the trip there. Can't say the same for you. Speaking of which, it's your last night here, Danny. Want us to turn around so you and Juliet can be alone?"

Everyone laughs, but Danny laughs the hardest. And then he changes the topic back to fucking football, and his workout regimen.

Luke swallows. The bob of his Adam's apple makes me thirsty.

"I'm going to have a beer," I tell Danny. It's half apology and half defiance.

His head jerks back. *"What?"*

I sigh. "It's just a beer, Danny. I didn't say I was going to shoot up."

He hitches a shoulder. "It just seems like a bad idea."

"So does pretending we're sleeping together," I mutter, "but that doesn't seem to stop you."

I grab a beer from the cooler and walk away. Not far, not dramatically. Danny barely seems to notice.

I take a few deep breaths, staring at the stars, wondering how the hell to straighten myself out. I think of my brother. How the world started to crush him, and how trying to make it stop ended him entirely.

"Hey," says a voice in the darkness, and Luke walks up beside me.

I force a smile. "It's your celebration. What are you doing over here?"

He shoves his hands in his pockets. "What are *you* doing over here?"

I glance up at him. This is the moment when I'd normally lie. If Danny had asked the question, I'd tell him I was looking at the stars because he wouldn't want the truth. "Thinking about my brother."

He steps closer. "You never talk about him."

I stare at the sand between us. With anyone else, I'd lie about this too. But I know it's safe, with him.

"These dealers were harassing him. I convinced him to go to the police and tell them the truth." I laugh. "You probably expected me to be the last person who'd suggest telling the police the truth."

"I guess it didn't go well?"

"He was shot in the head on the way out of the station. One of the cops told. And they never even looked for the guys who did it. Broad fucking daylight and they claimed there were no cameras and no witnesses."

"Having a shit life doesn't make every bad thing that happens inside it your fault, Jules."

I shrug. That may be true, but it sure doesn't feel like it.

He squeezes my hand and nods upward. "Look."

A star streaks through the sky. I close my eyes, but I want so many things from my life that I can't pick one of them fast enough.

"What did you wish for?" I ask him. "You've already won Steamer Lane."

He looks at me for one long moment. I think I might know what he wishes for, and I also know he'll never say it aloud. His eyes fall to my mouth and my breath holds, wondering if he's going to kiss me.

He wants to. I know he does.

"I'll tell you what I should have wished for instead." His voice is quieter than it was. "I should have wished that you get out of here. That you wind up doing what you love."

My smile is muted. I don't tell him why it won't be happening anytime soon. That it mattered more to me that he winds up with what he loves instead.

"You'll probably never be back here, after this weekend," I whisper, my voice breaking.

"Jules." His hand cups my face, forcing me to meet his eye. "I'll be back."

I shake my head. "By this time next year, you'd better be off on the pro tour, Luke Taylor. Don't come back to Rhodes."

I spin away and head toward the fire, choking back a sob.

Some people show love the way Donna does—by fretting and smoothing a hand over your hair, and by getting you an internship you don't even want. But me? I show mine in other, quieter ways the recipient will never be aware of. It's for the best. He'd never have accepted this love of mine if he knew what it cost me.

It's late by the time we get back to the house. The boys pack their stuff and eventually, unable to stand the tension, I go to my room and cry.

I wish I wasn't red-eyed when we get up to see them off. Luke looks away, his jaw flexing, when Danny kisses me good-bye. He shakes the pastor's hand and hugs Donna. I assume he will mostly ignore me, the way he did last summer. Instead, he hesitates and then pulls me against him. It lasts a second at most, but it's enough.

I cry for the rest of the day. And when I wake up after twenty-four hours of Luke gone, I know I can't live like this, that I can't keep pretending. I know, even when I told myself I belonged to Danny, it was Luke who kept my heart beating and my blood hot in my veins, and without him, nothing matters. I've got to find a way to get out of here.

23

NOW

When Cash's name flashes on the caller ID, I startle. Cash hates the phone. He won't even take calls from his mother, and I don't think I've ever once seen him dial a number. A few months ago, I'd have been thrilled by this turn of events. Weirdly, I just find this small pit of dread in my stomach instead.

I set my coffee mug on the kitchen counter and glance behind me before I pick up. "Cash?" I ask, my voice lilting at the end.

He gives a low chuckle. "That surprised to hear from me?"

"I've never seen you call anybody before." I turn to face the kitchen's entrance so I'll know if I'm being overheard. "I assumed someone was using your phone as a joke, or that you were calling to tell me Frank is dead."

"Frank is still alive and kicking. Asks about you every day."

I don't doubt he's telling the truth. I got to know Frank pretty well when I was opening for Cash. There were times when it seemed like he cared about me far more than Cash did.

My palm curves around the coffee mug, relishing its heat—

a tiny hesitation. There's a reason he's calling, and it's probably a bad one. "So, to what do I owe this honor?"

"You didn't reply to my text," he says. "You always reply."

I suppose he's right—our relationship has been on and off for two years, but I was always desperate to keep him on the hook.

Why was I so pathetic?

"Sorry," I tell him. "It's just been really busy here."

"Oh, yeah. It's, like, your aunt's house, right? Getting it ready for something?"

You would think he'd fucking know by now that she isn't my aunt, but I shouldn't be surprised. It's not as if I ever really thought he was listening in the first place.

"She basically raised me. And she added on this extension so she can house more foster kids, but it still needs a ton of work before the first two arrive, so I'm helping her."

"Cool cool cool," he says. He's already stopped listening. "So, I'm back in LA. We're all hanging out in the penthouse of the Beverly Hills Hotel. Come down and see us."

I wonder if he's already forgotten what I said about getting the foster home ready, or if he simply never listened in the first place. Maybe he just thinks he's so special that I would drop it all on his behalf. I probably would have, until a few weeks ago. But now, when I consider leaving, everything goes black, and the future looks like a space so dark I can't make out a single shape inside it. I guess, though, that it was always black. Cash was something I clung to, trying to find my way through the dark.

I dump my coffee down the drain and put the cup in the dishwasher. "Like I said, things are pretty busy. I don't see myself getting out of here until after the opening."

"I'll just have to come up there to see you, then."

I blink once, then twice, my mouth hanging open. Never would I have predicted Cash would offer to come here. It's the kind of thing I might have fantasized about a few months ago—having him show up and make it clear to everyone that I've finally moved on—but the reality would be disastrous.

He'd stride in with his tattoos and all those rings on his fingers, expecting everyone to fall at his feet. Donna would smile in that way she does when people tell her they miss Danny, a smile that seems to take every ounce of strength she has. And Luke would just stand there with his arms folded across his chest, towering over all of us, quietly condemning Cash, and condemning me for having chosen him. Or, worse, he'd throw a punch.

Donna's shuffling steps echo in the hallway, so I hurry to end the call.

"Don't do that," I say quickly. "You'd hate it here. I can come there for a night. Just give me a few days to set it up."

I wonder how the fuck I am going to explain this to Luke. I can't even explain it to myself—there is nothing in my heart but dread.

～

THAT AFTERNOON, I head to the grocery store while Luke is surfing. It's a sign of Donna's dwindling reserves that the refrigerator is so empty. That daily trip to the store used to be as routine as making her bed or brushing her teeth.

Heads turn and people stare. I recognize a woman who attended the church back when Danny was alive. Her mouth pinches as our eyes meet. She thinks the same thing they all do: no matter how it was reported, Danny's death was really my fault.

I load my cart with the sort of foods Donna used to cook, and I've just gotten in line when the store's sliding doors open and Grady walks in.

He's in khakis and a white Oxford buttoned nearly to the

top, as bland and officious as ever. I'd hoped these years as a pastor would soften him a little, but when his gaze zeroes in on me, it's clear they haven't.

His brow raises, and he waits. He waits the long six minutes it takes for me to check out before he blocks my path when I try to exit.

"Juliet," he says, his voice flat and unhappy. "Long time, no see."

God, I'd love to pull the rug out from under him. His carefully constructed life is a castle made of cards. I could wreck it with no effort at all, but not without wrecking my own as well.

I swallow. "I'm only here at Donna's request. For the opening."

His head tilts as his lips press flat. "I imagine you could have avoided that."

My heart is hammering but I force myself to act calm. "Your wife is on the board. I'd think you'd want to see the charity she's involved in succeed."

"As usual, you're over-valuing your own contribution. Danny's House will succeed with or without *you*."

I could point out that *The New York Times* and *Vanity Fair* wouldn't know this town or charity even exists were it not for me, but Grady is the kind of person who will set his own house on fire simply to prove it's flammable. I don't trust him not to burn me in any way he's capable of.

"I'm only staying through the gala," I tell him, steering the cart away, feigning boredom as my stomach starts to spin. "I'll be gone after that."

He grabs the side of my cart, holding me there. "Be sure that you are. I'd have no problem recanting my statement. I can blow up your entire sham of a life."

I suck in a breath. "Not without blowing up your own in the process."

His laughter is sharp, forced—as fucking fake as he is. "I

have no idea what you're referring to, but you're a known liar with a terrible reputation. Anything you say will be taken for what it is: a wild story meant to discredit me."

Fuck you, Grady, you absolute piece of shit.

He knows better than anyone it isn't a wild story, but that isn't the troubling part. The troubling part is that Grady *believes* he is safe now. He thinks he can destroy me without destroying himself.

And any hint that Luke and I are together again might be enough to make it happen.

24

THEN

AUGUST 2014

One week after the boys leave for summer training, the pastor has his stent surgery. It's an outpatient procedure, and he spends the rest of the week home, expecting us to wait on him hand and foot. Once it's over and Donna doesn't need me around to help, I'm going to leave. It won't be easy. I'll move first, and I'm hoping it will, perhaps, seem obvious to Danny that we aren't going to work out. He's not moving to LA and I'm not moving to San Diego. If it isn't obvious, I'll deal with that when it happens.

I call Hailey from the pharmacy while I wait for the pastor's prescriptions. "Did you still want to go to LA?"

She yelps. "Are you serious?"

I look around me again before I reply. "Yes. I mean, we'll need to find a place, and I don't have a lot saved. Do you?"

"Not a penny."

I wince. I was sort of hoping, naively, that she'd be able to pull her weight.

"What about your job this summer? And the graduation money from your grandmother?"

"I spent most of it. You know how that goes. But I'll find a job as soon as we get to LA. You won't have to cover me for long."

It's less than ideal. I have enough for perhaps three months' rent somewhere, that's it. "Okay," I tell her. "Let's look for something cheap."

Over the next few days, Hailey and I look online in our spare time, finally settling on a group house where they've agreed to let us share a room for twelve hundred a month.

On the pastor's first day back at work—we were told he'd be up and about, but he's barely moved from his favorite chair all week—I meet Hailey at a coffee shop halfway between us to be interviewed by our prospective housemates over Skype.

They're older, and male. I'd rather not live with men, but they seem nice enough, and Hailey tells me I'm being paranoid, so I reluctantly agree.

She squeals as she walks me out to my bike. "We're really doing it!"

We really are. I'm sad about leaving Danny, heartbroken by the possibility we might not even be friends when this is done, but also hopeful for the first time in a long while.

I want to drink. I want to dance. I want to be kissed by someone who's desperate to do it, not terrified. So I bike home, dreaming more of freedom than of what I'm giving up—of being able to hang pictures on the wall or stay out all night. I can eat potato chips for breakfast and Cap'n Crunch for dinner. I can sleep until noon. Not that those are things I'm necessarily dying to do. They're just things I couldn't *possibly* do, until now.

I get to the house, surprised to see the pastor is already home. I'll have to wait until Donna's alone to tell her I'm leaving, because the pastor always seems to be questioning my motivations—even suggesting a new song for Sunday's service gets a side-eye from him and a gentle, *"Is there something wrong with the song that was planned, Juliet?"*

I walk in to find him on the phone, and Donna sitting at the table, her hands clasped tight. "Oh, honey," she says, rising and throwing her arms around me. "I'm so glad you're here. Danny hurt his knee at training. He's been wanting to talk to you."

I never took my phone off silent after the interview. I pull it out of my back pocket—I have seven missed calls.

"The pastor's talking to the orthopedist right now, but I think he might need surgery."

I sink into a chair. Poor Danny. He worked out all summer, hoping this was going to be his season. I think he clung to the idea even harder, watching Luke's star begin to rise. "I guess there's still next year."

Her shoulders sag. "I don't know. Danny's worried he might get cut, and if he does, he'll lose his scholarship. We don't have enough saved to cover the difference if that happens."

"They can do that?" Danny has endured two years of practices and sitting on the sidelines, has given up weeks of his summer for training camp...all to lose his scholarship *now*? It would be so fucking unfair.

She nods. "He could get financial aid, obviously, but then he'd have loans to pay back before we could start our mission. I guess we'll just have to pray for the best." Her hand lands atop mine. "I sure am glad you're here though."

For a moment, I'd forgotten about my plans entirely. Plans I'm going to have to abandon.

Leaving is one thing. Leaving now...is too selfish, even for me. I just sent twenty-four hundred dollars via PayPal an hour ago—our deposit, our first month's rent—and I never even set foot outside the city limits.

I text Hailey to let her know I can't do LA after all, and she asks if I'm joking. When I tell her I'm not, she replies with a simple, *"Fuck you, Juliet",* and I don't hear from her again.

Which seems...fitting.

I've just lost my only friend. I'm remaining in Rhodes. I'm taking the internship.

I was right to bet on Luke rather than myself. From the moment I came into the world, I've been hearing, in one way or another, that it would be better if I hadn't appeared at all.

Today, at last, I agree. I'm never going anywhere.

DONNA FLIES DOWN to San Diego, spending money they don't have to do it. Between what insurance won't cover for Danny's surgery and the cost of the trip, they're stretched thin.

I remain behind to look after the pastor. I can't work much until Donna gets back, and I don't have a driver's license, which means I'm biking to the grocery store every day and balancing the bags on my handlebars to get them home. I clean and make dinner, and the pastor sees our meals together as a glorious opportunity to remind me about the importance of charity and gratitude, giving back and service.

I'm not angry about it, though. I feel nothing when he talks. I feel nothing when anyone talks. As if I'm encased in ice.

Danny's miserable, though the surgery went just fine. "I just don't understand why it happened," he says mournfully.

"What do you mean?" The *why* seems pretty fucking clear to me: he took a bad hit from the side; his knees were weak. It's hardly uncommon in football.

"I've done everything I was supposed to." His voice grows quiet. "You know, I watch my friends doing whatever they want for years, and I just thought my time would come. I thought I'd get rewarded for all of it. Like, maybe I'd finally get on the field this season and I'd play really well, and everything would change."

It seems impossibly naïve and yet...I get it. Half the movies ever made are about someone doing the right thing or trying harder than everyone else and winning in the end. In real life, though, you do the right thing and absolutely no one notices.

"Your father would say goodness is its own reward." My voice lacks conviction.

"I guess."

In his begrudging reply, I hear what he hasn't said: that it's not enough of a reward. That there are better rewards out there, and they're going to the people who haven't tried as hard as he has. "You could be more sympathetic, you know," he adds.

"Danny, I didn't mean to be—"

"I've got to go. My mom just made dinner. Oh, and she wants you to call and update her on my dad."

We hang up and I stare at the blank walls of my room. I'm so empty now that I don't even know what I thought I might put on that imagined wall in LA, what I cared enough about.

I wonder what it would be like to have one person in the world as concerned about me as the Allens are with each other and themselves. What it would be like to have one person say, *"Juliet, you don't seem happy. Are you tired? Is there something else you want from your life?"*

Except there is someone who cares that much. One person who put me above everyone else. He just couldn't show it to the world.

Maybe I'm not empty after all. It's just that the things I'd put on my walls and the things I'd like to sing about are ones I can't show the world either.

~

DANNY IS YOUNG AND HEALTHY. He's up and about within a week, so Donna returns, but life doesn't improve much.

My internship has begun and has turned out to be its own special kind of hell. The music teacher, Miss Johnson, is the type who'd make you hate anything she taught. My contribution involves making copies, straightening the room, and walking the bad kids to the principal, but she still acts like it's a burden to have me around. I just...let it happen.

The little I had to offer the world has been poured out onto the ground and gone to waste.

At home, the pastor isn't improving. He wheezes anytime he walks up the stairs. And increasingly, he just sits in his favorite chair and has Donna and I get what he needs. Grady is over frequently, lurking like the shadow of death over the house, salivating at the possibility that he might be able to replace the pastor once his mentorship is over.

"Do a bit of missionary work," the pastor advises him one night when Grady's been too obvious about his intentions. *"I could even handle the sermon on Sunday if you'd like,"* he'd said.

"Let yourself season for a while. When Mrs. Allen and I go back to Nicaragua in five years, you can take my place. Marry Libby too. No one wants an unmarried pastor."

Donna pats his hand. "Leave him alone, hon. Libby's the same year as Danny. But I suspect there will be any number of weddings two summers from now when everyone graduates."

She smiles at me then, and I go rigid, my hands gripping the kitchen counter. Yes, I knew this is where it was headed. It just always seemed very distant.

And two summers from now doesn't sound distant enough.

In late October, Danny is cleared to begin training with the team again, but things don't improve the way he'd hoped.

"That new freshman they brought in from Texas is starting," he tells me. "Two years I've been there and I never started once. And the guy got arrested over the summer for some drug shit, and it wasn't the first time. How is that fair?"

"It isn't." *Life isn't fair.* He lived among families with dirt floors and little food for most of his childhood. I'm not sure how he's only figuring this out now.

He's permitted to travel with the team when they play Fresno State, three hours away. The pastor and Donna decide not to go, in theory because of the drive, though I suspect it's simply that the pastor won't be able to climb up into the stands.

I think it would be better if I didn't go too. Maybe, if I pretend Luke doesn't exist, and if I pretend it for long enough, I'll finally stop missing him. But when Danny pleads with me to come, I don't feel I can say no.

It takes a series of buses and then a cab to get to the hotel in Fresno, so it's almost nine by the time I arrive. The team is just getting back from dinner when I walk in, but I can tell something's wrong. Danny isn't smiling as he crosses the lobby to me, and Luke simply turns on his heel and walks away, his fists clenched.

"Come on," says Danny, grabbing my bag, morose for reasons I don't understand. He already checked me in, since I wasn't old enough to get the room myself. My stomach is in knots, wondering if Luke told him about coming into the diner all summer, or if he mentioned his last night on the beach, when I thought he might kiss me. Nothing ever happened, but it sure doesn't look great that we kept it all to ourselves.

Using the keycard, he enters the room and sinks on the edge of the bed with his head in his hands. "I asked Scott, the offensive coordinator, to put me in because you were coming. He said no. They're not renewing my scholarship."

I take the seat beside him and squeeze his hand. "I'm sorry." I silently thank God I didn't leave for LA as planned. I guess that's my silver lining: I didn't get to go to LA, but I get to be here with him in his time of need—I get to repay a little of my debt.

"I don't understand." His voice cracks as he buries his head in his hands. "What did I do wrong? Why am I being punished?"

I think of the platitudes the pastor and Donna would offer now: *God works in mysterious ways; When God closes a door, He opens a window*.

I know how much I hate hearing them personally, how they feel less like an attempt to console and more like a warning that I've complained enough and it's time to stop.

I could suggest he *isn't* being punished, that hard things happen in life, and *his* hard things aren't even all that bad—Luke has suffered far more than Danny has—but it's not the time for that either.

"I'm so sorry, Danny. I don't even know what to say." I lean my head on his shoulder.

"Sometimes it seems like you're the only part of my life that's gone right," he says as he rises. He crosses to the mini-fridge and pulls out two tiny bottles of vodka, opening one and drinking it without a word, flinching at the burn.

And then he opens the other.

"What...are you doing?" I whisper. "You don't drink."

He slams the second one and reaches back into the fridge. "You want one? You were always wanting to drink with every-one. Here's your chance."

I frown at him as I kick off my shoes and fold my legs beneath me. "Maybe I wanted to have a beer at a party, Danny, but it's supposed to be fun. Not angrily drinking straight vodka."

"We're out of vodka." He fishes more bottles out. "Now I'm drinking straight gin."

My stomach tightens. I'm happy to sit here with him, and I'm happy to try to cheer him up, but I don't like where this is heading. "Please stop. This isn't you."

He sets the unopened gin on top of the counter. "I'm sick of always doing the right thing. It doesn't pay off anyway."

He slams the gin, then turns, crossing to where I sit and pulling me to my feet, kissing me so hard it hurts. His mouth opens and his tongue seeks. It feels foreign and awkward and forced. Something I don't want and even something *he* doesn't actually want. His grip is too tight, his teeth clank against mine.

I push away from him. "Danny, that hurts."

"Sorry, sorry," he says, pulling me back to him.

He kisses me again, more softly this time. It's still not what I want but I can't exactly complain about it.

His hand reaches up to grasp one breast, then slides to the button of my jeans.

I grab his wrist. "What are you doing?"

"I want this," he says as the button pops open. He pulls down the zipper. "I'm sick of always doing the right thing."

"I—" I stumble over my words as panic wells inside me. "I don't know if this is a good idea. You're mad right now, but when you stop being mad you might wish you hadn't done this."

"It didn't *just* occur to me." He pushes my jeans down to mid-thigh. "I've been thinking about it for months. When my parents said they weren't coming, I knew it was a sign."

He seems to be choosing his signs rather conveniently.

His fingers move against the seam of my cotton panties. "I promise," he says. "This isn't a spur-of-the-moment decision."

I still think it is and I...don't want to. With every bone in my body, I don't want to, but what am I supposed to say? We've been together for three years. *I'm* the one who said I wanted this, and I'm not a virgin, so it's not like there's anything to safeguard.

So, when he pulls me to the bed, I go. When he takes his jeans off, after a moment of hesitation, I step out of mine. I always imagined when I finally undressed in front of Danny, it would be sensual. Seductive. That just watching it would make him unravel. But this is awkward and methodical, as if we're undressing for an examination. My sweatshirt is still on when he climbs onto the bed wearing only his boxers.

"We don't have anything," I say, stalling and hoping for a last-minute reprieve.

He reaches for his jeans. "I got condoms from Luke."

Which explains the look from Luke when I arrived. His anger. *And fuck you, Luke, for having condoms in the first place. For judging me for something you've been doing for years, without fail.*

He climbs over me, and I press clammy palms to the mattress, trying to ignore the way my chest is tightening, the way my stomach rolls. Is it because of Justin? I guess I can't know for sure, but I don't think it is. There have been times with Danny when I was more than ready—like at the sorority house last year—but this? It just feels like something that shouldn't be happening.

He pulls my panties down before he removes his boxers. I think there will be more—I think he'll reach between my legs or into my bra because even *Justin* did that much, but he just reaches for the condom and then, after a moment of uncertainty, hands it to me. Like I'll know what to do. Like I've *ever* been a willing participant.

I swallow down a flare of resentment and hand it back to him. He hesitates, then tears it open and inexpertly, uncertainly, puts it on.

I'm still dressed from the waist up, and every light in the room is on when his weight settles over mine. I'm too warm in this sweatshirt, with his weight above me, and I begin to sweat. My stomach is so locked up I can't get a full breath.

After a moment of fumbling, he pushes inside me. I'm not ready, and it hurts, but what am I supposed to say? How could he ever *not* blame me for what happened if I told him what Justin used to do to make this better?

My mind goes somewhere else, pretending I'm not even here. I've got experience with this, with letting my mind wander until it's over. He suddenly groans, then stops, less than a minute in.

I'm slow to understand that...that was it. I feel used and relieved at the same time. I exhale as the knot in my stomach finally starts to unwind.

He rolls off me, painfully quiet. Maybe he's embarrassed? I want to reassure him that it's okay that it went the way it did and that we can try again in a while if he wants, but I don't. I can't stand to suggest doing it again. Not yet.

He glances down. "I guess I'd better get this thing off."

I nod, letting my eyes close as he walks into the bathroom. I once thought if he and I were sleeping together that it would bridge the impasse between us, but it's even wider now than it ever was.

When he reenters the room, he turns off the lights and climbs in beside me, pulling the blankets over us.

"Did you..." he begins, before trailing off.

It takes me a second to even understand what he's asking, because how could he possibly think I *came* from that?

"It's..." I begin, and then stop. "I think maybe it takes longer for girls."

His jaw clenches as he rolls onto his back, staring at the ceiling. "Did you finish with *him*?"

For a moment, I simply don't understand the question. "What?"

"Did you finish with Justin?"

It lands like a slap in the face. "God, Danny. I can't believe you'd bring that up *now*." I don't know if I'm more enraged that he would ask or embarrassed by the answer, but I have to lie because he will never, ever understand the truth—I'm not even sure I do. "Of course I didn't."

He slides an arm under my head. "I'm sorry. You're right. I shouldn't have asked."

And then it's silent. I don't want him to try again—the mere idea makes my chest constrict—but maybe he should because something needs to be salvaged here, and I think it's us. I think *we* need to be salvaged because I'm not happy, and I haven't been happy for a long time, and I don't know how much longer I can keep pretending this is all okay.

I drift off after a while, still wondering how to fix things. When I wake in the middle of the night, he's sitting up in the darkness with his face in his hands.

"Hey." I sit up beside him. "What's going on?"

His eyes squeeze shut. "I feel like I made a bad decision. We should have waited until we got married. My father's sick. The least I could have done is honor his values."

All the air seems to slip from my chest. I slept with him when I didn't want to because I thought I could improve a bad situation. But it only made things worse.

"Okay." I exhale silently, gathering my thoughts. *How do I fix this now? How do I fix this moment? How do I fix the two of us?*

He swallows. "It's not your fault."

I turn toward him, stunned. That he felt he needed to even say it aloud implies he thinks it *could* be my fault. After I fucking argued against this whole thing as much as I could. "Why would I think it was *my* fault?"

He hitches a shoulder. "You know, because you said you didn't want to wait."

"And how does me not wanting to wait make *your* choice my fault?" I snap.

"I just said it wasn't!" he explodes, tugging at his hair. "But I was trying to make you happy."

Thirty seconds of intercourse, no foreplay, and you're trying to say you did it for me? Jesus Christ.

It's my fault for not telling him, *"No,"* he thinks. It's my fault for wanting it in the first place. He pulled me out of the gutter and brushed me off, but I wasn't quite pure enough for him after all.

I climb from the bed, searching the floor for my clothes.

"Juliet, what are you doing?"

I step into my panties. He didn't even take off my fucking sweatshirt last night but this was my fault? "You were trying to make me happy? What about that would have made *me* happy, Dan?"

"Hon, stop." He throws off the covers. "It's the middle of the night. Where do you think you're going?"

I round on him. "I don't know. Someplace where people aren't blaming *me* for their fucked-up decisions. You brought this up tonight, and I even told you it seemed like a bad idea, and you pushed ahead anyway. And now you don't like what you did and it's too goddamn uncomfortable for you, so you're looking for a way to blame *me*."

He winces. I'd like to believe it's guilt but it's probably just that he hates profanity.

"Babe, wait." He jumps out of bed too fast and flinches in pain. If his knee is reinjured, I guess that will be my fault too. "Honey, I'm sorry, okay? You're right. You're absolutely right. Please just come back to bed. It's been a hard couple of months between my dad and my knee, and now the scholarship, and I'm just not thinking clearly."

"It's been a hard couple of months for me too," I reply. "You aren't the only one who's unhappy." My words are calmer than before, but I've still got one foot in my jeans, ready to finish dressing and leave. I stare at him, willing him to hear the truth in my words. To see that there are two of us here, two of us who matter.

His shoulders hunch, and he starts to cry. And for a moment, I'm frozen, torn between resentment and pity. He presses his face to his hands, trying to conceal it, but his body is shaking. He's never cried in front of me, and already I can feel my anger dissipating.

His father has heart problems, he's just lost his scholarship and his spot on the team, and now he's given up something he'd valued deeply. It's a lot.

I don't have the heart to stay mad. With a sigh, I climb onto the bed and hug him because, when you've been with someone for a sixth of your life, that's what you do.

But I just want out. And when I've been with him for a fifth of my life, for a quarter of my life...is that going to get any easier?

"**W**ell, I'm off," Donna says.

The reporter from *The New York Times* is back and has decided to expand the story. In theory, it's a good thing that she wants to meet with Donna. She's going to focus more on Danny's House than she'd intended to, which is what we want. Except I don't trust her. It's one of the reasons I negotiated with her in the first place, hoping a scoop about my background might be enough to shut her down. And Donna's never been media-trained. She has no idea how one offhand comment might unravel this whole pack of lies I've been telling for the past seven years.

"Be careful," I warn. "She'll act like she's your best friend and you'll find yourself wanting to tell her everything. Just imagine every word out of your mouth appearing in print."

She studies me for a moment. "I'm not sure I have anything in my head that I'd mind seeing in print," she says gently.

That's probably true, but it doesn't mean the way she might characterize my time in this house, and Luke's, won't cause problems. Laid out the wrong way, Danny's death might seem like the natural conclusion of those events rather than an unhappy coincidence.

Laid out the wrong way, it might look like we wanted him gone.

"She'll be fine, Juliet," says Luke, slamming the refrigerator door shut.

You wouldn't know a thing about that, Luke.

"What will the two of you do tonight?" Donna asks us, going through her purse.

Avoid each other. I've been steering clear of him for the past two days, ever since I saw Grady at the store. Luke probably thinks I'm fickle, that I came to his room simply to get laid. Let him think it. It's better than the alternative—letting down my walls, allowing him to continue shaking the past loose until it can't be put away. I'm going to lock myself in my room the moment Donna leaves and I won't emerge until tomorrow.

"We're going to rent a movie," he tells her. The look in his eyes is defiant. I nod, but there's no fucking way I'm watching a movie with him, and as soon as she drives off, I grab my stuff to leave.

"Where do you think you're going?" he demands. "We're watching a movie, remember?"

"You can watch it. I'm going to go read."

His arms fold across his chest. "That lie doesn't work with me, remember? Come on, Jules. Truce. I'll even let you pick."

Something softens inside me, though I don't want it to. How can he be so fucking kind to me? I wish he'd stop.

He sees that I'm weakening, and smiles. "You can pick something without a single explosion if you really want to punish me. Some movie that uses a description like 'rich tapestry' so you know absolutely nothing's going to fucking happen."

I find myself smiling against my will and walking to the family room with feigned reluctance.

I choose a movie about World War II, assuming there will be no romance, but within minutes I see my error: the main character and his fiancée are pining for each other, and that's nearly as bad as the sex scenes I'd hoped to avoid.

Because Luke and I...that's what we did, wasn't it? We pined for each other, for years. And I, at least, have continued to pine, all this time.

I sit rigid at one end of the couch while he sits at the other. I feel his gaze on me occasionally and ignore it. *Just get through the fucking movie, Juliet. Get through the movie, go straight to bed, and spend this last, final week pretending being so near him isn't tearing you apart.*

And then the soldier gets leave and meets his fiancée in a hotel. By the time he follows her into the shower, my skin is tight, overheated, too small for everything inside me. I'm breathing fast, and I know Luke sees it. I know he's remembering what I'm remembering: the two of us in that shower, in broad daylight. How one minute we were kissing, his hands sliding over my damp skin, and a moment later he was inside me. I knew I was cheating and I just couldn't stop it. We were like a train without brakes. I had no words, no ability to control it, nor any desire to, and after all this time, nothing has changed. How can it possibly not have changed, not have died, even now?

How can that still be all I want—him, naked and wet, pressed up against me, promising the world?

I jump to my feet, my heart hammering in my chest. "I don't want to watch this."

I just need to get away. I walk out the back door, into the yard, and within seconds he's behind me, and his hands are on my arms.

He spins me toward him, his face not an inch from mine. "Are you ever going to stop feeling guilty about it?"

"No." Tears slide down my cheeks. "Never. I'm never going to look at you without remembering what I did to him."

A vein pulses in his temple as he steps closer. "Except you can't look at me without wanting it again, either, can you?"

"Fuck you," I say, shoving him.

He presses me to the garage wall behind us and pulls my mouth to his, his hand on my jaw.

His weight crushes me, his scruff abrades my skin, and I want more.

I grab the waistband of his shorts and push them down around his hips. He's already hard, and he hisses when my hand wraps around him, too impatient for half measures.

He lifts me, pulling my legs around his waist before pushing my panties to the side and thrusting inside me.

My back arches and my head falls back toward the wall. He chases, seeking my mouth. I let my teeth sink into his lower lip, wishing I could consume him, eat him whole. I want to take in his smell, his taste, until they're the only things I know and remember.

"Has it ever been like this with anyone else?" He buries himself inside me. The words are a low growl against my ear.

No, it's never like this. Not even close. "Shut up," I hiss.

His hands grip my thighs, lifting me higher, making him go deeper. I gasp as he hits the exact right spot.

"Answer." He stops moving entirely, holding me pinned, still inside me. I'm so close. "Answer me or you won't come."

I wish I had more pride, but I'm too desperate for it now. "No," I admit, flinching.

His hips snap backward and forward so hard that I hear the echo of it inside the garage. "*Oh.*" My eyes fall closed. "*God.*"

Cash thinks I'm hard to please. I'm not. It's just that with him, I'm a husk. He has to work and work to find any part of me that still feels anything. Luke's the only person who can access all of me. He barely has to try.

A car engine hums in the distance. I'm so close to coming it barely registers. It's only when the wall behind me starts to vibrate—the garage door opening—that I realize what's going on.

I gasp. "Shit. That's Donna. You've got to stop."

His eyes are nearly black in the dim light. "No." He slams into me again and again. I know exactly how it will sound on the other side of that wall.

"She's going to hear," I plead. "You've got to stop."

"Then you'd better hurry up and come," he taunts, slamming into me again as her car pulls in.

His hand covers my mouth as I cry out. He thrusts once more and stills, biting my shoulder as his hips pump silently, squeezing me so tight I'll be bruised in the morning. He breathes into my neck as we stand frozen, waiting for the sound of the side door to open and shut.

"*Fuck*," he gasps when it finally does. He releases me, and my feet hit the ground at last.

"This was wrong," I say, pushing my dress down. I walk off, and this time he doesn't follow. But once again, there's a part of me that wishes he had.

26

THEN

DECEMBER 2014

Just before Danny comes home for winter break, Donna pulls me aside and tells me the pastor is having bypass surgery in January. She doesn't want Danny to know because he's already going through so much, though in truth, I think she's mostly worried he'll drop out of school. He's mentioned it more than once to both of us—a childish tantrum about being cut from the team that he's trying to pose as altruism.

She's going to be covering more of the pastor's duties at church—pretty much every aspect of the job aside from the Sunday sermon—and she needs me at the house to keep an eye on him when I'm not at my internship. She teared up as she explained the situation they're in. *"We don't own this house. We don't have anything saved. If things go downhill and they remove the pastor from his position, I don't know what's going to become of us."*

It's Grady she's worried about. Fucking Grady, always offering to *step up*, as if he truly cares about the pastor's recovery and isn't trying to get himself a fucking job at the end of the year.

I've only been able to work evenings and weekends this

year, so it's been an uphill battle to even replenish the money I lost at the end of the summer, and now I might be giving it up entirely.

But the hardest part is that it means...I'm staying.

And I stopped wanting to stay a long time ago.

WHEN DANNY GETS HOME, we meet all the guys at the bar Beck's mom owns, thirty minutes to the south. Surfing equalized them all, but that disappears when they're away from the beach. Caleb rolls up in his dad's Range Rover. Harrison has a Rolex. Fucking twenty-one-years-old and he's got a Rolex.

And I bet he'd give it up—I bet they'd all give up everything —to be Luke.

"I can't believe he's surfing Mavericks," says Caleb, shaking his head.

"What?" I whisper. My voice is dry, raspy with shock. Mavericks hosts some of the deadliest waves in the world.

Caleb looks from me to Danny. "You didn't tell her?"

Danny shakes his head. "No, because it's stupid. I was hoping he'd change his mind."

"It's all set," argues Caleb. "He's coming up after New Year's and we're gonna drive out to watch. I think he'll be okay."

Danny rolls his eyes. "He just started surfing again *two* years ago."

It's what I was thinking too. The difference is that I'm worried sick, but Danny just sounds pissed.

ON THE DAY after New Year's, Danny and I take the pastor's truck to a camping area just off the beach, only a few miles south of Mavericks. It's only the two of us, and the silence is deafening. I'm sick with nerves over both the prospect of seeing Luke and the possibility of him being hurt tomorrow. Plus, there's not much to say. Danny doesn't want to hear that I hate the internship, he doesn't want to hear about my songs.

He breaks the silence by again floating the idea of staying in Rhodes instead of returning to UCSD. "I hate leaving my dad like this. It doesn't feel right."

"He's not putting a lot of effort into getting better," I reply bluntly.

He nods. "Yeah, maybe but..." He trails off and my stomach sinks. I already know what's coming because he's implied some version of this several times. "I feel like I'm being punished for losing my way."

He's apologized a thousand times for what he said that night in Fresno, but he's still blaming me, and I'm sick of it. I'm sick of how he acts as if I'm a danger, the way he's wary even when he hugs me, and of his belief in a punitive God who lashes out for minor transgressions and is supposed to reward him for good behavior by making him the star of the football team.

But I think I'm mostly just tired of *us*, and I don't know how to escape it.

When we arrive at the campsite and I climb from the car, Luke is the first person I see. He's tan though it's January, in need of a shave as always, and his eyes glow brightly in the dim winter light. His gaze meets mine and I know he isn't holding Fresno against me. He probably never was—he was just upset about something he had no right to be upset about, and he didn't know how to handle it, which I understand completely.

It's how I felt all summer, after all, watching him walk away at night with a girl who wasn't me.

"Luke's first attempt at Mavericks!" Summer shouts, pulling up behind us, summing up in a single sentence why there's nothing to be excited about at all. Because the word *attempt* suggests a strong possibility of failure, and failure at Mavericks is likely to be fatal.

We unload the cars and Danny makes a point of setting up a pup tent for the two of us, a bit away from everyone else. Someone mutters, "Lucky bastard", and jokes are made about how the moaning tonight will be louder than the waves. Luke's nostrils flare and he walks away, going to the cliff's edge to stare at the surf.

I want to join him. I want to ask if he's scared. But it isn't my place, and I'd just wind up begging him to reconsider, which is the last thing he needs. I know I can't change his mind, but I could, perhaps, shake his confidence, and when he does this tomorrow, he'll need every ounce of confidence he's got.

Grady and Danny try to get a fire started while Libby unloads coolers and checks her lists. She's made chicken, pies, and appetizers. I suspect she's trying to prove what a good little pastor's wife she'll be, but it's been a struggle not to resent her excitement when Luke's life hangs in the balance.

"Oh, no!" Libby cries, removing a bag from the cooler. "There's no chicken in here."

She spent the whole damn morning on that chicken. Danny asks if it could be in another cooler and she presses a hand to her face, shaking her head.

"No, this is the only cooler I brought. Crap. I had it in there. I was shuffling things so the pie wouldn't tip, and I must have left it all on the counter. What a waste."

"Libby," Grady warns as if he's speaking to a child, "I'm sure we'll manage."

"I spent all morning on it, though," she says. "Like, the *whole* morning. And I soaked all the chicken overnight in buttermilk too. It turned out so well."

"God must be *very* good to us," Grady scolds, "if that's the worst thing that's happened."

Libby's head bows in shame, and I seethe. Grady's turning

her into someone less, a shadow of herself, and I think it bothers me because I worry I'm doing the same thing to myself. That I'm spending so much time denying the things I want that I'm gonna lose track of what they even are. That I'm denying everything I feel so often that I'll soon stop feeling anything.

"Does it have to be the worst thing that's happened for her to say something about it, Grady?" I ask. "All her work went to waste. She's allowed to be upset."

His mouth presses flat. "I was just trying to keep things in perspective."

I roll my eyes. "Yeah, let's all remember this moment the next time *you* decide to complain."

His eyes narrow. If I ever was unsure about this, I no longer am: Grady hates me. He hates me far out of proportion to anything I've ever said to him.

We roast hot dogs, and then the guys throw a football around while the girls watch. They're acting like this is a celebration when we might be driving back without Luke tomorrow. And Danny is bitter, for the wrong reasons.

"This is so stupid," he says, taking the seat beside me. "They're acting like he's Laird Hamilton. I could say I was gonna surf Mavericks too. *Anyone* could. It doesn't mean you start celebrating it like it's already happened."

I hate the celebrating because I think it will make it harder for Luke to back out tomorrow, the way he should. But it almost feels like Danny *hopes* Luke will fail, and that makes me mad.

"He's gotten really good."

"Sure," Danny says, his eyes rolling. "He's spent the whole summer surfing. Must be nice."

My fists clench. I want to point out how many summers *he* spent surfing. That the work he's been doing with his dad isn't what kept him from becoming amazing at it, and it isn't what kept him in bed every morning while Luke got up before dawn to get in the line-up. But I think part of the problem isn't so much that Luke is doing something Danny is not, but that he can feel my loyalties shifting, as if I'm on one of those rides where the floor tilts, and no matter how hard I scramble to maintain my footing, I'm inexorably sliding toward one side—Luke's. And Danny might not even realize it, but he's trying to pull me back.

~

THE NEXT MORNING, the sound of tents unzipping wakes me. It's still dark out, but once one of us is up, we're all up.

By the time I climb out of the tent, Beck and Caleb have got the beginnings of a fire going, and Harrison's pulling a grate and kettle out for coffee. Luke is pacing, looking out over the ridge as he waits for enough daylight to see the swell.

I go over to where he stands. "Do you feel ready?"

He turns toward me, the moonlight golden on his dark head, his perfect nose. "As ready as I'm gonna be."

"That isn't really what I asked," I whisper. I don't want to shake his confidence, but I also want him to know he can still back out. "You don't have to do this. Not one guy here would set foot in that water, so they're not going to say a word if you decide this isn't the time."

He regards me for a long moment. "Do *you* want me not to do it?"

No. Of course I don't fucking want you to do it.

But the question feels like more. It feels like he's saying, *"Declare yourself, Juliet. Admit you care about me in a way you shouldn't."*

And that's something I can't do, even if it's true. Even if I meant to end things with Danny months ago because of it.

"I just want you to know you don't have to. Only you can decide whether or not you're ready."

He turns away to stare at the ocean again. "Then it looks like I've decided. Go back to your boyfriend."

I hesitate before I give up and return to the tent, wondering if I might spend the rest of my life regretting not telling him the truth.

THE SUN IS BARELY out when we arrive at the cliffs overlooking Mavericks. We'll be watching from here since the tide has swept the beach away.

The guys argue about which board Luke should use. He's got a big wave gun now, ideal for the conditions. He doesn't want to use it because he's worried it will break and his logic sickens me. *If you're that worried your board will break, you shouldn't be out there in the first place.*

All the guys clap Luke on the back as he zips up his wetsuit. The girls hug him. I stand frozen, doing neither, and I'm the last one he looks at as he turns to start climbing over the rocks to reach the water.

He waits at the lowest rock until the tide rushes in before he jumps, and then he's paddling furiously, a tiny figure on a blue and green board, fighting his way through violent surf to reach the break. Soon he's inside what's probably a sixty-foot wave, working his way to the top, and my heart is in my throat. Am I the only one who understands how wrong this can all go? He's scaling something that could crush him in seconds.

"You want the binoculars?" asks Summer, and I take them with shaking hands, zeroing in on him. He looks like an ant in that wave even now, impossibly fragile.

I think of my brother, of how invulnerable he seemed when he left to talk to the police. They said he never even saw the shooter. That he walked out of the station and was on the ground seconds later.

Humans are so much more fragile than they seem, and you don't know it until it's too late. If Luke fails today—assuming he manages to survive the wave itself and isn't shattered in a thousand ways from that alone—he could still be held under for ten minutes if luck isn't on his side.

I hand her the binoculars. If these are his last moments, I don't want to see him up close. I don't think I want to see them at all.

Danny, beside me, is tense. "This was a bad idea." At last, there's concern for Luke instead of bitterness. "I should have stopped him."

I press my face to my hands, thinking of this morning. I should have told him not to do it. I should have begged him. I should have told him how I feel, either way.

"He's up next," someone says.

I peel my hands from my face just as he takes the next wave, paddling hard to get ahead of it, popping up at the top of the crest before gliding down.

It's a mountain of water, and he's flying over the surface as if it's something solid and unmoving, as if the energy beneath his board isn't rumbling like a freight train.

"He's got it!" someone shouts. "He's fucking got it!"

"Wow," Danny whispers. "He's really doing it."

But just as Luke enters the barrel, there's a bump and he's just...gone.

As if he was never out there at all.

Every exultant shout stops entirely, and everyone—even the strangers scattered across the viewing area—are staring at that one spot in the water where he disappeared.

"Fuck," Beck hisses. He looks to Caleb, then Danny.

They all stand, and suddenly it's chaos. Summer starts crying. The crowd is shouting, and the guys start toward the rocks, though I don't know what the hell they'll do when they get down there—they can't possibly reach Luke without boards. Even *with* boards they'd all just get sucked into the wave and drown with him.

Inside, my very bones are pleading with God to let him be okay, screaming it, but I'm locked so tight I couldn't say it aloud if I wanted to.

I will do anything You want. Just don't take him away from me.

Everyone is running, moving, crying...but I can't seem to unfreeze. I scan the water, desperate for any sign of him, sick to my stomach and numb all at once.

And then, like a miracle, Luke appears. He's bleeding from a cut on his arm and his board is gone but he's there, swimming back toward the shore.

A sob swells in my throat as the guys wade out to help drag him onto the rocks, but it's only when he climbs out and looks straight at me that the sorrow wins out, and I rise to my feet and run.

I have no idea where I'm going. I only know I feel completely out of control, that I can't let anyone see me like this.

I push through the brush with tears streaming down my face, and when I'm out of sight, I press my face to a tree and cry like a baby. I don't even know *why*. He's okay. But my tears aren't just over the terror of those last few minutes. They're about all the things I want from life that I'm not going to get. Luke, most of all.

A twig snaps behind me. I turn to find Luke marching toward me, wetsuit hanging off his hip bones, water glistening on his skin, still bleeding.

"What the fuck, Juliet?" he begins.

I round on him, suddenly livid. It enrages me that he took the risk he just did. *How could he?*

"You fucking scared me!" I cry. "Do you have any idea how devastated I'd be if—"

Before I can say another word, he's closed the distance

between us, one hand wrapping around the back of my neck as he pulls my mouth to his.

It's not a sweet, gentle peck on the lips. It's as if I'm his only source of oxygen, as if he'll die without it. Something desperate, something magical, is pulsing in my blood, blooming as his hands grip my jaw, framing my face in his palms.

"I thought I was going to die, and the only thing that mattered, the only thing I wanted, was you," he says against my mouth. "You were all I fucking thought about."

He pushes my back to the tree, the saltwater on his skin seeping through my clothes. I groan as his hands slide down my sides to drag my hips closer, and I let my fingers dig into his hair, the way I've wanted to...always.

This is what existed between the two of us whether we were touching or not. This is the source of my sharpness with him, the source of his narrowed eyes as he watched me at dinner, and the rage leveled *at* me as often as it was leveled on my behalf.

I register the large, solid weight of him against my abdomen —this too is different from Danny, and thrilling. If there's a voice of conscience inside me, whispering, *"This is wrong,"* it's too faint to make a dent.

I wasn't empty when he left, the way I thought. I was *broken*. And now I'm a bird free of its cage, soaring through the air, and I never, ever want to go back.

"Juliet!" shouts a voice, and it takes us a minute to register that it's *Danny's* voice.

Luke is still pressed against me, still holding my hips, his breath coming as fast as my own. He flinches and steps away, his gaze locked on mine as he shouts his reply. "She's here!"

The horror of what I've just done sinks in. "Luke...I'm sorry."

His nostrils flare. "Don't you dare take it back."

He turns and walks away, down the hill toward camp, and

only seconds later, Danny is before me, his shoulders sagging in relief as he wraps an arm around me. "What happened?" he asks.

"I don't know. I just freaked out."

"Why are you wet?"

I think of Luke's body pressed to mine. The fever of it, the urgency.

"I tripped," I say. "I'm fine."

He slips his fingers through mine, taking me at my word.

And he really shouldn't. Because nothing is fine. I'm not sure it ever will be again.

LUKE and I don't say a word to each other for the rest of the morning. But his eyes meet mine as Danny and I climb in the truck, and there's a question in them: *What are you gonna do, Juliet? Are you going to end things with him now that you finally understand?*

"I don't know," is the answer. I don't know what to do. I promised Donna I'd help. I can't just abandon them now.

But God knows I might not be doing them a favor by staying, either.

27

NOW

I find Donna on the front porch, on the morning of the opening ceremony. She stares at the small stage that's been set up in the yard, something melancholy in her face as she gazes at it, at her dream coming to fruition.

"It's going to be perfect," I assure her.

"I know. It's just a happy occasion and a sad one at the same time."

"Why sad?"

She sighs. "The idea of this house...it's what got me through those first years after Danny died. It felt like I was moving toward something, with Danny. He was still with me."

Her mouth pinches closed, trying to hold in her tears. She's been moving toward this with Danny. And tomorrow, once the house is officially open, it'll be over. They'll be parting ways. I know exactly what she means. I feel it, too, the way I am about to close the door on a part of my life I hated and loved at the same time. The gala's a week away, and I'll leave after that. Where did the time go?

"There will always be more to do here," I tell her. "The kids coming in will need so much from you."

She smiles through her tears and squeezes my hand. "I know," she whispers. "And I know I'm being silly. I just felt like it was us and Danny, taking one last trip together, you know? And there will be other journeys, but he won't be with me for them."

She goes upstairs to get dressed because the caterers will be arriving soon, and I start unloading the dishwasher, my stomach tied in knots.

I have done my best to keep these entities separate—Luke, Grady, the press. Today, they all come together. Today, people will be discussing Danny's life and perhaps his death, creating a fuller picture...and fuller pictures are dangerous.

Luke enters the kitchen. My body blooms to life at the mere sound of his footsteps, but I force myself to ignore him until he steps up beside me with a dishtowel in hand, standing closer than he should.

"Stay away from me today," I tell him, slamming the dishwasher shut before turning to face him. "I don't want people thinking the wrong thing."

He throws the towel on the counter and leans toward me so only I can hear what he's saying. He's like a space heater—I can feel the warmth of him when he's not even touching me.

"My sheets smell like you," he says against my ear, his fingers grazing my neck as he pushes my hair away, "and I have your claw marks on my ass. I could follow you to your room right now and have you begging me to fuck you in *seconds*. It wouldn't even be an effort. So, explain, exactly, how it would be the *wrong* thing for anyone to think."

I shiver at his nearness, goose bumps climbing up my arms, core clenching.

He walks out of the room, not expecting an answer. I'm so tired of pushing him away, I'm so tired of trying to make him hate me, but God knows it matters today most of all.

When I go to my room to get dressed, I lock the door

behind me because he's right—I've never said *no* to him once, even when I was with someone else, and seven years later I still can't manage it.

I cannot be trusted. I guess I already knew that, though.

∼

BY THE AFTERNOON, the sun is blindingly bright, with no breeze to offset it. The caterers all try to remain in the kitchen as much as possible, and the audiovisual guys are drenched in sweat as they tape down power cords in the front yard.

I emerge from my room just before the ceremony in a beige Dries Van Noten sheath and matching heels. It's the most prim, conservative clothing I own, but Luke's gaze still feeds on me like I'm wearing nothing at all.

The board members arrive and come inside to escape the heat while seats begin to fill. When it's finally time for all of us to file outside to the reserved rows in front, I follow them out... and come to a stumbling halt.

Why the fuck is the reporter from the *Times* here? I expected local press, but an event like this would only merit a line or two in her article at most—so she must be here for something else.

Is she hoping someone will break?

It's a gathering of the people who knew Danny best, many of whom were with him when he died, and perhaps she's hoping one of them will say something about it, that they'll peel back another layer from the mystery of what *really* happened to him.

There were thirty of us in the house that weekend. Thirty people drinking and chatting and having conversations with Danny that I wasn't privy to. Thirty people who might have overheard my final moments with him and kept it to themselves all this time, who had suspicions about me and Luke they finally want to voice.

Luke's sitting at one end of the first row, so I head toward Libby, sitting at the other, and he watches me. There's something warm in his gaze, even after what I said this morning, even after the way I've behaved since I got here. As if he knows I'd give anything in the world to be able to sit by his side during this. That I'd give anything for us to be able to hold hands, just like Grady and Libby are, and not have anyone find it troubling.

Libby smiles at me as I sit. "How are you, hon?"

I force a smile. "Fine. You guys did a great job."

"*You* did a great job. It's your money and fame that made this what it is."

I shake my head, unwilling to take the credit. This wasn't charity on my part. It was penance.

Grady says a prayer and then Donna steps up to the microphone, looking tiny and worn in the bright sun. Her blue eyes swim with tears before she's said a word.

"Just before we left for Nicaragua," she begins, then her voice gets rough and she has to stop to clear her throat. "Just before we left for Nicaragua when Danny was five, we stopped to pick up fast food. He had a bit of a tantrum because I wouldn't let him get a soda."

I smile. Anyone who's ever seen a kid in a restaurant knows there's usually a tantrum thrown about soda.

"When we left, there was a man huddled outside the restaurant asking for help. Danny wanted to give him our food, so we did." She stops again, her hands gripping the podium so hard they're nearly bloodless. "Our stomachs were growling later, and his father said he hoped Danny had learned a lesson from it. And Danny said...Danny said, *'I can do a bad thing and still do good things.'*" Donna brushes at the tears running down her face. "So, when you remember my son, when you think of this house, just know that you, too, can make mistakes, but as long as you can still find a little bit of love inside yourself, it isn't too late." She smiles at me. "That's what this house is for. For all the children who are certain they are bad and unlovable. So that they can find the good that's been in them all along."

Tears stream down Donna's cheeks, and the ache in my chest can no longer be held in. I press my face to my hands as I start to cry. She just used this moment, her moment and Danny's, to tell me to forgive myself.

Libby squeezes my knee before she walks to the stage, and then someone takes her seat and an arm wraps around me, too heavy and too perfect to be any arm but Luke's. I press my face into the stiff fabric of his jacket and cry like a kid against his chest. I thought it was best that we stay apart here, today, when people are watching. When someone might put it together.

I'm glad he didn't listen to me.

28

THEN

JANUARY-MARCH, 2015

I don't know what the pastor's bypass surgery was supposed to accomplish, but it didn't work. He comes home less mobile than he was, and far crankier. Donna rents a hospital bed for him and puts it in the family room—it's supposed to be temporary, but he makes no effort to get himself back upstairs. Slowly, she moves more and more of his things down to the first floor until we've all accepted that this is the way it's going to stay. Danny learned about the surgery after the fact, but he has no clue how bad things still are.

The pastor shuffles out of the house a few times a week—to speak at church on Sunday, to perform the odd funeral or wedding—and Donna does everything else: she supervises Grady, manages Sunday School, the church women's group, the charitable outreach and Bible study. She pays the bills, oversees the Sunday bulletin and refreshments, and all the church correspondence.

She's good at it, tirelessly checking her lists, making her calls, and running back and forth from the church to the house. She's come into her own, at last, but I am wilting: stuck with the awful Miss Johnson by day, stuck with the pastor bitching about gratitude at night while he treats me like a servant. I haven't worked at the diner in nearly two months, and I'm wondering if they'll even take me back when this ends. *If* this ends.

In the middle of February, Danny calls to say that Ryan's aunt has a house in Malibu available for spring break.

"You've got to come," he says.

I don't know who'd look after the pastor while I was gone, but the more important point is that I don't think I should be in the same house as Luke, ever again.

There isn't an hour that goes by that I'm not thinking of him. Every time I get home, I think of him sitting at the kitchen table, watching me cook. Every time I pass the diner, I think of him walking in the door, of the way he'd watch me come toward him with the bagel or Danish he didn't order, the way his gaze felt palpable as I poured his coffee. And then I think of the way he kissed me at Mavericks, and how I was liquid, boneless, and burning alive all at the same time. How in the brief span of that kiss, I remembered what it was like to feel alive.

I want to see him so much I could weep. And that's precisely why I shouldn't go.

"I doubt I could get out of my internship," I reply. "Your break won't be the same as the school district's."

"Juliet, that internship isn't even *paid*. Who cares if you miss a week?"

I'm...stung. "I didn't realize you thought so little of it."

He sighs. "Come on. I didn't mean it like that. I just meant... it's flexible, right? They've got to understand it isn't your first priority. I'll have my mother talk to her friend. I'm sure she can arrange it."

When I want to do the wrong thing, the Allens get in my way. But then I try to do the right thing and they're in my way too.

No wonder I feel so trapped.

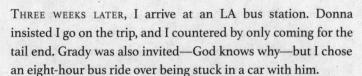

THREE WEEKS LATER, I arrive at an LA bus station. Donna insisted I go on the trip, and I countered by only coming for the tail end. Grady was also invited—God knows why—but I chose an eight-hour bus ride over being stuck in a car with him.

I walk outside into the balmy air and look around. There are tall buildings, mountains, and millions of people no one knows, and for a moment I find myself desperately wanting to stay. To just grab another bus and head into the city and make it my home. It would be a fresh start, a place where I can be anyone, where I can reinvent myself.

Luke's Jeep glides to a stop in front of me with Danny at the wheel. I guess Luke is surfing, or didn't care about seeing me.

We head toward the coast, and I stare at all the shops and restaurants as we pass them, trying to quell my longing. No one would know me in any of those places. No one will have heard the pastor talk about the bruised girl who wasn't safe, who couldn't count on a hot meal, who was scared to go home.

I'd just be...a girl.

I force my gaze to Danny. "How's the surfing here?"

He shrugs. "Bad surfing is better than none. The house is kind of a dump, though," he warns. "We're sleeping on the floor."

"That's okay," I reply. It's not the house I'm worried about. It's Luke. I have no idea what to expect from him when I arrive: will he fault me for staying with the Allens after that kiss? Will he try to do it again? And what will I say to him if that happens?

"There's no pool or anything," Danny continues. "We've just been using the neighbors'."

"They don't mind?"

He laughs. "I'm not sure they *know*. The family's in France for spring break. The girls are following their travel on Instagram and very jealous."

We enter Malibu and take a left into a development along the coast. I'd always assumed Malibu held nothing but mansions, but the ramshackle house Danny pulls up to—two lots back from the beach—is a one-story relic of earlier days, with a gutter that hangs askew and two different bird fountains in the front yard filled with algae and rainwater. Definitely not a mansion. I stare at the wooden walkway along the house's side, the one that would lead me to Luke, and my stomach spins with a sick sort of excitement.

Danny guides me inside, where I find shag carpeting, Formica counters, linoleum floors. Someone has pushed the coffee table off to the side of the room and replaced it with a keg. There are red plastic cups and people I've never laid eyes on wandering through the kitchen, and then the side door opens and a bunch of guys file through, laughing and loud, throwing sandy towels on a chair by the door.

Luke is the last to walk in, wearing a wetsuit hanging off his waist. His gaze locks on mine and I can't seem to look away. Nothing has changed. The pull toward him is as strong as it ever was, and I'm not sure how I ever hoped it wouldn't be.

Danny's arm wraps around my waist and Luke walks straight to the fridge and grabs a beer. He's had half of it before he even turns around to face me again. "Jules," he says quietly. There's a storm in his eyes—this thing hasn't died for him either.

He grabs a second one as he heads to the shower.

By the time he emerges again, pizza has arrived.

Luke sits across from me and Danny and eats while a girl hangs all over him.

I didn't know it would be this hard. I didn't know that I'd struggle to even *look* at anyone but him, that I'd want to throw over the whole fucking table to get that girl away. It's always bothered me, seeing him like this, but it's far worse now. I know he's not mine. I know he never will be. But do these girls even see past the surface? Is it all because of his face, his body? Or do they understand his secret sweetness—that lost look he gets on his face sometimes, the one that makes me want to curl up in his lap and ease it away?

I don't want them to have noticed—those things are all mine.

"I'm so fucking sick of pizza," says one of the guys, which is when I realize I was staring at Luke again. I've got to stop.

"Juliet can cook," Danny offers. "You got some experience cooking for a crowd all summer, right?"

Before I can reply, before I can reluctantly agree to do the same shit I do every night, Luke slams his beer bottle down.

"She's not here as the help, right, Dan?" he asks. "If she's the housekeeper, our bathroom could use a good scrub, but you'd better offer her a salary first."

Danny laughs, good-natured as ever. "Of course she's not the housekeeper, but she's like my mom. She loves to take care of people." He turns to me. "You don't mind, right? It's not like you'll be surfing all day."

There's no way to gracefully tell him, *"No"* in front of everyone. There's no way to say, *"I thought this was my vacation, too, and as it happens, I fucking hate to cook."* But Luke, in his own way, was standing up for me. I've hung him out to dry before, with Aaron Tomlinson and Donna. I'm not doing it again.

"Are *you* going to help?" I ask.

Danny's eyes widen. He glances at me, waiting to see if I'm joking. "Uh, sure? I guess? I mean, I'll be surfing all day and you might not have much to do, but..."

"I'll swim."

He laughs. "Babe, the water is cold as hell. Believe me, you don't want to swim."

My resentment grows. Why am I even here, then? Why am I sleeping on the fucking floor and not drinking and not having sex and not going in the water? Is it all so he can show them all what a great little lady he's wrangled for himself? *She cooks! She cleans! She spends eight hours on a bus just because I ask her to!*

"Super," I say between my teeth. "Then you surf, and when you're done and you want to cook, you let me know. Otherwise, we're ordering pizza."

Luke's mouth twitches. A smile he couldn't quite hide. It feels like a pat on the head.

"Where's your drink, Juliet?" Ryan calls and I glance at him.

"You're right. My drink *is* missing, Ryan. I'd better rectify that."

I go into the kitchen and make myself a rum and Coke, but Caleb sees me wincing and pours me a margarita from the pitcher he just blended up. I take a walk on the beach with the girls who came here with Beck and Caleb, and slowly, I relax. I was worried I'd feel like a loser, as the one person here who isn't in college, but most of the conversation is about sex, the guys' drunken antics, and how little interest either of them have in surfing...I can understand most of that.

I almost see how I could even belong somewhere, in a house that wasn't the Allens'.

By the time we get back, most of the guys, including Luke, have gone out to a bar. Danny waves from the table where he's playing cards with Grady...who's saying something about sin. Naturally.

"Why is he even here?" I ask under my breath.

Caleb grins and grabs my drink to refill it. "He's just worried we might need someone to tell us what the Bible *really* thinks about homosexuals. You can never be reminded too often."

I laugh. It's kind of a revelation to be around people who say the wrong thing, who think the wrong thing and don't feel bad about it. In the Allens' home, I'm the outlier, the one who doesn't share their faith and doesn't care the way I should. Here, though, I have the potential to be almost...normal.

If only Danny saw it that way.

"Sweetie, you'd better slow down," he says, walking over as I take a seat with my second margarita.

I slowly lower my glass. "Why?"

"I just don't want you to do something you regret," he answers.

I'm sick of being treated like I'm a child in need of guidance, the misguided girl from a bad home who still needs his help. He's trying to protect me from myself, but maybe I'm not so evil that I *need* to be protected from myself. Maybe I'm just like everyone else.

As the night wears on, couples slip off to dark corners, or to the beach, and the drunks pass out in chairs or on the floor. I *keep* drinking, childishly defiant until I'm slurring my words and feeling like I just need a good cry. Only then do I go to the air mattress we're sleeping on and pass out.

I wake in the middle of the night to find the house is dark and silent and the room is spinning, Danny's arm draped over me, heavy and suffocating.

I'm still drunk, but my thoughts feel clearer than they ever have before.

Danny has no idea what I need, and he doesn't care. If I tell him I'd like to surf, he'll say it's not a good idea. And if I say I want to dance, or drink, those won't be good ideas either. It's as if the mere act of me wanting something for myself is enough to *make* it a bad idea, and I just need to get away.

I crawl from the room because I'm drunk enough that I suspect if I try to stand, I'm going to trip, which is exactly what happens the minute I enter the living room.

I wait and make sure the crash hasn't woken anyone before venturing out the side door.

"Juliet," Luke croons, his voice like hot syrup pouring over my skin, six-plus feet of warm muscle blocking my path. "Where do you think you're going?"

"Shhh," I say, overloud. "I'm going swimming."

He laughs. "It's three a.m. Also, that water is cold as fuck."

I keep walking. Now that I've decided to live my own life, I'm not allowing anyone, not even him, to stop me.

He walks alongside me. "Haven't you ever seen Jaws? A hot girl swimming late at night—guaranteed great white attack."

I frown at him. "Then go away so you won't have to watch."

"What's gotten into you?" he asks. "Since when do you sneak out to swim late at night?"

"Oh my God," I groan, running my hands through my hair. "You're as bad as Danny. Jesus Christ. I'm almost nineteen, and I can't even walk out of a vacation house without a million questions about my safety and motives!"

I'm too loud now, but we're close enough to the beach that it's drowned out by the crashing waves. I can see him clearly in the moonlight—his arms crossed over his chest, biceps bulging, an amused smile on his face.

He's laughing at me.

"Fuck you," I say on an exhale and start walking again.

I go down to the shore. The water is so cold that it burns. There's no way I'm going in. Another attempt at independence foiled. Inexplicably, I feel like I'm going to cry.

"Is this big and bad and dangerous enough for you, Jules?" Luke asks. His smile is a slight thing, belied by the misery in his eyes. He's closer than I realized.

There's a lump in my throat growing, and growing, so fast I can't seem to make it stop. It's not about the fucking water. It's simply as if this past miserable year has finally caught up with me, along with the miserable years preceding it. The world has been crushing me a little more with each passing day, and I feel pinned under its weight. That ache in my chest and throat gives way at last, not in quiet, subtle tears but huge rolling sobs that make my shoulders shake.

He pulls me against him. "Jules. Stop. It's okay."

His hand runs over my hair as he shushes me, then he pulls

me back to the sand to sit beside him. "You remember what I said last summer, about you needing to be willing to leave the cage?"

I nod, still too upset to try to speak.

"It was what I thought the day we met. Watching you at the Allens'—it reminded me of this lady on our street who got a macaw. You know—the big blue ones with all the feathers? But she treated it like a little bird. She didn't let it fly, she kept it in a small cage, fed it the same shit. It started to lose its feathers, but she kept right on treating it like a regular bird until finally it died."

I look up at him through my tears, waiting.

"You're the bird," he says softly, his fingers brushing my mouth. "You're something wild and magnificent, and he has no idea how to take care of you, so he spends all his time making sure your cage is secure because he has no idea what else to do. And that's why this kills me, Juliet. Because I think I *do* know how to take care of you, and I want to take his place so bad that it fucking hurts to look at you sometimes."

My heart hammers, ready to burst.

His mouth lowers and I don't stop him. His lips are soft, his skin is warm. A thrill starts deep in my gut and seeps through my bones. I've wanted this for a very long time, since it first happened last winter. Since the first day he walked into the diner.

I've wanted nothing but him for going on two years, and I can't say no.

My mouth opens beneath his and he groans, pushing his fingers through my hair.

I slide my palms under his shirt and over his chest, the beautiful expanse of skin I've wanted to touch a million times and could not. And now I am. It's really happening and I can't move fast enough. He lays me back in the sand and pulls me against him so I can feel the effect this has on him. He's hard as a rock and he's not ashamed of it or blaming me for it. His eyes are bright, feverish, and he's not ashamed of that either. He wants this so much he's going to combust, just like I am, and he thinks that's a *good* thing.

His fingers slide lower, between my legs, beneath my loose shorts, inside me.

"Oh, fuck, Juliet," he rasps. "You're so ready."

Is there a part of me that thinks I should stop him? Of course. But there's a bigger part of me that knows I could no sooner stop this than I could stop a freight train or the planet's orbit around the sun.

He doesn't remove the shorts but continues to drag his fingers back and forth, dipping inside me, swirling around my clit. It's different than anything I've felt before, electric and raw. His mouth is at my neck, his teeth sinking into my skin, his hand moving faster, and then out of nowhere I shatter, crying out, digging my nails into his arms.

I feel the hard press of his erection against my hip and reach for him blindly, sliding my hand beneath his waistband. He's throbbing, so big my palm doesn't quite wrap around him.

"Jules," he groans, breathing heavy. It's a question, one I answer by pulling him above me and pushing his shorts down.

"Yes," I whisper.

He checks my face one more time before he tugs off my sleep shorts and lets his weight settle, his cock nudging between my legs. I shift just enough that he can push in.

Luke is careful. Agonizingly slow. Checking on me to make sure I'm okay. He stills for a moment, flinching, when he finally bottoms out, then captures my mouth, his tongue tangling with mine. I'm stretched tight but it's perfect at the same time.

And the perfection of it is such a relief.

I don't need to let my mind wander, the way I did with Justin and Danny. I'm not counting the seconds until it's over. I want it to go on and on forever, just like this.

He grunts as he bottoms out again. "*Jules*. Fuck."

He moves faster, his breath rasping, his kisses desperate and savage as he tries not to come. And then, at last, he does, with three violent thrusts and a quiet gasp against my neck.

He collapses against me, and I never want him to pull out. I never want this to end but...*oh my God, what am I going to do?*

How do I face Danny in the morning after this?

Luke's eyes open slowly. "Don't." He holds my chin, forcing me to meet his gaze. "Don't ruin this."

I nod through my tears. I don't want to ruin it either, I really don't. But I'm not sure how we move on from here.

He rolls off me, and I sit up, still drunk...but also sober at the same time.

"I should go," I whisper.

He sits up beside me and winds his fingers through mine. "Jules, you've got to end it with him. This thing with us has been there since the beginning, and it's never going away. You know that."

Except the pastor is sick and Donna needs me, and I've spent almost every penny I have, so even if I was willing to abandon the Allens, I'm not sure how I'd do it.

He kisses me and I try to let my answering kiss respond in kind. I try to let my kiss say, *"Luke, I love you so much I'm sick from it, so much that you've ruined my happiness, because no matter how good my life is I will always want you. And I will always want you more than all the rest. But walking away isn't nearly as easy as you think."*

We walk back to the house in silence, my body light and heavy at the same time. When I reach the bedroom, I crawl onto the air mattress and look at Danny's face in the moonlight. He's so peaceful, so innocent. He trusts me, and I'm not sure what makes me feel worse: the fact that I cheated or that I might be the person who destroys that innocence.

I believed I loved him, I really did. And I guess I do love

him, but not in the right way. I love him like a brother or a best friend. I just didn't know, until Luke, that I was supposed to feel more.

Is it better or worse to pretend it didn't happen and keep it all to myself? Am I even capable of pretending now? Luke is in my blood. I can still taste the saltwater on his lips, hear his exhale in my ear, his body slick with sweat and gritty with sand. I can still feel the way something inside me unfurled when I was beneath him, some hungry prisoner who'd kept quiet a little too long.

I don't know how I can live without it anymore.

I WAKE TOO EARLY in the morning. It's just past dawn and the guys are already making a racket, getting ready to surf.

Luke's in the kitchen, the ubiquitous wet suit hanging off his hips. I take in his lean body, the hollows in his broad shoulders, his firm stomach, and all I can think of is my hands in those hollows, my body arching into that stomach, and the way he looked at me, as if nothing in the world mattered more.

My hair's a rat's nest, my mouth kiss-swollen, my eyes half-asleep, but when he turns, he looks at me like he's never seen anything better. And like he'd very much like to repeat what happened last night.

Danny's hand lands on my shoulder like a bucket of ice. I have to stifle my desire to shudder in response, but Luke stifles nothing. His eyes drop to that hand and his mouth flattens. *Don't do this, Luke. Please don't.*

"You not surfing today, Dan?" asks Ryan, wandering through the swirl of tension in the room without a clue.

"I'll come out later. I'm going to hang here with Juliet for a while."

Luke's eyes flicker over me again, possession in his gaze. "She should be surfing too."

"I can't surf."

"I think you could do anything you set your mind to," he replies.

I'm pretty sure he's not talking about surfing. My heart gallops in my chest as I look away.

When Danny finally leaves, after breakfast, I gather my stuff to shower. The bathroom is disgusting, with three days of hair and filth that no one has touched, so I walk to the neighbors' house, the one whose pool they used last night. I unlatch the child lock at the top of the tall wooden gate as Caleb's girlfriend instructed me and discover a clear rectangular pool gleaming in the sun. Above me, the house has multiple decks overlooking the ocean, but I ignore them in favor of the enclosed shower around the corner from the pool.

I linger under the heated spray, soaping myself, shampooing twice, shaving carefully. Everything feels sensual today, reminding me of Luke's hands on my skin, his weight above me. To Danny, I've long represented something bad, something he needs to keep at a distance, covered from view. Luke made me feel priceless, seductive, and desirable in the best possible way.

After I dry off, I climb into the rich family's hammock on the second floor, swaying in the breeze.

Caleb's girlfriend showed me the family's Instagram—the beautiful wife, her adoring husband, and their two little girls grinning in front of Parisian landmarks.

How do you get a life like that? How do you get to be with the person you love and have children with him, and take off for Paris instead of your vacation home in Malibu?

I fall asleep in the hammock with my hair still wrapped in a towel, dreaming that it's my house and that Luke's the husband who wants to whisk us away. I don't even care where he takes me.

I AVOID LUKE THAT EVENING. He goes to the neighbors' house to swim and I remain behind with Danny, not drinking.

When Danny and I go to bed, I lay on the air mattress facing the ceiling, wide awake. I can't get comfortable because even the smallest motion on my part makes the entire mattress roll like a boat in a storm. I'm not sure I'd be able to get comfortable anyway—with every memory of Luke, of him touching me and kissing me, comes a sick pulse of shame.

I also can't escape the desire to do it again.

Eventually I rise, taking my blanket with me. I'd sleep better in the neighbor's hammock than I would here. I enter the living room and find Luke on the couch. His gaze is on me, and though I mean to keep walking out the door, he holds out his hand and I'm drawn to it, unwillingly. He pulls me down beside him, his muscles tightening as he wraps himself around me. We fit together perfectly, two objects that were made only for the other. I inhale the salt of his skin, let myself bask in its heat.

He's already hard and we've been here for seconds. I'm instantly wet at the very idea of repeating last night. His hand slides between my thighs and inside my sleep shorts and he exhales against my neck—quick and sharp—when he discovers it for himself.

I rise, grabbing my blanket and heading for the door, and he follows.

Last night was unplanned. We were drunk and it could all have been written off as a regrettable mistake. But this is as intentional as it could possibly be. His fingers tighten around mine as if he's worried my conscience might make a sudden reappearance, but there's no need.

I don't simply want this. I *need* this. I need everything from him I can get, and I know there might never be another chance. I'll end things with Danny eventually—I have to, after what I did and what I'm about to do again—but me and Luke? That will never happen. It would destroy Danny, and Donna too. This has got to be the last time.

We step off the wooden boardwalk and into the sand. He leads me to a dark corner, where the bayberry hedges cast shadows, blocking us from the moonlight's glare, and then he tugs me against him and kisses me as if it's all he's thought of since last night.

His hand slips between my legs again. "You've been wet like this the whole goddamn day, haven't you?" he asks, his mouth moving over my neck.

I nod and he pulls me down to the sand and kneels between my legs as he pushes them apart. His finger runs down the center of my chest.

"One day," he says, "we are going to do this where I don't have to worry anyone will walk in on us. And then I'm going to get you naked in my bed and keep you there for days."

I open my mouth to reply, but that finger he just ran along my chest is pushing inside me and whatever I was going to say becomes a quiet moan.

He tugs my shorts over to the side and then slides down, pressing a gentle kiss between my legs before his tongue starts to move.

It's different than intercourse. It's different than anything else. It's slick and hot and soft all at once, and when I groan, he reaches beneath me, grabbing my ass to pull me closer to his face, his tongue flickering mercilessly. My toes tense, my feet arch. My whole body is coiled tight as a spring, and when it releases, I cry out, stunned into carelessness, shocked into utter disregard for anything but this.

"I—" My words trail off. "I don't even know what to say."

I sound drugged.

He climbs over me. "Jules," he says, and it's the plea in his voice, the desperation in it, that wakes me up. He's pressed rigid against his shorts, the fullness of him resting on my abdomen. "Can I—"

I reach for him, pushing the shorts down, and in one surging thrust he slams inside me.

"God," he whispers. "*Yes*."

It's different than what he just did with his tongue, and as satisfied as I thought I was, I can already feel my belly tightening, my muscles clenching around him. Those nerve endings wake to life again and my hands slide down to grip his ass. "Go slow," I beg.

"You're gonna come again?" The words are a grunt, disbelief, hope, and desperation all at once.

I gasp at his next sharp thrust. "Yes."

"Fuck," he hisses, and somehow I know he's not expressing disappointment. He's simply struggling not to finish too soon.

His mouth moves to my neck, and his hand slides beneath my t-shirt to palm my breast and then pinch my nipple. And all the while he's moving inside me, and I'm so slick and so full that I can feel a second orgasm coming faster than I ever imagined.

When it hits, I sink my teeth into his shoulder to stifle my scream, and with a series of jabbing thrusts he joins me, groaning against my neck as he lets go.

I'd give anything, anything in the fucking world to stay just like we are. To fall asleep like this, and wake like this, and have it all turn out okay. For a moment he lets his weight sink into me. *Relax. Yes, stay*. But then he rolls beside me and pulls me to his chest.

"A room," he says. "We'll run off and have a room of our own. No, fuck it. We'll have a whole house."

I laugh quietly. "I thought of that today. I went to the neighbor's place to take a shower and then I laid in their hammock and imagined it was ours."

"We'd have a house just like that, but with way better waves than these. An oceanfront home facing the Pipeline, maybe, and every morning I'll go surf and you'll sleep in, and then I'll come back and make you breakfast."

I laugh. When he dreams, he dreams big. Neither of us could even afford an oceanfront *shed*.

"That sounds like a pretty easy life for me. Am I at least responsible for buying the groceries?"

"No. You can't because I'll have burned all your clothes."

I giggle again. "If you've burned all my clothes, can I even go outside?"

"You make a good point. Okay, I'll put up some hedges for privacy so you can go into the yard, but no farther." He pinches me. "You can finally open that copy of *Wuthering Heights* you kept claiming to read for school. Now ask me what we'll do after breakfast."

"Okay, what are we doing after breakfast?"

He rolls above me. "You've been sitting there eating pancakes naked for thirty minutes. What the fuck do you think we're doing?"

I'm still laughing when he pushes inside me again, surging harder and harder like a storm coming in. And when I'm close, when my body stiffens and I'm sinking my nails into his back because I need him to tip me over the edge, he gasps against my ear.

"God, I'd do anything to have that," he says, and for a single blissful moment, when I'm blind and senseless and stunned by the force of my orgasm, distantly aware of his hoarse cry as he joins me, it feels as if it all came true.

As if there is another life in which we moved to Hawaii and never let the world come between us. Where we'd sway in a hammock, wondering if we should take our twin girls to Paris. And ultimately decide we were too happy where we were to ever leave.

29

NOW

There's a small reception after the ceremony for Danny's House.

Caleb, Beck, and Harrison are here, as handsome as ever but world weary now. Caleb has some kind of tech company, Beck's still at the bar, and Harrison's an attorney. Somehow, I'd pictured them happier in adulthood than they are, and it was kind of them to come out for this on a workday, especially when they live to the north, but I sort of wish they hadn't. That *New York Times* reporter seems to be roving from group to group. She'll get to them eventually, and God knows what they'll say.

"It was a nice ceremony," Harrison says. "Danny would love this. And it's a much better way to remember him than..." He trails off.

"Than what?" I demand, my voice sharper than I intended.

His eyes widen. "I shouldn't have brought it up. But you know...the night he died, he just wasn't himself. He argued with Luke, he—"

"He was drinking," I say firmly.

They're too polite to point out that the bad mood came first.

"Well, anyway, I'd like to remind you all that *I'm* the one who said Juliet and Luke would be famous," Caleb announces with a grin.

"Anyone who heard Juliet sing knew she'd be famous," Beck counters. "But Luke, not so much. That asshole still can't surf."

My eyes widen until I hear Luke's laughter behind me.

"True," Luke says. "But I still surf better than you, Beck."

They shake hands, and I'm about to excuse myself when Luke clears his throat. "But in all seriousness, I guess I've got one of you guys to thank. Those boards I was able to buy from the GoFundMe donation made all this possible. So, who was it? Which of you fronted the three grand?"

They all look at each other, confused.

"Believe me, I'd be taking all the credit now if it was me, but I was working as an unpaid intern," says Harrison. He turns to Caleb. "Was it you?"

Caleb's brow furrows. "Where the hell would I have gotten a spare three thousand dollars, asshole? I was working as a *lifeguard*."

They both look at Beck, and Caleb laughs. "We know it wasn't *you*. You were borrowing gas money from *us*."

"It had to be one of you guys," Luke says. "Juliet made this big, embarrassing announcement around the bonfire basically insisting everyone donate, and the money was in there a few hours later."

They look at each other, and then Luke looks at me, and I see something shift in his face. A question, one he dismisses then calls back. *"She had no money,"* he's telling himself. *"It would have taken every penny she had."*

"I'd better check on Donna," I say with a forced smile. "I'll see you guys at the gala, right?"

I don't even remain long enough to hear their answer. I cross the yard toward Donna, who's talking to a stunning woman in a nicely tailored suit. I realize, belatedly, that the girl is Summer, all grown up. She's ditched the bleached blonde hair and heavy self-tanner, lost a little of the baby fat.

Is she here for Luke? She always liked him, and I'm pretty sure they slept together. *Of course she's here for Luke.*

She throws her arms around me. "You're more gorgeous than ever," she says, then turns to Donna. "I was so jealous of Juliet, back in the day. She was the only girl in the group that was taken, and she was still the one they all wanted."

My smile falters. "That's not true. But anyway—"

"Oh, it was definitely true. My God, the way they all mooned over you at night. And then you started singing and it was game over for me and Rain."

My gaze darts to Donna, wondering if she knows what Summer's really saying. It wasn't that everyone wanted me, it's that Luke did.

"Just look at all of them over there," she continues. "How did they manage to get even more attractive?"

I glance at Luke across the yard, in a blue shirt, now slightly unbuttoned, tie loosened. He's so lovely. She wants another shot. How could she not?

And in the meantime, the reporter is with Libby and Grady, and Luke's talking to the prep school guys about that donation. I'm beginning to think this day can't get worse.

"So good to see you," I tell Summer, squeezing her hand as I walk away. I want to stop everything that's happening right now. I want to pull a fire alarm or call in a bomb threat, and I know as I walk into the house, frantic and lost, that even those things might not stop what's already in motion.

I go to the kitchen and sink into a seat. I fucked up, during that interview. I fucked up by refusing to mention Luke when she was bound to find out that he lived here with us for two summers. It's highly suspicious, that omission of mine, a neon sign saying, *"Check out this clue I've left for you."*

I close my eyes and press my face to my hands, briefly imagining that I didn't come back to Rhodes in the first place, imagining all the choices I *could* have made that would have led to a different outcome. And finally, I let myself dream of the outcome that was always the most improbable, the one I fall asleep to at night during my weakest moments. The one I'd have given up almost anything for and still would: Luke and I, together, swaying in a hammock outside the beach house we share.

"You're sure you don't want to go to Paris for spring break?" he asks.

The breeze from the ocean ruffles his hair, and I reach up to push a hand through it. *"I'm sure."* I can't imagine anything better than where we are because I've seen the entire world now, and it was meaningless without him.

"Juliet?"

I startle, my head jerking up, resentful that I've been pulled out of my reverie, guilty I was there in the first place.

The reporter stands there, her head tilted, her eyes slightly narrowed.

She followed me into my fucking home. She must be feeling pretty sure of herself to just walk in here after me.

"Yes?" I ask, rising, my voice brusque. A *you-have-no-right-to-be-here* voice, as if this woman has ever cared about boundaries.

"It was a very nice service," she says, but there's something more guarded in her demeanor than there was the night we met. "I'm surprised you never mentioned Luke Taylor lived here too. Especially given how close you were."

I lick my lips and smooth my dress, stalling for time. "Whether or not Luke wants to discuss living here is his business, not mine. It didn't seem like it was my place. And we were hardly 'close'."

She raises a brow. "He was in several altercations on your behalf. Sounds pretty close to me."

Altercations, she said. *Plural.* Who even knows about most of them except him and me? This has gone off the fucking rails and all I can do is deny it. "I have no idea what you're talking about. If Luke got into any fight because of me, he was doing it on Danny's behalf, not mine."

"So you're denying you were close," she states. "Even though you were the one who begged him not to make that risky jump right before Danny died."

Who told you that? I guess it could have been anyone. It might have even come from the police interviews when it happened.

"Several of us begged Luke not to make that jump," I snap. "I wasn't even the first. I can't imagine how any of this is relevant to an article about Danny's House, and you agreed the article wouldn't focus on Danny's death."

She gives me a thin smile. "The article is about *you*, Juliet. And to be honest, the most striking thing I've found so far is how desperate you are *not* to talk about Danny."

I stare at her, my mouth dry.

I was so careful for so many years and now I've ruined everything. I just keep making it worse.

I walk past her, flinging the door open. "Because I don't want the speculation to hurt Donna. And this is still a private residence," I say over my shoulder, stepping over the threshold, "so get the fuck out of here before I call the cops."

Outside, the crowd is dispersing. I'm relieved to see that Libby and Grady are gone. Donna stands with Luke, Summer, and the rest of the guys. I've got no choice but to join them.

Luke glances at me. "There's a new bar at the beach. We're all driving over there. You want to go?"

I have no desire to listen to them rehash the past while Luke studies me, trying to find something in the words I don't say, the answers I don't offer.

"No thanks," I reply stiffly.

"You should," he says, looking to Donna for help. "You've barely left."

But Donna simply smiles at him. "Go ahead, Luke. We'll have a nice night in, just the two of us. I think Summer needs a ride though, don't you?"

"Yes," says Summer, brightening. "My sister dropped me off. Do you mind?"

Luke glances at me once more before he shakes his head. "No, of course not."

"That's nice, seeing them together," Donna says as Luke and Summer walk away. "Don't you think they're a good match?"

No. I don't think that. Not at all. I feel like I'm going to be sick.

"She's not really his type."

"What do you mean? She's gorgeous. And doesn't she surf too?"

Yes, and she'll have her hand on his fly before they've even got their seat belts on. "I don't know."

"Oh, honey," Donna says, hugging me from the side, misinterpreting my tone. "You *know* what it's like to be in love. You've had that. Don't you think Luke deserves that too?"

Yes. Yes, he does. And I want him to be happy. I want him to move on. But I don't want to watch it happen.

DONNA and I snack on leftovers from the reception in lieu of dinner and watch several dumb sitcoms with laugh tracks. And the whole time, I stew. Luke's been gone for a long time. Caleb and Harrison have wives now—I doubt they're still out drinking—and Beck owns a fucking bar...he probably had to leave for work.

So it's just Luke and newly gorgeous Summer, reliving old times on the beach or in the back of his truck.

Donna goes to her room and I go to mine, and I hate myself for the fact that, on this day, when we celebrated Danny, I'm only thinking of Luke. I wonder if Danny is somewhere witnessing this, and if he's as disgusted with me as I am with myself.

Eventually, I hear Luke in the hall. I wait for him to go through his night-time routine, the sounds I've memorized: toilet flushing, water running, lights switched off, his retreating footsteps. Instead, my door opens and closes.

He sits at the end of my bed and puts his hand on my leg. "I know you're awake," he says quietly.

I say nothing until I'm sure my voice will hold up. "Did you kiss her?"

Silence.

"Get out," I hiss, but he does not.

He pulls the sheet down, stretches out over me, and lets his weight push me into the mattress as he whispers in my ear. "Would it bother you if I did?"

"Get out," I growl, and attempt to throw him off, but he doesn't move at all.

"Answer the question."

"No," I snap. "It wouldn't bother me."

"You're a liar." His hand slides beneath the sheet, up my thigh, beneath my shorts. "I thought so." He laughs, and I stiffen as his fingers slide inside me.

"Get out," I hiss for the third time, but he's already removing my shorts.

"I didn't kiss her," he says, sliding down the bed, his hands on the inside of my thighs, pressing them open. His tongue flickers between my legs.

I gasp, and there's a huff of breath against my clit as he laughs. It infuriates and excites me at the same time, and it barely takes him two minutes to make me come exactly the way he knew I would, arching upward, digging my hands in his hair.

He climbs back up my body, shoving his pants down, already certain I won't say *no* to this either.

"Admit you were jealous." He pushes inside me.

I meet his gaze and say nothing, but I grip him tight just in case he's considering walking away.

"Admit you're the one who gave me the money," he says, his mouth running over my neck, his hand sliding beneath my tank to pinch my nipple. I arch into him, wanting more.

His hand fists in my hair. "You're still in love with me," he says, thrusting harder.

I clench around him. I'm so close to coming. I'm so close to breaking open in a hundred different ways.

Yes, I was jealous. Yes, I made that donation. Yes, I'm still in love with you.

Those words swirl inside me, begging for release. I bite my lip as I come to keep them from escaping.

30

THEN

MARCH 2015

"Where'd you go last night?" Danny asks when we wake. The sun's barely rising, but the house is already in motion. I'm still not clear on why they all surf so early in the day.

I swallow. "I couldn't sleep. The mattress sinks every time we shift."

He sighs. "Yeah. This was a cool idea, but I wish we'd just stayed with my parents. I've never eaten so much pizza in my life."

It feels like a subtle dig, a *"You could have cooked for us but you didn't."*

Only guilt keeps me from saying something back.

I fall asleep after he leaves, and when I wake, the sun's been out for a long time and there's music blasting in the kitchen. I make a sandwich and head to the beach with Caleb's girlfriend, shivering in my hoodie. When I've seen spring break in movies and on MTV, it was clearly never in Malibu. We'll be lucky if hits seventy today.

Danny exits the water just as I arrive. "You want to go to the house with me?" he asks, but he isn't even asking, really. He fully expects me to do it.

"I just got here," I reply.

He stands there for a moment, waiting for me to give in. Of course he does. I let him think he could dictate my schedule for years because I just felt lucky he wanted me, and now...I don't feel lucky. I'm angry I ever did feel lucky. I'm angry he encouraged me to think it.

When he gives up and walks away, I drop into the sand next to the other girls. I haven't even gotten fully seated before Luke's head turns and he rides a shitty little wave into shore... coming straight toward me.

My stomach tightens as he walks out, easily ripping the leash off his ankle and tucking the board beneath his arm. There's something in his face that wasn't there before: possession. He knows that I'm his, even when no one else does. I'll jump if he tells me to jump. I'll beg if he tells me to beg. I'll walk out of the house with him in the middle of the night and let him fuck me, again and again, after claiming it can't happen anymore.

"Come into the water," he says, looming over me. A command, not a request, his eyes daring me to say, *"No."*

I have no desire to try surfing again. It was hard and the water is cold, and I'll look like an idiot, especially next to him, the surf champion. Except...it's a chance to be near him, and I will suffer anything for that.

People talk about love like it's peaceful, but it isn't, at all. It's turbulent and anxious. It's euphoria and despair. It's the willingness to brave cold water and humiliation and stab the people who love you in the back. I'll do all those things for Luke.

While I struggle into a borrowed wetsuit, he gets me a board—thick foam, several feet longer than his.

"I'm that pathetic, huh?" I ask.

His brow furrows. "It's a beginner's board. What else would you start on?" But even as he asks the question, I see the answer dawn in his eyes: that Danny didn't bother putting me on something buoyant when he tried to teach me. That he sent me into the much bigger surf at home on a six-foot board, and then acted like it was a lost cause before I'd even tried.

We walk down to the ocean, side by side. He secures the leash to my ankle once we're far enough out and we start to paddle, but I'm making no progress whatsoever. "I'm even bad at *paddling*, Luke," I wheeze, exhausted.

"Stop," he says. "Just relax."

He glides ahead of me and grabs my board between his toes, towing me out. I've nearly doubled the weight he's pulling and he shows no sign of it. His shoulders rotate, leisurely bringing his arms into the water, that pronounced hollow in them the only sign he's doing any work at all.

When we get to the break, we sit up, straddling our boards.

His eyes flicker to my mouth. He's thinking about last night. I'm thinking about last night.

"We can't do that again," I whisper, biting my lip. "It just isn't right."

"Grady saw us walking in. He just asked why we were up. I told him we couldn't sleep."

I try to remember. Were we touching each other on the way in? Talking about it? No. We wouldn't have been. We were careful. Mostly.

"We're not going to be able to sleep tonight either, Jules," he says, and I know it's true. The pull he exerts on me is like the tide at its worst. It can drag me under easily no matter how hard I fight.

"I know. But it still has to stop."

His eyes fall shut in silent argument, and then open again. "Lie flat. When I tell you to paddle, go for it. As hard as you can."

A wave seems to have appeared out of nowhere. I've got no idea how he even knew it was coming. But now that it is, I'm newly terrified of making a fool of myself.

"I'm not sure I want to do this," I whisper. "I'm really bad."

"No. You're a beginner. There's a difference."

"Maybe I should just ride it on my knees."

He raises a brow. "Do you already have a fucking back-up plan for failing before you've ever even tried?"

I laugh. "Yeah, I guess I do."

"Paddle."

Before I can respond, he shoves my board hard toward the shore. I paddle simply because he told me to and because I'm terrified of what will happen if I don't, and then he's shouting, "Get up!" and I'm doing that too.

I'm almost fully up when I lose my balance and go over the side. But when my head pokes back through the water, he's reached me, smiling as if he's proud, even though I completely fucked it up.

"That was great. You were perfect. This time, just keep your eyes forward."

With Danny, I tried three waves. After the third, he'd said, *"Are you sure you want to do this?"* and I told him I didn't. What I meant, though, was that I didn't want to keep failing.

He'd seemed relieved. And I don't think he'd have been relieved if I'd done it well. What he really wanted was not for me to learn to surf, but to stay on the shore, pretty and bone dry, remaining the failure who was just lucky to have him.

"Paddle," Luke says, close to my ear, and he shoves me again.

This time, I manage to stand up. My balance wobbles with the vibration of the wave beneath me and I have a moment where I'm certain I'm about to lose it, but I manage to reset myself. I'm not doing all the amazing tricks Luke does—I'm not carving into the wave horizontally, just going straight forward

—yet it's still thrilling. The wind beats against my wetsuit, sends my hair flying, and it's like I'm on the most spectacular roller coaster ride, one I've created myself.

It's only when I turn back to smile at Luke—amazed at this small triumph—that I lose my balance entirely and go over the side. But I'm still smiling when I emerge.

"I did it!" I shout.

His eyes are so full of light, his smile so wide, that it hurts my heart. I catch another wave, and another after that.

And after the third wave, he's still smiling, but there's something more serious in his gaze too.

"Leave here with me," he says when I reach his side. The words are quiet, but certain.

A startled laugh escapes my chest. "*What?*"

"Don't go back. Stay in LA tomorrow and don't get on the bus. I've got enough saved to get us a place."

I sit up, straddling my board as my eyes fill with tears. I want, so badly, just to say, "*Yes.*" To say yes without exploring the insanity of it, without thinking about all the ways it could fail.

"I can't," I whisper. "That would...destroy Danny. It would destroy his whole family."

"We can keep it a secret," he says. "Just for now. I'll get you someplace to stay and then finish out the semester. There's not even two months left. No one has to know we're together for a while."

"You'll still have a year of school to go."

He shakes his head. "I'm just going to finish up the semester. I've got two more competitions coming up. I place in either of them and I'll have enough between what I've saved and sponsors to go on the tour. For us both to go on the tour, if you're willing."

There are so many holes in this idea of his, but for a moment I let myself consider it: Luke and I in an apartment somewhere near the beach, where he can surf and I can come home to him every night. Luke, coming into a diner to see me on his way to work every morning, where neither of us has to hide. Curling against him at night while we watch TV, or sliding beside him in bed, bare legs to bare legs, bare chest to bare chest. Falling asleep and waking up and never wanting, for a moment, to be away from him.

It's so perfect it makes me ache.

Except I don't know how I could leave the Allens with the way things are right now.

"Luke, I can't. Donna's relying on me."

His jaw clenches. "Of course she is. There will always be something with them."

The air in my lungs leaves on a slow sigh. Yeah, the situation with the Allens just seems to get worse and worse, and I'm more enmeshed than ever, but it isn't their fault. It's just life.

"There has to be an end coming," I tell him. "They've had a bad run this year. The pastor's had two surgeries, and Danny hurt his knee. They saved me when my life was at its worst. I can't just turn my back on them when they need something from me."

I see the hope woosh out of his eyes. "Juliet, I'll wait for you forever. But if you leave it up to other people, that's exactly how long it will take."

I go in after that, returning Summer's wetsuit to her and heading to the house.

Caleb throws something at my head when I walk in. "Heard you did pretty well out there, newbie."

Danny's in the kitchen making a sandwich. He sets the knife down. "You surfed?"

I nod. "Luke took me out." I feel like I can't even mention Luke's name without giving myself away.

"On *his* board?" he asks.

I shake my head. "No, he grabbed some huge board, like nine feet long."

Danny hitches a shoulder. "That's great, hon." His tone says something else entirely, though. It says, *"That doesn't really count,"* perhaps, or *"Oh, that's cute you think you surfed."* But no one listening could accuse him of it. He's the master of sucking the life out of my tiny accomplishments, of making sure my wings stay clipped, without ever appearing to have done it. I'm not sure how I'm just seeing this now.

I think back to him telling me my song was *"sad"*. To him warning me that *"college is a lot harder than high school"* when I considered applying. Suggesting a solo at the regional music festival would be too competitive for me.

Maybe none of it had to do with me at all.

"It *was* great," I reply, this tight thing in my chest beginning to grow. "I wished I'd done it years ago."

I grab my shower stuff and head to the neighbors' house, and as I rinse away the sand, the entire morning, that sadness seems to swell in my throat until I can't stand it anymore.

God, I wish I could just have told Luke, *"Yes. Yes, let's run away. Yes, I want to spend all my nights with you forever."*

He offered me every single thing I want in the world, but what kind of person would I be if I accepted? What kind of person am I already, with the things I've been doing, with the lies I told? Even now, confused and guilty, all I want in the world is more time with him.

I hear the gate shut outside, footsteps, and then the shower door is flung open.

Luke stands there, naked but for the swim trunks hanging off his lean hips, his eyes moving over me like I'm something he's been starved of for too long. When he steps inside, letting the door shut behind him, I close the distance as if we've been magnetized. As if I'll die without the sleek, sandy feel of him pressed to my bare skin. His hand cups the side of my face, thumb smoothing a path over my cheek, eyes flickering over my face. His brow scrunches, and I know he can tell I've been crying, but he says nothing. *He knows why. He always knows.* My hand goes to his shorts, pushing them down his hips, distracting him from his thoughts and my own.

He lifts me up, holding me against the wall. My legs wrap around him, pulling him closer as he slides inside me. "I haven't asked you once if this is okay," he says. "Like, without protection."

"I think it's fine," I gasp.

"You know why I didn't ask?" His teeth slide over my earlobe like he's skimming them over an artichoke peel. "Because a part of me wanted it to happen. I'm that desperate to get you to leave, Jules. I know it's wrong, but that's the truth. It would mess up our entire future and I don't even care."

I realize only as he says it that I'm just as desperate. That a part of me *wants* my hand forced. "Give me a week," I beg. I tighten around him, close already.

"Thank God," he whispers. "One week. I'll come get you."

His mouth finds mine as I fall apart, silencing the noises I make. His eyes are dreamy as he finally pulls away and sets me back down.

"One week," he says, and his smile is so sweet that it makes my eyes fill with happy tears.

"One week."

I KNOW, as I walk back to the house, that I should be anxious and guilty, and it's not that those feelings aren't there, but right now I'm so thrilled, so overwhelmed by the possibilities, that there's no room for anything else.

It's the end of trying to be good all the time. It's the end of an internship I hate, and cooking dinner for a man who never stops thinking I owe him more. It's having a room or even an apartment where I can hang things on the wall and set my own schedule.

But best of all, it's Luke. It's Luke when he sleeps and when he wakes and all the hours in between. I'll probably spend the rest of my life missing Donna, and feeling bad for the way I handled things, but Luke is my sun, my moon, my tide, and I'm tired of fighting his pull.

It's our last night, but I don't drink. I'm already drunk on hope, and every time I look at Luke, I know he is too.

We barely even speak. It's just a smile, a knowing thing in his gaze.

"One week," he whispers by my ear, just before I go to bed.

"One week," I repeat.

I fall asleep dreaming of it, once again pretending the warm shoulder wedged into my back isn't Danny's. I'm dreaming of it still when a phone rings in the middle of the night. The mattress rolls so suddenly that I fall right off the side as Danny reaches for the call.

"I don't understand," Danny says into the phone.

I sit up. Over the mattress, his shocked eyes meet mine. "Okay," he says. "We're on our way."

He puts down the phone, his voice barely audible. "It's my dad. He had a heart attack. We need to get up there."

We pack as quickly as we can. Grady offers to drive us, since he was going back today anyhow. My gaze meets Luke's as we're walking out the door, just before dawn. He's wondering what happens now. I wish I had the answer.

We make the drive to Rhodes in near silence. Sporadically, Grady says a prayer, or suggests God has a plan. It annoys the shit out of me, but Danny doesn't even seem to notice.

"I don't understand," Danny says out of nowhere. "I thought he had the surgery to avoid this. Why didn't anyone tell me he was sick?"

Grady glances at me in the rearview mirror as if this is entirely my fault.

"You and I could take over for him," Grady suggests to Danny. "I can handle the counseling and sermons, you could handle the management of everything else."

My eyes roll. How like Grady to use Danny's family tragedy to move himself up in the world, and frame it as charity.

When we arrive at the hospital, we're told it's family only, so Danny goes back to his dad and I sit in the waiting room with Grady, the two of us uttering not a single word to each other. The guilt eats at me: I shouldn't have left Donna to care for the pastor by herself. And how the hell am I going to leave in a week? When the pastor gets home, he's going to need so much more help than he did, and Grady will be gunning for his job with all he's got.

And just when I think I can't take it anymore—the silence, my guilt—the doors slide open and Luke walks in.

My shoulders sag in relief as our gazes meet. I assumed he drove back to school after they cleaned up the house this morning, and I shouldn't want him here now but, *oh my God*, I do.

We don't discuss what is going to happen to our plan because it isn't the time. He doesn't hold my hand. But his arm is beside mine and he's here and that's enough.

Grady has returned to his aunt's house to shower when Danny and Donna emerge, gray-faced, to go to the cafeteria during the nurses' shift change.

Donna hugs us both. "I'm so glad you're here," she says, and I try not to ask all the questions that would absolve my guilt: *Was she there when it happened? How much did she have on her plate because I left?*

We sit together, picking at rubbery burgers and pieces of sweet potato pie.

And we haven't finished half of it before Donna gets a call telling her the pastor is gone.

I'VE ONLY SEEN Danny cry once before, but this is different. He *becomes* his grief, holding on to me like he'd drown if I removed his arms. So I don't. He falls asleep like that, beside me on the couch, and even when my whole body hurts from his weight, I let him stay.

Donna comes in to cover us with a blanket. "I'm so glad he has you," she says.

Luke just looks at me. He's exhausted, despondent. Any plans we made...they won't be happening soon.

The pastor's buried on Wednesday. That it's done so quickly only makes the shock of it harder to absorb. How does a person eat his dinner and read his wife an article in the paper on Saturday night, and become a distant thing you can't even touch, far beneath the grass, by Wednesday at lunch?

Afterward, people pour through Donna's house, offering their condolences. I take all the dishes they bring, and Luke helps me stack them in the freezer and rearrange chairs and offer people something to drink. They smile at him, but it feels different when they look at me. I was the orphan they wanted to warn the pastor about, wasn't I? I was the girl who was going to do nothing but cause problems and look at that...I left Donna to care for the pastor alone when he was sick, and he died. They think it was selfish that I went on a trip I didn't want to go on in the first place.

I have no idea what all this means for Donna. The church isn't going to continue paying for them to rent this house, and I know she doesn't have much saved. Danny's already said he's not finishing the semester, and she was too drained and upset to argue.

But if they have to move, maybe they won't even have room for me. Would it be acceptable for me to leave then? Or do I still need to stay by their sides, somehow, until they've recovered from this newest tragedy? I'm alone in the kitchen, pondering all of this, when Grady appears.

"I hope you're pleased with yourself, Juliet," he says. He has two tiny white spots on either side of his nose, his thin lips pressed tight.

He's blocking my path, and all that stands between us is the big casserole in my arms. "I don't know what you're talking about."

"They're moving me," he says. "To Oakland. This church should have been mine, and instead they want me to keep *assisting* someone."

"How exactly would that be my fault, Grady? Do I look like I carry a lot of sway with the church?"

"*You* had the pastor write them. You convinced him to write them and tell them I'm not ready. They told me he'd said as much."

"I can't imagine what makes you think I had any sway with the pastor either." I step past him toward the counter. "Maybe he just thought you weren't mature enough yet. Or maybe he knew you were the kind of person who'd *confront* someone after a funeral."

He grabs my arm and the casserole crashes at my feet, splattering me in sauce and noodles and shattered glass.

"What the—" I begin, but before I can finish, Luke has crossed the kitchen and grabbed Grady by the lapels.

"Who the fuck do you think you are, grabbing her like that?" he demands, shaking Grady hard. "I ever see you lay a finger on her again and you won't live to tell the tale."

The crash of the dish has drawn a crowd to the kitchen, but it's Luke grabbing Grady that they've stayed for. And Danny is among them.

"I don't know what's going on," he says, gently scolding all of us, "but this isn't the place for it."

Luke's jaw grinds as he nods at my feet. "It splattered all over you. Go change. I'll clean this up."

Maybe it's just that I know how he feels, but it seems like Luke used to be better at hiding things than he is now. People are probably wondering if his concern is misplaced.

Grady, glaring at me as he walks away, seems certain of it.

AFTER EVERYONE'S GONE, I heat up the lasagna someone brought. Danny blinks back tears when his mother asks him to say a prayer in the pastor's place. His hand slides over my own as the prayer ends, and Luke watches, swallowing hard.

That life I imagined with him feels like it's further away than ever.

Donna asks me to cut up one of the pies that was delivered once the lasagna is cleared, though I doubt anyone will eat it. I put on coffee and cut up the pie. I'm playing the role I always played and it's never felt more fake than it does now.

When we're all sitting, Danny lifts his fork and puts it down. "During our last conversation, I told Dad something." He turns to face me, his eyes bright. "I told him I was going to ask you to marry me."

My fork freezes in mid-air. I want him to stop talking, but it's already out there, this thing he assumes I want.

"He was glad. He said he'd prayed for that since the day I brought you home." He smiles at me, blinking back tears. "So I want to do it, Juliet. I know he won't be there to see it, but it's the last thing I promised him I'd do. Mom?"

I watch, astonished, as Donna crosses the kitchen and grabs an envelope tucked between the flour and sugar. She hands it to Danny, smiling at me through her tears and he shakes a tiny, tarnished silver ring out of it. It belonged to his grandmother—Donna's shown it to me before.

He reaches for my hand. "Juliet, will you marry me?"

My heart is thundering in my ears, and I feel like that bird Luke once told me about. Too large for its cage, its wings unable to stretch—flapping frantically until it finally stopped trying. Except I'm wiser than that bird in one way. I know without even trying that I'm never getting out of the cage.

Luke watches, all expression drained from his face, as I tell Danny, "Yes."

31

NOW

It's coming to an end. I have six days until the gala, and once I leave here, it's all behind me. I've let down my guard a bit, though I shouldn't. I just want one last chance to pretend these things are mine.

I go to the store with him. I follow him around the house like the lovesick girl I've always been. He's folding laundry—I offer to help.

"I still have your sweatshirt," I admit as we fold. "That UCSD one you loaned me the night I ran from the sorority house. I guess I should give it back."

"No," he replies, "you shouldn't. It's yours."

Luke and I work together on the kids' rooms without being asked. We hang pictures and fill dressers. We make breakfast and dinner, side by side. And when we're sitting across from each other at the table, I can almost believe this is our life. I allow myself to go for long stretches of the day forgetting it's going to end, filled with a lazy, delighted sort of contentment. Cash texts to ask when I'm coming and I don't bother to reply.

It's the feeling of hopefulness, and it's not real, but I let it happen anyway because I know I won't feel it again.

Donna and I hear him hammering in the backyard one morning and follow the sound. He's hanging a hammock between two of the trees.

"Do kids even like hammocks?" Donna asks.

His eyes hold mine and I smile. "Everyone likes hammocks."

In the afternoons, Luke surfs, and I play guitar in the backyard. I'm trying something new, music that's more real and honest than anything I've created since that first album. I've been hiding for a long time, submerged. I've been singing about life seen from the bottom of the ocean, but here, now, I'm singing about the world as it is when you've just come up gasping for air.

At night, I slide into Luke's bed when it's late enough, when the street is silent and the house is pitch black, and he's always waiting for me. I press my nose to his skin and just inhale. I hope he doesn't notice.

"Jules," he begins one night as I climb over him, and I know, just from his tone, that he's about to ask some question I don't want to answer.

We aren't anything. It's not going anywhere and it won't continue.

"Don't ruin it," I say, cutting him off.

He tenses. I know him. I can feel his desire to argue in the tightness of his muscles, in his sudden silence. My mouth moves to his neck, hoping to distract him, but he remains rigid beneath me.

"Get on the floor," he finally replies.

I still. "What?"

"Get. On. The. Floor."

I don't know if he's punishing me for the way I refuse to let this be anything more than it is, or showing me how full of shit I am—because he can *prove* it's more. He can prove I'm his.

I slide onto the floor, on my knees. He stands, shoving his

boxers down and grabbing his cock, bringing it to my lips. "Open wide," he demands, and when I do, he thrusts inside my mouth, weaving my hair through his fingers.

"Take the whole thing," he grunts. "All the way to the back of your throat."

He's treating me like a whore, and I'm soaking wet anyway, participating eagerly because I'm so turned on.

He uses his hand to move my head, faster and faster, going far enough to trigger my gag reflex.

"You love this, don't you?" he hisses. "You'll do any fucking thing I ask, any hour of the day, but you can't tell me the fucking truth a single goddamn time."

He's swelling in my mouth, moving faster. I groan around him, squeezing my thighs together as the ache between them grows unbearable.

"Swallow all of it," he grunts, and then he explodes in my mouth with a sharp inhale, a quiet cry.

He remains like that, breathing heavily for a long moment before he finally unwinds his fingers from my hair. I don't know what happens now...if he's still mad, if he wants me to leave.

Why isn't this enough for him? That I'll leave, that I'll stay, that I'll lie beside him all night, twisting in the sheets, just in case he wants to fuck me later?

"Get on the bed," he finally says, sliding out of my mouth. "And take off the shorts."

Because even when he's mad...he'll do anything for me too.

THE GALA for Danny's House is being held at The Obsidian, this dreamy all-white hotel that sits right on a beach to the north of us. It feels a lot like the wedding Donna wished she could plan for me and Danny, the "*Wouldn't it be amazing if we could afford that?*" dream that was way out of our price range.

On the morning of the gala, Luke drives me and Donna to the hotel to help set things up. I check us into the three-bedroom suite I've rented so that we don't have to drive all the way back to Rhodes when we're done, and Luke carries our bags in while Donna and I go to the ballroom.

There are floor-to-ceiling windows overlooking the ocean, and a terrace wraps around the outside so guests will be able to flow easily in and out of the space.

"We're cranking the air conditioning," the hotel liaison tells us, "but it won't be this cold in here once it's full of people."

I text Luke and ask him to bring a sweater for Donna. He returns with the cardigan she wore in the car and one of his hoodies for me, so big it will fall to a few inches above my knees. I shouldn't accept it but here I am, letting my foot off the gas again. I pull it over my head and inhale deeply. It smells like him.

He catches me and his mouth curves into a pleased, lopsided grin. "It's yours," he says, holding my eye. *Everything I have is yours*, is what he means. God, I wish I could say it back.

We follow the coordinator as she points out where things will go, and Libby whispers the names of guests in my ear—a lot of Silicon Valley, tech-rich couples who could probably buy and sell me easily. They've already made large donations or have offered to match the final sum.

That *New York Times* reporter, no matter how little I care for her, wasn't wrong: Danny's House is turning into something that might be repeated all over the country.

Luke and I are the ones who brought it the exposure, yet Hilary Peters still doesn't want us around.

"I didn't expect to see you here," she says to me with a tight, displeased smile on her face.

Luke moves closer. It makes no sense that he still wants to protect me—he's seen how readily I put myself first.

"Of course they're here," says Libby, wrapping an arm

around my waist. "They're the whole reason we're able to do this."

Hilary's smile grows sharp. "Their contributions are a drop in the bucket compared with what's come in over the past few weeks."

"And those contributions are coming in because *Juliet and Luke* brought us the publicity," Libby counters in a surprising show of backbone.

I fight a smile.

Hilary acts like she hasn't heard this, but Libby and Donna exchange a glance when her back turns. I'm glad they're both keeping an eye on the situation because Hilary is exactly the sort of woman who will say the right thing to Social Services, then stomp all over some powerless kid she happens to dislike.

We're led to the tables where the silent auction will be held and start taping down bid sheets and setting up the displays. There are toddler ballet lessons and themed baskets. There are also trips, from the mundane—Napa bus tour—to a glamorous private home overlooking the Sea of Cortez, chef included.

We're still there when the hotel staff come to set up the stage for the band and a parquet floor for dancing. Donna stands with Luke, fretting as she watches them. She calls me and Libby over. "Do you think it's big enough? Thirty by thirty sounded big on paper but look at it."

"Let's see," says Luke, pulling me by the hand.

I shouldn't. I shouldn't willingly let him grab my hand in public, much less dance with him, but he's smiling in that way I can't resist, and it's all so effortless and easy. I'm like a bedsheet floating off a clothesline as he leads me across the floor. I could no sooner walk away from him now than that sheet could stop floating and fold itself into four square corners.

Libby grabs Donna and spins her too.

"He's singing 'Jingle Bells'," I call over my shoulder to Libby and Donna. "I can't believe you don't know any other songs."

"I know lots of other songs," he argues before launching into "The Wheels on the Bus", loudly. Donna starts to sing along, and Libby and I are laughing so hard we're nearly bent over.

"You're proven your point. We need a bigger floor," says Hilary sharply, cutting into our silliness.

We stop dancing, still trying to control our giggling, and that's when I see Grady. He's standing by the ballroom doors with a garment bag over his shoulder, staring at me and Luke.

Me, wearing Luke's sweatshirt.

Me, happy and flourishing.

I drop Luke's hand fast, but not fast enough. The room is still freezing, but I can already feel the sweat trickling down my back.

32

THEN

JUNE 2015

I figured Harrison came from money, but I didn't know he came from *this* kind of money. His parents' house, with its multi-million-dollar views of the Pacific and the cliffs, is the equivalent of three regular homes. It has a pool and two kitchens, two laundry rooms, and so many bedrooms that, though there are thirty of us, no one needs to sleep on the floor.

I haven't seen Luke since the night of Danny's proposal three months ago, when he watched me say, *"Yes"* in stunned silence. He was gone the next morning, before I woke.

I think he understood that I didn't have a choice, that I couldn't take one more thing away from them when they'd just lost so much, and he appears to have moved on just fine—he won a shortboard contest in La Jolla and finally secured enough major sponsors to go on the tour, though he nearly lost all of them when he got into a fistfight at the next competition.

I'm happy for him, but when I close my eyes, I still picture the plan we made: LA, living together, him coming in to see me at work every morning after a day of surfing, curling up next to me at night. We'd have been broke, the place would have been a dump, and I still can't imagine anything better.

I spend a lot of time telling myself to *stop* imagining it, but this weekend is just going to make it harder.

The guys are on the deck discussing the storm coming in when Luke arrives. "There's the hero of the hour!" Caleb booms, clapping him on the shoulder. "Nice work, man."

Luke smiles and thanks him, but then his gaze lands on me with something bleak in his eyes that wasn't there before. I was wrong, then, when I said he was doing just fine. He was reckless when he won at La Jolla. I wonder, now, if that's my fault. I glance away, but not fast enough. Grady is watching, already angry. I still can't believe Danny invited him after the way he acted at the funeral, but he's always been better at forgiveness than I have, and as he pointed out—we couldn't invite Libby without asking Grady too.

"How are the waves?" Luke asks.

"There's no way, bro," says Liam, nodding toward the churning ocean. It's a small strip of beach, set between two cliffs, each of them littered with jagged rocks at the base. The break is far out, and the wind is pushing the waves hard to the south. Simply trying get out there would mean getting thrown into the rocks. "Maybe it'll calm down a little tomorrow, but right now that's a death wish," Liam adds.

Luke continues to survey it, though, and my stomach drops. He is desperate to get away from me. I already knew I shouldn't have come, but now, watching him, I'm certain this weekend was a big fucking mistake.

We all get settled into our rooms. Danny and I are given a master bedroom with a king-sized bed in honor of our upcoming wedding. We exchange an awkward glance as Harrison sends us in.

Currently, I share a bedroom with Donna, in the two-bedroom apartment we moved into after the church kicked them out of the house. I'll switch over to Danny's room when I become *Mrs. Allen* mere weeks from now, though I can't begin to imagine what our nights will be like, with his mom sleeping across the hall. The situation is temporary anyway—a stopgap until we leave this fall. The church has agreed to let Donna set up an orphanage in Nicaragua. There have been objections to it, people lobbying the church not to send *"hard-earned American dollars elsewhere"*, and deep in my evil little heart I'm *hoping* they succeed. Because what am I qualified to do in Nicaragua? Nothing. So I'll have to cook, clean, and do the laundry all day for the kids, and at night I'll have to sit with Danny and Donna, pretending I'm grateful to God for letting me do it.

"The room is amazing," Danny says to Harrison when we get back upstairs. "Way bigger than anything Juliet and I will ever have."

Luke pales. Swallowing hard, he walks back to the sliding doors. "You ever try jumping off that?" he asks Harrison, nodding at the cliff to the south.

Harrison laughs. "No. I actually enjoy my life. I'd like it to continue."

A muscle flickers in Luke's cheek. "If you jump with your board at just the right moment and angle it right, I bet you could get past all that and paddle out."

"Luke," I say before I can stop myself. "*No.*"

There's way more anxiety and desperation in my voice than I want to betray, but everyone is too busy agreeing with me to notice. I step toward him but catch myself before I go farther.

"She's right, man," says Beck. "Think about it...Even if you survive the jump and even *if* you manage to paddle out and don't get swept into the rocks, how do you get back in? You're still facing the same problem you were on the way out."

Luke swallows. "I think if you rode in through the center of the channel and timed it right, you'd be fine."

"That's a really big *if*," says Danny.

Luke glances at me, and before he even says a word, I already know exactly what he's thinking and what he feels:

that he wants to surf, and that he's angry about so many things, and that if it doesn't work out...it just doesn't fucking work out.

"I can do it," he says.

"Please," I whisper.

He looks at me for one long moment. Too long. "It's good, Jules."

A simple thing, those words. Only I know what he's really saying: that he understands the risks, and that I've made my decisions and now he's making his.

He grabs his wetsuit out of his bag and goes to change.

"Someone needs to stop him," Libby says. "This is stupid, even for him."

The guys glance at each other.

"It *is* stupid," Liam finally says, "but if anyone could pull it off, he could."

Panic tightens my chest, but the rest of the crowd shrugs in reluctant agreement, and when Luke emerges, there's a weird combination of anxiety and excitement in the air. They all do things someone else has suggested is ill-advised, and Luke is a far better surfer than any of them. He surfed Mavericks, after all. Telling him he can't make this is like telling an Olympic athlete he can't break a record—none of them feel qualified to say what he can or cannot do.

"Wish me luck," he says before taking one last look at me and disappearing downstairs.

My stomach drops to my feet.

We gather on the deck, and a minute later we see him walking out to the beach with his best board, the one he used to win at La Jolla—yellow, white, and black striped—like he thinks it will make him invulnerable. It won't. That fucking board could snap in half the second he hits the water if he lands wrong.

"This is crazy," Libby says firmly. "He probably won't even

survive the jump. Make him wait until tomorrow. The weather will be better, and he can surf then."

"The weather's not going to be better tomorrow," says Beck.

"That's not the point!" I cry. "Make him stop!"

Don't they see he's acting like someone with nothing left to lose?

"Juliet, even if we wanted to stop him, we couldn't," says Beck. There's sympathy in his gaze, sympathy that wasn't there when he addressed Libby just a moment ago. It's almost as if he knows exactly what's going on here.

It's Mavericks all over again but worse this time. Luke isn't doing something he knows other people have succeeded at. He has no clue what could happen. And I didn't try to stop him at Mavericks, but I still remember those moments when I thought he was gone. I still remember how deeply I regretted not trying to talk him out of it.

"No," I say, dropping Danny's hand and taking off at a run.

Danny shouts at me to stop, but I ignore him, running down the stairs and chasing Luke across the sand.

I know we've got an audience and I just don't care. Nothing matters to me as much as convincing him to stop.

The gravel slides under foot as I scramble up the cliff behind him. He's halfway there by the time I catch him.

He glances over his shoulder at me, his face stern. "Go back, Juliet."

"I'm begging you." I gasp for air from running out here and climbing. "Don't do this."

Something flickers in his eyes. I'm not sure if it's pity or concern, and I don't care as long as it means he's listening to what I'm saying.

It disappears as fast as it arrived, and his eyes grow cold again...it's how he steels himself against me.

"The difference between us is that you're scared of death

and I'm not." He turns to start climbing again. "If I was, I'd never get out of bed in the morning."

He easily scrambles up the last rocks to reach the top only using one hand, while I struggle to follow.

"There is a world of difference," I huff, "between a calculated risk and what you are doing right now. This isn't a calculated risk. This is suicide."

He reaches down to pull me up over the last big rock, and for a moment we're standing close, his hand still on my arm, but then he releases me as if by force, walking forward to the cliff's edge. I look down. Far, far below us the water churns, charcoal gray and ominous. He'll have to jump ridiculously far to make it, and the odds of it happening, without him either getting hit by the board or breaking it in the process are slim to none.

He walks back to me. His face is too serious, too determined, for me to hope he's changed his mind.

"I haven't loved many things in this world," he says, "but I loved you from the minute I saw you, and whether it's today or seventy years from now, I'll love you with my dying breath."

And then, without hesitating or calculating, he runs toward the edge of the cliff.

I want to scream but the sound is locked in my throat. I want to run to the edge to see if he made it, but my limbs won't work. *I'll love you with my dying breath.* I didn't even get a chance to say it back.

I'm frozen, too terrified to look. If he's gone, if he's badly hurt, I don't know how I'll even...

A cheer erupts from the people on Harrison's deck. I walk to the edge, my legs shaking like a new foal's, and I sink to my knees when I get there, unable to stand even a moment longer.

He's paddling toward the break, and though he's survived the jump there are still no guarantees. I clutch my stomach, worried I'm going to be sick.

The break is farther than it first appeared. By the time Luke reaches it, half the house is down on the beach, watching, shouting encouragement he can't possibly hear. Rocks and gravel slip underfoot behind me, and then Danny comes up to one side and Libby to the other.

We watch in strained silence while he lets several moderate waves pass, his gaze focused on the horizon.

"What's he doing?" Grady asks from behind us. "Those look like decent waves to me."

I roll my eyes.

Danny, as always, is kind. "He's waiting for that," he says, pointing to a blue swell in the distance.

I'm not sure how he knows it's different from anything else, but he's right. It gets bigger, and Luke lies flat on his board and starts paddling—slowly at first, and then faster as it closes in. As always, he makes it look easy, but he's moving fast and he's timed it perfectly: the wave is probably twenty feet overhead by the time it reaches him. Small, by Mavericks' standards, but far more dangerous because he's surrounded by cliffs on both sides. It's surfing a huge wave, while maneuvering through a deadly obstacle course, all at the same time.

"Holy shit," whispers Danny.

Even over the roar of the surf, the excitement from everyone who remained on the deck is deafening as they run down the stairs to get closer.

Luke carves across the wave and then takes a sharp turn at the last moment to angle himself down the center of the channel, just skirting the rocks. And when he finally steps out of the water, the guys standing on the beach hoist him on their shoulders as if he's just won the Superbowl singlehandedly.

"Thank heaven," Libby says under her breath, turning with Grady to head to the beach.

Danny grabs my hand to stop me from going after them. "Why the hell did you follow him up here?" he asks me under his breath. "We already tried to talk him out of it, and he made it clear he wasn't going to listen to any of us."

"I don't know." I stare at the ground, unable to meet his eye. "I was just positive he was going to die, and I needed to know that I'd tried to stop it."

"Since when do you care so much whether Luke lives or dies?"

I shake off his hand, shocked by the callousness of the question. "If you think I'd be ambivalent about someone's death, then I don't know why you're marrying me."

He sighs. "I'm just not sure why everyone's making such a big deal out of it. They're acting like he's Jesus. He's just got a better board than the rest of us do."

My jaw falls open. "Do me a favor," I snap, moving away from him, "and don't act like the only thing he's got that you don't have is a good *board*."

I hurry down to the beach without him, wanting only to see Luke with my own eyes. I stand at the edge of the crowd, drinking in the sight of him—wet hair pushed off his face, unwilling smile pulling at the corner of his mouth, eyes lighter than they were. I'm still not over the terror, still furious that he did it in the first place and will probably do it again, but I'd go through the rest of my life content if I could just keep seeing him as he is now, whole and safe, and unspeakably beautiful.

The moment ends quickly, of course, because there's something restless and agitated in Luke, something that's never satisfied. Our gaze finally meets as he cuts through the crowd to climb up the cliff again, and my eyes fill. I squeeze them shut before the tears escape, and when I finally have my shit together, he's gone.

"If nothing else, maybe this will keep him out of a fight," Beck says quietly.

I glance at him. "You make it sound like he fights all the time."

His arms fold. "His sponsors have threatened to pull the plug twice already, and he just got signed, Juliet. It wouldn't take much."

We watch from the beach as he jumps again. It seemed so unplanned the last time, but from this vantage point I at least know that he's timing his jumps, waiting for the precise moment the swell explodes against the cliff face.

He rides a second wave in and goes back for a third. A group of us remain on the beach, watching him. It would take just one bad jump, one mistimed wave, for it to all go wrong, but night is falling so I know he won't do it again. I sit with my knees to my chest, a tight ball of fear, until he finally steps into the sand and removes the board's leash from his ankle.

Thank God.

As we return to the house, I release air I think I've been holding in since he first suggested this bullshit, and my stomach starts to slowly unknot itself. This afternoon has taken a year off my life.

Soon, everyone is celebrating, acting like Luke's victory is their own, a weird testosterone-fueled sort of relief.

The music is jacked up to max volume, shots are poured, the keg is tapped. I sip at the margarita handed to me, but I'm not celebrating anything. I'm just trying to shake off my terror from earlier, and the fear that he might try again tomorrow.

Danny's drinking, too, but it isn't making him jubilant like it is the rest of them—he's just growing more melancholy. Donna calls to see if we made it here safely and to ask if we'll be back in time for dinner Sunday.

"We might be earlier than that," Danny says gloomily. When he ends the call, he looks around the room. "I wonder what my dad would say if he could see this now. I don't think he'd be impressed."

"Well, if there's actually an afterlife, maybe he's gained a little perspective."

He sighs wearily. "What's that supposed to mean?"

I know I should back off, but I don't especially feel like pulling my punches right now, not after what he said to me on the cliff. "When I picture God, I picture someone who's a little more accepting of human frailty than your father was."

He snatches his beer bottle off the table as he rises. "I think you should stop drinking, Juliet," he says, walking away, dismissing everything I've said as the byproduct of a single margarita.

I silently fume as I return to the kitchen. The girls are whipping up appetizers, laughing and drinking and celebrating, just like the guys are, and I feel lifeless in their midst. I begrudgingly start cleaning when all I really want to do is go to our room and sleep until this whole fucking weekend is over.

Liam jumps on the counter to get our attention.

"I think a toast is in order!" he shouts over the music, which someone promptly lowers. "Because our boy here did the unimaginable today and lived to tell the tale."

The crowd shouts and claps its approval. Luke is sitting on the couch, knees spread wide, head back against the cushions. His grin is sheepish, far less impressed with himself than everyone else is. "Just got lucky," he replies.

"Bro, there was no luck involved. That was solid gold talent," says Caleb.

"Don't count me out yet," jokes Ryan, the only one of them who barely surfs. "I haven't even tried yet."

Caleb laughs. "I'm counting you out, dude."

"Or me," adds Grady. It's the first joke I've ever heard him make. "Who knows? Maybe I'll be amazing at it."

Caleb raises a brow. "Sure, Grady. Never stop dreaming."

"Give me a couple of years of surfing in Nicaragua," Danny says, and he is *not* joking. "Maybe I'll catch up, though I'm never going to have the money for a board like Luke's."

The smile leaves Luke's face. "When are you going surfing in *Nicaragua*?"

Danny crosses to where I stand and wraps an arm around my waist. Given how much we've bickered today, it feels like he's doing it simply to make a point. I have to fight myself not to push him away.

"We're moving there," he announces.

My lids flicker closed, a half second of unwillingness.

"My mom is opening an orphanage and Juliet and I are going to help."

The room goes quiet, aside from the music that's still playing. Danny wants everyone to celebrate this news the same way they celebrated Luke's triumph, but it's the wrong crowd for that. No one envies us. They don't want to be in our shoes. And plenty of people in this room—Luke especially, based on the look on his face—think it's fucking insane.

He rises, looking only at me. "Are you serious right now? How long would you go for?"

I stare at the floor while Danny answers. "I don't know," he says. "Probably for good. You guys will have to come visit though. Seriously, the surfing there blows California out of the water."

Harrison places a quiet hand on Danny's shoulder. "That's great, man. I hope it works out."

"Tell me something, Danny," Luke says, still staring at me. "What *precisely* does Juliet get out of this deal? Or are you just assuming the pleasure of cooking and cleaning for you is enough for her?"

My heart thuds loudly in my chest. I squeeze my eyes shut, praying that this moment just ends. Or that it hasn't happened at all.

Danny stiffens, and his arm around my waist tenses until it feels more like a shackle. "I'm not sure you need to worry about *my* fiancée, Luke."

"Someone fucking needs to," Luke snaps.

Beck jumps to his feet, moving between them.

"Stop," I whisper, because it's all I can get out. I pull away from Danny and walk blindly out the door, down the stairs to the beach as tears run down my face.

Despite the storm coming in, it's a beautiful starlit night. I feel nothing at all looking at it. I feel nothing at all most of the time, now.

What a fucking disaster this is.

Luke and I, rushing to stop the other or defend the other, all fucking day. Everyone must have noticed it. What will I say if Danny asks? And I'm not sure it's ever even occurred to him that I don't want to go to Nicaragua. If he finally asks me tonight, point blank, am I still going to lie?

There's a shift in the air behind me. I look over my shoulder to discover Luke approaching. "You shouldn't be out here," I whisper when he steps beside me.

"Why?" he demands. "Because you can't control yourself when I'm around? Maybe that ought to tell you something, Juliet."

I shove my hands in the pocket of my hoodie, hating that he's right. "Luke, I'm doing my best." My voice cracks.

His hand wraps around my forearm, turning me toward him. "No, you're not. Your best would be to say 'Danny, I love you, but not in the way you want.'"

"You think it's that easy? You think I can do that to Donna? This wedding is the one thing that's kept her going the past few months."

"It's never going to be easy," he says, his voice softening. I bury my face in my hands and he pulls them away, holding them tight in his own. "You don't want to hurt him, but he'll spend his entire life trying to make you happy and it'll eat him up that he can't do it. It's already eating him up. You saw how he was tonight."

"God, Luke," I cry, "I wish you hadn't come here. I convince myself things feel okay, and then you walk in the room and I realize they're so far from okay that I must have been crazy to think otherwise."

He pulls me into him, and his hands slide over my hips as he buries his face in my hair. "I can't fucking stand this. If I thought you were going to be okay, if I thought you were getting what you wanted in the end, I'd walk. It would hurt, but I'd walk. But Jesus...Nicaragua? Living as a missionary? Name one thing about that whole scenario that's for you, that's what *you* want."

I'd like to come up with something that proves he's wrong, but my brain is empty. I can't think of a single thing about it that appeals to me. "Not everyone gets a happy ending, Luke. Not everyone gets what they want out of life."

"You think I don't fucking know that? I know better than anyone alive that not everyone gets a happy ending. But at least I'm not handing mine away. At least I'm willing to fight for it."

His breath skates over my face, his eyes on my mouth, and my heart takes on that irregular pattern it always does when he's too close. I think I'd give up a decade of my life to have him kiss me again, but I shake my head, warning him off.

He releases me. "I'm going to leave now," he says.

I watch as he turns away, heading for the shore. I wish I could film this, film every minute of him walking and laughing and sleeping and surfing, so I could hold onto him once he's gone.

He gets roughly ten feet away and turns to look back at me.

"Fuck it," he says, reaching me in five long strides before grabbing my face and kissing me hard. I don't stop him. I breathe in the smell of his shampoo, the salt on his skin, taste his lips and try to memorize all of it—his smell, his size, the tightness of his grip.

"Choose *me*, Juliet," he whispers. "Please fucking choose me."

And then he walks away and doesn't look back.

I cry until there's nothing left. I'll need to look for Danny now, I guess, and apologize for what I said about his father, and then reassure him that the lukewarm response he got about Nicaragua doesn't mean anything, that this future he's planning is all I could ever want.

I've got many, many years ahead of pretending the things Danny and Donna want are the things I want too. I know I owe them that much, but it seems like a very long life without Luke. Long and utterly pointless.

I walk slowly toward the house, my teeth clenched with the effort to hold myself together. I freeze at the sound of creaking wood when I reach the back porch and turn. Danny is in a rocking chair by the stairs, watching me.

I step toward him, uncertainly. We were too far away for him to overhear us, and it's too dark to see anything from here, but he's never been one to sit by himself. "Hey. What are you doing down here?"

He climbs to his feet. "Waiting for you to explain why you were kissing my best friend."

I sag against the wall. Of all the possible things that could have happened—me hurting him by leaving or calling off the wedding—this is a hundred times worse.

I could claim I was drunk, but I don't know what he's heard, and the truth is probably coming out no matter what I say.

"Danny," I whisper. "I'm so sorry. We were talking about Nicaragua and it just...happened."

"Talking about *Nicaragua*?" he demands with an unhinged laugh. "Was he offering you the luxurious lifestyle of a guy with *two* sponsors instead? Newsflash, Juliet, getting a sponsor doesn't mean he's rich. He won't be living any better than us."

"Of course not."

"How long has it been going on?" His voice cracks and the pain in it destroys me. This would be easier if he were simply enraged right now.

"Nothing is going on." I'm a liar to my core. "I haven't seen him or even spoken to him since he was here for your dad's funeral."

He holds a hand over his face. "I'm so stupid. I'm so fucking stupid. You've always loved him, haven't you? Fucking always. And he's always loved you. *Luke* was the one who got into fights over you. Luke was the one rushing off to your rescue, and I thought he was just a good guy."

"Danny—"

He laughs. "Your tears last winter when he surfed Mavericks. God, was it going on then too?"

"No! Of course not. You and I were in the same tent, and he was with one of the other girls. You know that."

"Do you love him?" he asks. "No, don't answer. I don't want to hear a single word from your lying mouth right now."

He starts walking away, and it feels vital that we don't leave things like this, that I somehow make him feel better. But the only way to do it is by swearing Luke means nothing to me, that I want to stick with the plans we made. I can't do that.

"Where are you going?" I ask.

He stares at me. "I don't even know."

I hurt him. I hurt him just the way Luke predicted I would.

I have no idea what I'm supposed to do. My first instinct is to get Luke, but he's still out there somewhere and I doubt he's even got his phone. I need to know how Danny and I are resolving this before I discuss it with him anyway.

I can hear the shouts of the guys playing beer pong inside, and drunken screams of the girls upstairs, singing at the top of their lungs to Rihanna. I can't stand to face any of them, so I walk up to the second-floor deck and enter our room from the sliding glass door.

I hurt Luke, I hurt Danny, and soon I'll have hurt Donna too.

I just fucking ruin everything I touch.

I curl up on the bed, beyond tears. There's nothing to be done at this point but wait and see how it's all going to turn out.

DREW

> Just landed! I'm sending my hair and makeup team for you and Donna, FYI. I knew you'd forget to book people 😊

> OMG. You didn't need to do that. The fact that you're attending at all is more than enough. But thank you.

> Are you kidding? I owe you EVERYTHING.

My megastar friend is giving me way more credit than is due—she was twenty times more famous than me when we met, and she remains so—but I just happened to help her at one of the lowest points of her life.

She's at the happiest point now—madly in love with her husband, her baby boy. Her happiness has gone on for years and shows no sign of going away, but it's hard to imagine having an amazing thing come into your life and actually getting to just...keep it. Just getting to stay happy. That's not how my life has worked. That's not how most people's lives work.

Luke surfs that afternoon, so Donna and I have the suite to ourselves while the hair and makeup team do their work.

When the team is done, my hair is blown out to long, sleek perfection, and I've got red lips to match my red dress—strapless and fitted, perfectly suited to a James Bond-style villainess, which is how half these people see me now anyway.

I walk into the living area to find Luke freshly showered, tugging at the collar of a tuxedo shirt just as Donna walks in from the hallway with a bottle of champagne in her hands.

"Oh, Juliet, you look stunning. Doesn't she look stunning, Luke?"

His eyes drift over me for one long moment. There's desire there, but also something sweeter, as if he feels exactly what I do—the hit of straight joy I get simply watching him walk in the room. I try to grip the moment, seal it into my memory. Later tonight, I'll think about this look on his face and imagine that nothing ever went wrong between us. I'll imagine he was simply my bored husband, waiting for me to emerge from our room and remembering all over again why he chose me.

"Yeah." He coughs. "You both do."

Donna hands him the bottle of champagne. "Juliet's friend Drew sent it up. I was hoping someone in the hall could open it, but since you're out of the shower, I'll allow you to do the honors. Summer's coming tonight, by the way."

I stiffen, nails digging into my palms. Luke's gaze lands on me and he barely hides a smile. "I'm not sure she's my type," he tells Donna.

"Oh, Luke, don't you think it's time you settled down? Wouldn't it be nice to come back from your trips and have someone there waiting?"

His eyes meet mine as he hands her a glass of champagne. "I've thought about that on occasion. I wouldn't mind getting a little place on the beach. A deck with a hammock. The whole thing."

It hurts, hearing my stupid little dream parroted back to me when I'll never be the one in that house waiting for him.

We finish our champagne and take the elevator downstairs together.

"Juliet!" Drew squeals, exiting the elevator beside ours and throwing her arms around me.

Drew's husband, Josh, greets me in a far more subdued manner. "Juliet," he says, placing a hand at the small of Drew's back, "good to see you."

Heads start to turn, and it's a relief to not be the interesting one for once.

"Donna, Luke," I begin, "let me introduce you to my friend Drew and her husband Josh."

"Luke Taylor," Josh says, his jaw dropping. He's married to one of the biggest stars in the world and his brother is a famous guitarist, but I've never seen him look awestruck until this moment. "Holy shit, hon. How could you not tell me a surfing *legend* was going to be at this thing?"

"I'm so proud of them both," Donna says, wrapping an arm around each of us. "You know, Luke lived with us several summers in a row, in college."

"Wait a minute," says Drew, turning to me with astonished eyes.

My stomach drops. I already know what she's going to say, and I wish I knew how to stop her.

"Is *he* the reason you were at Pipeline Masters?" she asks, as I knew she would.

Oh, Juliet, how could you have forgotten this? How could you be so careful about so many things but allow this one to slide?

Luke stiffens. "You were at Pipeline?"

"There was a big party there," I reply weakly. "I stopped by."

Drew laughs. "I love how Juliet tries to make it sound like she was there to *party*." She turns to me. "Dude, you weren't even *drinking*. You were hiding out on the dunes with a pair of binoculars that entire—" At last she sees the look on my face and stops talking.

Donna reaches for my hand. "I had no idea you were at Pipeline," she says, and I'm saved from replying by Hilary, who marches herself into the center of our circle with another of her tight, displeased smiles.

"Have any of you seen Libby?" she demands. "She's supposed to be monitoring the silent auction tables, but she's nowhere to be found, which is *exactly* why it's a bad idea to entrust personal friends with important roles."

I've fucking had it. I take a step forward but Luke beats me. "Donna and I will see if we can find her," he says. "And, Hilary...alienating the people who pay your salary isn't a great move." His words are polite, but his tone and the chill in his eyes send a clear message. He takes one last look at me, a too-long look, before he leads Donna off in search of Libby.

"I'm sorry," Drew whispers. "Was he not supposed to know?"

I shake my head. "It's okay." But I feel like it's all spilling out, one secret after the next and, really, there's only one left. The worst one. "Let me see if I can find Libby."

I walk away, pulling out my phone and looking for Libby's name. When our text chain appears, I feel sick all over again about how one-sided our friendship became: it was always her reaching out, her congratulating me, and me replying every third or fourth time with a heart emoji or something similarly distant.

One more person I disappeared on.

> Hey, just making sure you didn't go into labor.
> Hilary is looking for you. Is everything okay?

LIBBY

> No, not really. But I'm nearly there.

She walks in the door a minute later, and I cut across the room toward her.

"What's wrong?" I ask.

She looks over her shoulder. "Here, walk with me," she says under her breath. "I'm supposed to be working in the auction part of the room."

We start walking. The air seems to whistle out of her chest, and with it, she deflates. I hadn't realized, until now, just how tired she looks.

"Grady got a call this afternoon and said he had to go back to talk to the police," she continues.

"The police?"

She nods and looks around her quickly. "Some reporter gave them all this new information about the night Danny died. She's suggesting they reopen the investigation."

I grip the table closest to me to stop the room from spinning. "What?"

"Oh, honey, I'm sorry. I shouldn't have broken the news to you like that. I just...they're making something of the fact that Grady and Danny argued. And I guess Grady was seen coming back in the middle of the night—I didn't even know about that. I mean...they can't possibly believe Grady would kill someone, would they?"

The room is too loud and too bright. My knees begin to shake.

If the police even *suggest* Grady was involved, I know exactly what he'll do. The very thing I've dreaded for the past seven years.

He'll tell them the truth.

"I need to—" I whisper weakly, moving away from her without even finishing the sentence.

I walk blindly toward the other side of the room, hands pressed to my stomach, my heart beating wildly. I don't know how to fix this but I'm still desperately hunting for a solution. I

think of Luke so many years ago at Harrison's house, glancing
up at the cliff and saying, *"You ever try jumping off that?"* Right
now, I'm looking for a way he can jump and survive. I don't
think there is one.

I have no idea what Grady and Danny argued about, but it
hardly matters because Grady *does* have an alibi for those hours
on the beach. And Luke doesn't.

*That fucking reporter. I should have known. I never should have
come back.*

"I can't wait to peel that dress off you later tonight," Luke
says from behind, leaning down so I'm the only one who'll
hear.

I turn, looking around us before I answer. "We can't.
Donna's going to be in the suite."

"You think she'd care at this point? She just wants us to be
happy."

He tugs me toward the dance floor. It seems like a bad idea,
in front of all these people, and an especially bad idea when I
should be figuring out how the hell to get him out of this mess I
made, but I can't resist. The clock's been ticking for us, ever
since we arrived, and it's moving faster by the moment. If the
cops are talking to Grady right now, this might be my last
chance to be near Luke at all.

"I didn't figure you for a dancer," I tell him, stalling. "Or a
guy who'd own a tux, to be honest."

His mouth twitches. "I'm full of surprises, sweetheart."

His hand slides from my hip to the small of my back. People
will talk if they're watching, and I should probably back away,
but I can't seem to. I should probably tell him about Danny's
case getting reopened and I don't do that either. I suspect he'll
just make things worse. He was always too goddamn honest. I'll
have to solve it on my own. Somehow.

"Are you going to tell me why you were at Pipeline?" he
asks, tugging me closer.

"I just was."

I start to pull away from him and his grip tightens around my hip, pressing me against him. "Can you just, for once in your fucking life, tell me the truth? You didn't just *happen* to be there."

"It doesn't matter why I was there," I whisper, but my voice cracks.

It doesn't matter that I was in Tahiti for the Tahiti Pro and in Australia for the Pro Gold Coast, and that I have gone to as many of those as I could possibly attend and hidden it so he wouldn't know. It's all resting there, right on the tip of my tongue, but then he turns me...and I stop dancing entirely as Cash walks toward us. Cash, who never made any effort to see me, is *here*, cutting across the dance floor, in a tux. He's smiling, but there's a dangerous look in his eyes I recognize. He hasn't seen me in six weeks but still thinks he's got the right to be angry that I'm dancing with someone else.

I stop moving, and Luke turns, already wrapping a protective arm around me when he has no clue what's happening. And then he recognizes Cash—and that arm tightens.

"Cash?" I whisper. "What are you doing here?"

He raises an eyebrow and folds his arms across his chest. "I *thought* I was here to surprise you." His head jerks toward Luke. "Who the fuck is he?"

Luke is still and silent, and then the arm that was wrapped around my waist releases me as he steps forward, his fist striking Cash so hard and so fast that Cash can't even brace himself.

He stumbles backward, into the crowd, knocking over dancers, but Luke isn't done. He dives at Cash and knocks him to the ground while the dance floor turns into chaos. People scatter, and Cash's bodyguards spring into action, grabbing Luke from behind and pulling him away. Beck steps in as Cash climbs to his feet to make sure the fight ends...but the damage is already done.

Luke just hit Cash with no provocation and there were many witnesses, including Donna, who stands a few feet off the dance floor. Her eyes are wide, confused, and then her shoulders sag as if she's finally figured out what's been so obvious to everyone else.

"Call the cops!" Cash yells.

"No." I step forward. "Let's just go."

Luke reaches for me. "Where the fuck are you going?" His fingers are on my skin for the very last time. *Memorize this, Juliet.*

"Let me handle it," I reply, shaking him off.

"Juliet, if you leave with him, we're over," Luke says.

I swallow hard. These weeks with him have been thrilling and painful, and I think maybe I've stored up enough memories to get me through a few more years.

"I know," I reply softly. I mean to sound careless but I don't. I sound like I'm on the verge of falling apart.

I cross to where Cash stands and slide my arm through his. God, his timing couldn't be worse. I'll get him out of here and then figure out how to fix things with the police. "Let's go elsewhere."

"Fuck that," he says. "I'm pressing charges."

I raise a brow. "Cash, you're not the only one who can press charges. The whole world saw you dragging me off an elevator by my hair, and there's so much more I can say. So should I call the cops on *you* or should we start walking?"

He stares at me, dumbfounded. For all the dozens of times he's hit me or thrown me against a wall, I've never once suggested I'd turn on him. "You wouldn't."

I laugh. I never said I loved him. I never even said I *liked* him. He just assumed it was true and took my silence as proof. "Watch me."

A vein throbs in his temple as he grudgingly turns toward

the ballroom's exit just as the doors open and my stomach drops farther than I thought it possibly could.

Two uniformed officers are making their way toward me. Four others are heading toward Luke.

"What on Earth?" Donna asks, walking up beside me. "It was just a little fight."

Except they're not here because of the fight.

They're here because Grady told them everything.

They keep walking until they're nearly to where we stand, and then one of them turns to the security guards surrounding us and holds up a piece of paper. "We have a warrant," he says, and nods to the guys behind him. Several of them walk to Luke, and one of them comes to me.

"Luke Taylor and Juliet Cantrell," he says, "you're under arrest for the murder of Daniel Allen."

34

THEN

JUNE 2015

I startle awake to find every light in the room is still on, and Danny is not beside me. The house is silent for the first time, which means it must be late. I rub my eyes as I look at the clock. It's 3:30. Would he have...left? Would he have gone home? Is he back in Rhodes right now, telling Donna everything? I don't know how I'll face her again when this all comes out.

I go to the front deck to look for his car, and it's still there, right where we left it.

Upstairs, the living room is an absolute disaster, a wasteland of red plastic cups and beer bottles, but there's no one up here. I search the decks, the couches in the basement, the hot tub. I even look inside the bed of Danny's truck. I call and he doesn't answer.

Where the hell is he? I walk out to the beach, using my phone's flashlight once I'm down there. In the distance, I see a blanket I recognize from the basement couch, someone moving inside it.

He's out here with another girl?

My shock turns into relief in seconds. If he's out here with another girl, so be it. I *want* it to be him. There's a reason I've still got my ring on, after all. If he'd come back to the room begging me not to leave him, it would have bordered on the impossible to do it. Finding him with another girl right now would give us a clean end.

The huddled figures startle and blink into the light as I approach.

"What the fuck?" Ryan demands a voice, sitting up.

"Sorry," I whisper. "Sorry. I'm looking for Danny."

As I lower the flashlight, the figure beside him, scrambling to pull the blanket overhead, is illuminated: Grady.

I stumble backward in shock.

Grady, with all his bitching about *"the gays"* at the beach. Grady, always threatening to call the cops on them for no good reason.

"Sorry," I say, turning away, walking rapidly in the direction I came.

I can't wait to tell Danny about this.

My stomach ties into a knot as I remember he's missing, that he might never get over what I've done. That we might never be friends again, after tonight.

God, I hate that I hurt him. He has flaws, but we all do, and he never meant any harm. I begin to shiver, wrapping my arms around myself as I walk.

"Juliet," Grady calls. I turn to find him running toward me, still buttoning his goddamned shorts. "It wasn't what it looked like."

My laughter is thick with disbelief. "You might sell that better if you weren't *undressed*."

He reaches me and wraps a tight hand around my wrist. "Wait. Please. Seriously...I don't know what I was thinking. I'm not gay. It was just...I was half asleep, and I'd had that beer earlier, and I didn't even know what I was doing. I'm not gay."

It's the lamest explanation for cheating I've ever heard in

my life. One beer and some fatigue doesn't make you walk out to the beach with blankets and blow the captain of the football team if you didn't already want to.

"I couldn't care less if you're gay," I tell him, jerking away. "I *do* care that you're cheating on Libby, but you're not my issue right now."

"I'm not gay! It was so stupid. Please don't say anything to anyone."

I throw out my hands. "Grady, I don't give a shit. Danny's missing. He didn't come back to the room last night."

Something grows hard in his face. "After your *fight*, you mean."

I blink. "What?"

"I'm just glad he's finally figured out what's going on with you and Luke. I suspected it from the beginning."

I stare at him. "There is nothing going on between me and Luke. Jesus Christ, Grady. I tell you Danny's missing and this is where you want to go with it? If you're not going to help find him, go back to your date."

I march off, and after a moment he follows. "You're sure he didn't just go home?"

I roll my eyes. "Of course I'm sure."

"Should we wake everyone up?"

I bite my lip. There could be a completely reasonable explanation for the fact that he's missing. If I wake everyone, I'll probably have to tell them what happened and he wouldn't want that. Or maybe he would, but that's his choice, not mine. "No, not yet."

I leave Grady and continue to walk, but at five a.m., when the sky morphs from charcoal to violet, I can see the beach clearly enough to know it's completely empty.

I return to the house, praying I find him curled up in bed and furious with me, but the room is also empty. Which means I need Luke.

I tap on his door and there's no answer, so I open it, bracing myself for the sight of him with someone else. He's alone, thank God, sprawled face down with a pillow over his head, naked from the waist up. "Luke," I whisper, placing a hand on his shoulder.

He pulls the pillow off his head and turns to look at me, still half asleep.

"Juliet?" he rasps, rolling over before sitting up. "What's wrong?"

"Have you seen Danny? He never came back to our room, and he's not in the house, either."

His nostrils flare, and I can read his thoughts so clearly: *I'm in love with you and you're enlisting my help to find your missing boyfriend?* He rubs a hand over his face. "Did you try his phone?"

"He didn't answer." Eventually I'll need to tell him about the fight and everything Danny knows, but suddenly this all feels...serious.

He glances at the clock and turns his head toward the beach, though his curtains are drawn. "Did the weather improve? Maybe he got an early start."

I shake my head. "Luke," I whisper, my voice breaking, "I've been looking for him since three. I'm scared."

That's the moment when I see something like worry creep into his eyes. "Fuck. Okay."

He goes next door to wake Harrison. Within a minute or two, the whole house begins to stir.

"Đamn, y'all start early," Liam grouses, walking out of his room in nothing but shorts, his girlfriend behind him.

He sees us standing in the hall and comes to a stop. "Who died?"

My chest tightens, and I don't know if it's superstition...or presentiment.

"Danny's missing," I reply. "He never came back to the room."

Liam's girlfriend frowns. "I heard him last night outside, yelling at someone. Who'd he fight with?"

They glance at each other, at the floor...anywhere but Luke. He was the one who argued with Danny in front of them. He was the one who may have wanted what wasn't his. They already know it must have been him.

Harrison places his hand on my shoulder. "I'm sure he's okay. We were all drinking. He probably just passed out in the wrong place."

If he knew about what Danny saw...would he still say that? Or would he be thinking we need to call the police? Because that's what I'm thinking right now.

"Juliet already checked the beach, but maybe we should check again," Luke suggests.

Liam starts putting on his shoes. "I'll go up to the top of the cliff. The view's better from there."

Caleb and Beck go with him while the rest of us continue onto the beach.

Fix this, fix this, I plead to God, well aware it's useless.

Ask and ye shall receive? I've been asking for years, and God has not lifted a fucking finger on my behalf. I'm asking and asking now, when it's never mattered more, when it involves someone more worthy than me of God's attention, and all I get is fucking silence.

We trudge through the sand, and I come to a dead stop at the glint of white and yellow in the water.

"Luke," says Harrison, "isn't that your board?"

We all stare.

Half of Luke's favorite board bobs calmly, trapped in the rocks. My stomach plummets, as if some much wiser part of myself already knows what's about to unfold.

"Yeah," Luke says hoarsely. "Looks like it."

"He wouldn't have tried to surf," says Harrison. "Right? He argued *against* it yesterday. And no one could have done that in the dark."

Let there be another explanation. Any other explanation.

Luke's eyes catch mine. "I think we need to call the police."

Any minute now, Danny could walk out here yawning, wondering what the fuss is about. But I nod, my hands shaking so badly I have to hand the phone to Harrison.

I walk away while he's talking to them. And turn to see Caleb walking down the cliff, Danny's shoes in one hand.

The shock of it is a sonic blast, a force that levels me, and I sink into the sand, dizzy and dazed. The guys are wide-eyed, saying things I can't hear.

Danny jumped with Luke's board. In the dark. He probably wouldn't even have been able to see where he was landing. There'd have been little chance of him surviving even if the board didn't break.

But it did.

I rock in place with my knees against my chest, and Luke tells Libby to stay with me as they go to the house to wait for the police, but I can't really process it.

"This can't be happening," I whisper again and again. Was he trying to prove something to himself, or had he just given up? I guess it doesn't matter—either way it's my fault.

I need to call Donna. But oh my God. How am I ever going to tell her this?

"I'm going to get her a blanket," Libby says and then she's gone.

The waves crash and the wind picks up again, and when it settles, Grady speaks. "This is your fault," he whispers, his voice broken.

I blink, uncomprehending. "What?"

"Your little love triangle with Luke and Danny," he hisses, brushing at the tears on his face. "Danny catches you together and suddenly *disappears*, and the only piece of evidence that remains is Luke's surfboard. Luke, who's constantly starting fights on your behalf and who fought with Danny over you *last* night. Surely even you can put those pieces together, Juliet."

I stare at him. For a moment, I'm simply too numb, too destroyed, to understand what he's saying. Yes, I know it's my fault, but then...that word *"evidence"* catches in my brain.

Evidence. Luke's fights. Luke's arguments.

He's blaming Luke. And he's trying to make it sound like this was *intentional*. "What the fuck, Grady? Danny's—" My voice breaks and I have to swallow hard to hold it together. "Danny may be dead and you're sitting there creating conspiracy theories? Maybe you should have gotten a little more *sleep* last night."

It was the wrong thing to say.

His eyes narrow. "Conspiracy? Tell me how I'm wrong. We all saw them argue last night and watched Luke take off after you. Then Danny catches you with him and a few hours later he's dead and the only piece of evidence is Luke's smashed board in the water. A child could see what happened."

My stomach drops. It's insane, but when he spells all this out for the police, they're going to agree with him. Every fucking thing that's happened is pointed straight at Luke.

The police will look at the incidents he's been involved in. They'll look at the part where he threatened to drown that kid.

They'll hear from everyone in the house about the argument last night between Danny and Luke, about how they heard Danny shouting at someone on the beach. Then half of Rhodes will come forward to mention Luke defending me after the pastor's funeral.

Luke, who was out on the beach last night for hours, with no alibi. Luke, whose surfboard is the only evidence they have. Even if they can't pin it on him, he'll lose his sponsors for sure.

"Grady," I plead, "you know Luke would never do this.

Please don't tell anyone about my conversation with Danny. He was being...irrational. He sensed we were drifting apart and he was saying all kinds of crazy stuff."

"Danny wasn't crazy, and don't you dare try to imply he was. The only thing that was crazy was that he didn't see it sooner. I kept telling him and he wouldn't listen."

Oh, God. What has Grady been saying and for how long? And why did Danny never ask me? Why didn't he just end things?

If he'd ended it, if he'd never met me at all, he might be with someone like Libby by now. Someone who'd love to be a missionary's wife. And Luke...he'd be unblemished. All his altercations, prior to me, were as a juvenile. Ancient history. He'd be surfing, accruing sponsorships, sleeping with a different bikini-clad girl every night.

Maybe I'm just as poisonous as my mother said. Maybe I've ruined people's lives—my brother's, Danny's, Donna's. But I refuse to add Luke to that number.

"Tell me what to do," I beg. "You know Luke wouldn't have done this, but he's got a record. Even if it comes to nothing, he'll have lost all his sponsors by the time it's done. This is going to ruin his life."

He scoffs. "Look how fast your tears dry when we start talking about Luke."

I want to apologize. I want to grovel. I want to say anything that will convince him to help. But I'm making this worse every time I open my mouth.

"Grady, Danny even said something about making the jump if he had Luke's board. You heard him. Punish me all you want, but you know Luke didn't do this. Don't tell the cops Danny saw me with him."

He stares at me, pale, dry-eyed, and calculating.

"I want you gone," he says at last. "If you want me to keep all this to myself, I want you out of Rhodes. Permanently. And don't think for a moment I'm going to let you walk into the sunset with Luke after everything you've done. You leave, and you cut off all contact with him."

I can't. It will hurt Donna and Luke, but it will *kill* me.

"Grady, I'm not going to say anything about last night—"

"Last night didn't happen, do you understand? Imply otherwise, ever, and I will ruin you and Luke both. I just want you gone."

"How am I going to explain that to them?" I ask, my voice breaking. "They'll be so hurt."

"What would hurt Donna more? You leaving or her finding out *you're* the reason Danny's dead?" His mouth presses tight. "As for Luke, just tell him you can't look at him without seeing Danny's face. If you were a better person, it would probably be true."

THE SEARCH and rescue team arrives, and when I start to call Donna, I'm crying too hard to get through it. Beck takes the phone and tells her what's happened.

The police ask us to follow them to the station. I'd normally ride with Luke, but suddenly every step I make seems suspicious. Will they wonder why I woke Luke first? Will they make something of the fact that I rode with him to the station? Will they see what now, out of nowhere, seems completely clear to me: that I was with Danny, but Luke is the one I've been leaning on. That I was marrying Danny, but Luke's the one I told things to and turned to when I was upset, again and fucking again.

So, I ask Harrison to take me instead, ignoring the confusion on Luke's face as he watches me head toward the BMW. At the last minute, though, I turn and walk over to where Luke stands. He's so fucking honest—so unexpectedly, unnervingly, unreasonably honest.

I need him not to be, today.

"Don't tell them anything about us," I whisper. "Don't tell them you liked me. Don't tell them about our conversation last night. Just don't...drag me into this." By which I mean *don't drag yourself into this*, but I can't say it. He has no sense of self-preservation whatsoever, but he will preserve me, and today I'm using that to its full advantage.

"Okay," he says. There's a flare of hurt in his eyes, a clench of a muscle in his jaw. Good. *Be hurt and confused, Luke. It'll just make it easier for you to believe I want nothing to do with you once this is through.*

I press a hand to the ache in my chest at the thought.

I don't know how I'll stand to do it.

WHEN WE ARRIVE at the station, they tell us Danny's body was found. Luke's leash was around his ankle.

I sink into a black padded chair, my legs shaking too badly to hold me up. I knew it already, but it's different, hearing it confirmed. I bury my face in my hands, telling myself to wake up.

Nothing changes.

He's really gone. Did I make him happy these past few months? I'll never know. I only know he's gone now and it's all my fault.

Donna calls me, her voice choked with tears, so stunned she can barely form words. "Juliet," she whispers, "how am I going to live without him?"

My eyes squeeze shut. *I don't know.* I don't know how any of us will ever move on. We weep together until someone comes to get my statement.

I'm led back to a desk, thinking the entire way of the last time I was in a police station. How they quietly blamed me and asked me to sell Luke out over something so much more minor. I think of how they set my brother up to die before he'd even left the building. No matter how nice they seem, I can't afford to trust anyone.

If I lie and Grady doesn't, it'll look like I'm helping Luke cover up a crime. Maybe a really good lawyer could poke holes in that version of events Grady presented...but we can't afford a really good lawyer.

So, when the cop arrives, I take small truths—that Danny was drinking, that he was jealous of Luke's board—and spin them into a story about what happened that bears little resemblance to reality.

"I understand Luke and Danny argued," he says. "Do you know what it was about?"

"I have no idea," I reply.

Lying comes easily, but I guess it should. I've been doing it for years.

THE DAYS LEADING up the funeral are a blur.

The church has rescinded its offer to support Donna's mission in Nicaragua and she's too broken to care.

I sit on one side of her during the funeral, and Luke sits on the other. I haven't met his eye once.

Afterward, there's a reception held at the church. Donna is surrounded by people trying to console her and feed her. Libby would like to do the same for me, but Grady is always hovering nearby with a look that frightens me.

He's only gone along with this because I'm holding something over him. What if he figures out one day that he doesn't have to be ashamed of who he is? What if it comes out anyway? He wasn't exactly being *careful* that night. If he gets caught with someone else, will this whole thing fall apart?

I let my gaze rest on Luke for a moment, that face I love so much. How much further would I go to protect him? I'd go as far as necessary. If I could think of a way to eliminate Grady entirely, I'd probably do it.

The old, bad Juliet is front and center right now, as if she never left. I'll need her, going forward.

Luke crosses the room to me. "Can we go somewhere to talk?"

Grady is watching. I need to just...get this done.

"No," I reply. "And stop trying to pull me aside like this. People are already talking about how I followed you when you took that first cliff jump. You're making me look bad. I'm leaving for LA tomorrow. Don't call me, don't text me. This is done."

All the color leaves his face.

"You can't be serious right now." I've never heard his voice so hoarse, so empty.

"I will never look at you without seeing what I lost," I lie, my throat constricting so tight I can barely get the words out.

I take one last look at his shocked, heartbroken face and walk straight out of the reception hall, unable to hold it together for another moment.

I don't know how I'll survive without him, but for his sake, I'm going to figure it out.

35

NOW

I was homeless when I moved to LA. The first time a guy tried something in the shelter, I punched him in the throat so hard he reported me. I lied on job applications, shoplifted food, dated a club owner to get gigs, and slept with a producer to get a demo made. I was ruthless and calculating, twenty-fours a day, and I felt absolutely nothing about it.

Something had hardened in me the day I walked out of the church and left Luke behind. It was the moment I gave up hoping I'd ever be good, or loved, or even happy. I decided to simply survive, nothing more. It made things easier.

Now, as I meet Luke's bewildered gaze as we're marched out of the ballroom in handcuffs, I know I need to find that thing again. I will hurt anyone I have to—even Donna, even Luke— in order to get him out of this.

Donna runs alongside me. "Juliet, what's going on?"

In an ideal world, I'd tell her the whole, terrible truth before she hears Grady's version, but I'm not sure mine sounds much better, and I'm scared she won't do what I need to if she knows it.

"Luke didn't do anything," I whisper. "I know this looks bad, just believe me...Luke had nothing to do with it. You've got to get him out of this. Find Harrison. And get Drew to call her attorney."

I'm not sure if she will. I wouldn't, in her shoes.

Luke and I are taken in separate police cars. I don't utter a single word and I don't cry. I hold my shit together and try to decide who I'll call when they book me. My agent, someone at the label, my manager, Luke's agent? Who stands to lose the most money from our arrest? Who'll work hardest to fix this? I'm not sure.

None of them will work hard enough.

Everyone in the station turns to stare at me as I enter—I guess it's not every day you witness the arrest of a celebrity in a floor-length satin dress—and I stare right back, looking for one person who can help me. I'm photographed and fingerprinted, and all the while, the only thing I'm wondering is who I can fuck, threaten, or bribe into helping Luke out.

"We'd like to talk to you about the night Danny died," the cop says.

"I want to make my call."

"It's just a few questions."

I stare him down until he hands me the phone.

I call Ben, Drew's attorney and my friend. I don't think he practices criminal law but he's smart as hell. Between him and Harrison, they'll at least be able to get Luke released on bond until we can figure something out.

He answers on the first ring. "Juliet, say nothing," he warns. "Drew already explained and I'm on my way. Your friend Harrison is probably there by now. We'll fix this."

Donna did what I asked. For the first time since this went down, tears threaten.

I swallow hard. "Don't worry about me—"

"When I told you to say nothing, I meant say *nothing*," he

growls. "Yes, I know who you're worried about. We're handling it. Just hang in there and keep your mouth shut."

Ben sounds confident, but Ben always sounds confident. And he might just be trying to shut me up.

I'm deposited in a room with poor lighting and a two-way mirror. Metal chair, cheap wood table, just like they show on TV. I assume that any minute now, two detectives will walk in to play *good cop, bad cop*. One will offer me water while the other one throws chairs.

I wait and wait, but no one enters, and I finally rest my head on my folded arms and try to come up with a back-up plan in case Ben and Harrison fail. I've got nothing, though. In the end I just think of Luke beside me, swaying in a hammock, telling me it's all okay. And that's when I finally start to cry.

I'm not sure when the tears give way to sleep, but I'm jolted awake by the sound of the door opening. I have no idea how much time has passed.

"You're free to go," says a guy in a uniform.

I stare at him, waiting for stipulations. Waiting for him to tell me Ben posted bail or that I've got to appear in court in an hour. "Just like that?"

He arches a brow. "Were you hoping to stay?"

I'm led to the processing desk, where they return my clutch and heels. Harrison is waiting at the end of the hall, still in his tux.

My mouth opens and he shakes his head, warning me not to say anything yet. It's only when the door shuts and we start walking down the hall that he speaks. "Luke's fine."

"But is he *out*?"

He shakes his head again. "Not yet, but I think he will be."

"I don't understand," I whisper. "If they had enough to arrest us, what could have changed?"

"Their evidence is entirely circumstantial. Luke's leash around Danny's ankle proves nothing. Grady told them about your affair with Luke and your fight with Danny on the night he died—that gave them motive, but they don't have that anymore, either. Donna took care of it."

I stop in place. "Donna?"

"She told the police that she spoke to Danny that evening and he said he was going to take the same jump Luke did."

I was sitting right next to Danny when he spoke to Donna. There was no mention of the jump at all.

My brow furrows. "*What*? That's not—"

He cuts me off with a warning glance and a hand on my arm. His smile, though, is gentle. "She loves you and Luke like you're her own, Juliet."

"*She lied*," is what he's saying. She learned tonight that Luke and I were together, and that Danny jumped because of what *we* did, and she still lied to save us both.

But does it mean she's forgiven us too? I can't imagine anyone would be capable of it.

He leaves me at the entrance to the lobby, telling me he's got to handle some stuff for Luke. I walk out alone to find Donna waiting. She rises, holding out her arms, and I go straight to her like the child I still am, on the inside. The scared fifteen-year-old who isn't sure anyone has ever cared about her.

I have my answer at last. She cared. All along. Just like Luke did.

"I'm so sorry," I whisper.

She hugs me close. "I'd do anything for my children...*all* of my children. I'm not stupid. I know there's a lot going on I'm unaware of. But the one thing I know beyond a shadow of a doubt is that neither you nor Luke would ever have intentionally hurt my son. This wasn't your fault, Juliet. We weren't fair to you. I realized that long ago."

"But I—"

She shakes her head. "You needed us, and we used that to our advantage. I wanted a daughter, and Danny wanted an easy love story, something uncomplicated, but that's something you can't have with a complicated girl. We walked over you and you never said a word."

"I had nothing to complain about. You saved me."

She squeezes my hand as she blinks back tears. "Oh, we hammered that one home, didn't we? We told you in a thousand ways how lucky you were, just so you'd stay in your place." She leads me to a chair and sits beside me. "I suspected you and Luke had feelings for each other. If I'd been better and stronger, I'd have let you go, but I wanted what was best for me more than I wanted what was best for you. You loved him right from the very start, didn't you?"

"I'm sorry," I whisper. "I loved Danny, too, but it was different."

She wraps an arm around me and my head falls to her shoulder. "I know, honey," she says, and I can hear the smile in her voice. "Why do you think I asked you both to come back here to help me?"

We sit like that for a long time, and inside me, a window opens. There was never a single sermon the pastor gave that made me believe in something bigger than myself. But a love like Donna's, forgiveness like Donna's, is too huge, and too lovely, to have ever occurred by chance.

Maybe I still don't believe in God, but I believe in her and Luke, and right now...that feels like enough.

It's three in the morning when Libby walks in. I sit up straight, tense. She gives me an uncertain wave as Harrison ushers her into the bowels of the station.

I'm not sure what she's doing here or what I'll tell her if she wants to talk on the way out. I'm sure Grady has given her a very different version of what happened that night, and maybe

I should just let her think it. She's having his kid in a matter of months, after all—my warnings would come a bit too late.

She's only in back for about a half hour when Harrison walks out with her.

"Your friend Ben's still back there, but things look good," he tells us. "Why don't the two of you get some sleep? I think he'll be released by morning."

Donna looks from him to me. She knows just by the set of my jaw that I'm not going anywhere. "I think we'll stay a bit longer," she tells him.

We retake our seats, and Libby sinks into the chair beside mine. "So," she begins. "Interesting night."

My laugh is shaky. "Yeah, I guess it was."

"I'm sorry," she says, and her eyes fill with tears. "I told them the truth."

I swallow. *Fuck.* Maybe this isn't wrapping up the way I thought. "Which truth is that?"

"That night? When Danny died?" She stares at her hands. "It was Grady he was yelling at on the beach. I know everyone thought it was Luke, and I let them think it because it would've looked bad if it all came out."

Donna and I glance at each other. "If *what* came out?" she asks.

"Grady was the one lobbying against you going to Nicaragua. I didn't agree with him, but I knew he was doing it. A lot of people knew. He held meetings, he organized a letter writing campaign, and Danny found out. I really thought Grady just wanted the money to stay here, but now...I don't think that's what it was." She swallows. "Grady told me last night that you'd been blackmailing him. That you made up some story about catching him on the beach with Ryan in order to keep him quiet about you and Luke. It wasn't made-up, though, was it?"

My shoulders sag. I want to lie to her but I can't, not when she's asking me outright. "It wasn't. I'm so sorry. I'd have told you if I could have. Grady said he'd pin what happened on Luke if I said a word."

She's quiet for a long moment. "I think I already knew. Not about that night on the beach. But I've found things, in the house, on his computer and his phone. He always had an excuse, but...I think I sort of knew." She laughs quietly, to herself. "You know who I think he might have really loved? Danny. I never understood why he hated you so much, right from the beginning. And it was always Danny he wanted to be around, back then. Not me."

Of course. I'm not sure why it never occurred to me before —the way he hated me from the start, how I never understood why he always wanted to hang out with us. Him suggesting he and Danny could run the church together after the pastor's heart attack. And then, apparently, going out of his way to keep Danny *here*.

"So what will you do?" I ask.

"She'll come home with me, of course," says Donna. "I'm going to need some help. We fired Hilary, you know. She allowed Cash to attend—a man who'd assaulted you, our biggest donor. She hardly seems like the kind of person we'd want making decisions for our kids. Now, Libby, if you don't mind driving me home, I'd be grateful. Juliet, can I persuade you to leave with us? It could be hours still."

I want to make sure he actually gets out. That nothing else goes wrong. "I'd like to stay...unless you think he won't want me here?"

She tilts her head. "Why wouldn't he want you here?"

So many reasons. Starting with the fact that he just spent the night in jail because of me. "I told so many lies, Donna," I whisper. "I lied to you, but I lied to him even more. And I hurt him. Again and again."

She pulls my hand away and tucks it into her own. "Honey,

you did it for him. He's going to understand that. And he's going to understand it was the wisest thing you could have done."

I swallow. "It wasn't though...I mean, it was all for nothing. I probably just made it worse."

She smiles. "Could you have gotten one hot-shot attorney, much less two of them, seven years ago? Could you have afforded *any* kind of attorney back then, either of you? I'd have been in no condition to help, and Luke would have lost all his sponsors no matter what we did. How can you possibly say it's for nothing?"

I bite my lip. "I just have a feeling it's not going to work out."

"Juliet, you don't have that feeling because it's not going to work out. You have that feeling because you still don't believe you deserve a happy ending. Just this once, for me, have a little faith."

I rise and hug her for a very long time. People are the thing that will grind your trust down to nothing. But they're also how you to discover a small seed of something inside yourself again, something soft and hopeful and full of love, something that will grow.

I felt that once. And tonight, Donna's helped me see it's still there.

I hug Libby, and the two of them start walking away, but then Donna turns, her eyes twinkling. "Oh, and, Juliet, when he's released and it all works out just the way I said, take a day or two, will you? We've still got that room at the hotel, after all. I'll see you both once you've gotten some rest." And then Donna, the former pastor's wife, *winks* at me. And Libby, the current pastor's wife, stands behind her with wide eyes, mouthing, "*Oh my God*"...before she gives me a thumbs up.

~

THE STATION IS RELATIVELY quiet over the next few hours. I feel ridiculously conspicuous in this red satin dress but eventually doze off and dream of Luke curled up against me.

"This is the most uncomfortable hammock I've ever laid on," I tell him.

"It's not too late. We can still go to Paris."

I press my lips to his neck. He smells, oddly, like Windex. *"I think we just need to buy a new hammock."*

"Jules," he says, but it isn't *dream* Luke. It's real Luke. My eyes blink open to find myself splayed over two chairs, him kneeling in front of me.

His face is drawn, his jaw locked hard. He spent the night in prison because of me, and I wonder if he spent it dwelling on just how much he's suffered at my hands, year after year. He had to watch me agree to marry Danny after I told him I'd run away with him, after years of wanting me from afar and doing anything he could to take care of me. And then he had to watch me walk away, acting as if he'd never mattered in the first place.

"Come on," he says, rising.

I stumble to my feet and follow him outside, blinking into the too-bright sun. He walks around to the side of the station and I follow, my stomach sinking fast.

He's staring at his phone. It feels intentional, as if he's doing it simply to shut me out.

"Luke?" I touch his elbow. "I—"

"This is our car," he says, as if I hadn't spoken, nodding at a Kia swinging into the parking lot. His voice is cold, distant. He's treating me like a woman who broke his heart, or nearly got him charged with murder, or who spent seven years lying to him. And I'm all those things, so why shouldn't he? I swallow hard as I slide into the back seat.

"The Obsidian?" the driver asks.

Luke nods, staring out the window, his jaw still clenched. "Yeah. Thanks."

The driver glances at us in the mirror, his eyes widening with recognition when they meet mine. I can just imagine what kind of story this will turn into, if it isn't *already* a huge story, and I no longer care. I just need to know where we stand.

"Luke," I whisper, "can we talk?"

His eyes close. Even the sound of my voice is unbearable to him.

"Not here," he hisses, never looking my way.

We continue in silence, through neighborhoods where children are walking to the bus stop and through some town where people stand twelve-deep in line for coffee before we finally turn toward the beach.

Donna was wrong. He isn't going to forgive me. I press my face into my hands and take deep breaths through my fingers. How will I survive the next few days? How will I survive the next years, the next decades?

"We're here," Luke says as a valet opens his door.

I step out after him, ignoring the stares as I follow him into the lobby. He keeps moving, straight to the elevator, and it's only when we're both inside that he finally looks at me.

His mouth opens and he shakes his head, saying nothing.

We get to the suite. I walk in and he follows, letting the door slam behind him.

My eyes fill as I turn to him. "Luke, I'm sorry. I'm so fucking sorry."

He pulls off his jacket and throws it on the couch, tugs the already loosened bow tie free. And then he presses his hands to his forehead before sliding them into his hair. "Jesus fucking Christ, Juliet. What the *fuck*?"

I brush at the tears that have begun to fall. "I know. I know. I'm so sorry."

He stares at me, his eyes bright with rage. "Do you have any idea what I've been through? Do you have any idea what the past seven years have been like, trying to get over you?"

Grief strangles me. I can't even reply, but simply press a hand to my throat.

"You know what I did after you walked away at Danny's funeral?" he demands. "I drove back to that fucking cliff, planning to jump."

I inhale, sharp and fast. I knew he'd been hurt by what I did, but my God, if he'd jumped...

"I thought and thought, and only two things kept me from doing it—the fact that it would hurt Donna and the possibility that *you'd* come to your senses."

"Luke, I thought I was doing what was—"

"I waited for you to come back to me for *years*, Juliet!" he shouts, starting to pace. "That's how long it took to convince me it was done. And it was all a *lie*? Why didn't you just tell me?"

I dig my hands into my hair. "Because you wouldn't have gone along with it if you knew! You'd have confronted Grady, you'd have gone to the police, you'd have fucked it all up, and even if you didn't wind up in prison, you'd have lost every sponsorship you had! I had to do it. Surfing meant everything to you."

He stops pacing and stares at me, his nostrils flaring. "No, *you* meant everything to me. Surfing's just what I do for a living."

I lean against the wall behind me. He thinks I messed up and maybe I did. Or maybe I kept him out of jail. I can't take any of it back, so all that's left is to make sure he knows the truth before he walks away.

"I wanted you to be happy more than I've ever wanted anything for myself. If you think the past seven years weren't awful for me, then you don't understand this at all." My voice breaks. "If you think the past seven years haven't *killed* me, then you can't possibly love me the way I love you, the way I've loved you since you first walked into the diner, because when you love someone like that, yes, you'll fucking lie *to* him and *for* him—"

My words die off as he closes the distance between us, pinning me to the wall with his hands framing my face. "Don't try to tell a man who's waited ten years for you that you love him *more*."

His mouth lands on mine, then, hard and soft at once, angry and gentle. I hold onto his waist just to maintain my balance, just to keep from losing myself or sliding to the floor.

He needs to shave. I need to shower. But I'm wrenching his belt loose and he's unzipping my dress.

"I'm so fucking mad at you right now," he says, his hand fisting my hair to jerk my head up to his, "and I've also never loved you more."

His mouth returns to mine, and I get it, at last. He's going to forgive me. He was always going to forgive me. I can be flawed, I can do terrible things, and his love for me will always be bigger than that.

He groans as I reach into his boxers and wrap my hand around him. "Bed," he demands, unclasping my bra.

I pull him toward the room clad in nothing but my thong. He pulls his shirt overhead while I climb on the mattress, spreading my legs wide as he kneels between them.

He fists his thick cock, already dripping. "Are you ready for me, Juliet?" he asks, sliding a finger beneath my thong and inside me, his eyes gleaming. "Of course you are. You're fucking soaked. You always are."

He pushes the thong to the side and moves over me, then thrusts. We both groan, and for once neither of us has to silence it.

He begins to move, sinking his teeth into my shoulder as I gasp. It's desperate and frantic, and when I finally clamp down around him, unable to hold out a moment longer, he is only seconds behind me. "Fuck," he hisses. "*Yes*."

He groans as he lets go at last, then collapses above me, pressing soft kisses to my face, to my neck.

"I love you," I whisper. "I love you so much."

"It's about time I didn't have to drag it out of you," he grumbles, and when I laugh, he finally offers me a reluctant smile. "I love you too. But I'm guessing you knew that."

"I'm sorry. I'm sorry we were apart. I'm sorry it took us so long to get here."

His lips press to my head, his arms pull me closer. "I don't care how much time it took, as long as you're mine in the end. I told you I'd wait forever, but I'm glad I didn't have to."

I want to keep talking to him. I want to tell him everything, but I guess we've got all the time in the world for that now. We both agree we're going to get out of bed and shower in a minute, but instead—with the breeze billowing through the curtains and the roar of the ocean in our ears—we drift off to sleep.

It's every bit as good as I dreamed it would be.

I WAKE ALONE. I roll toward the balcony, where Luke stands in nothing but a pair of shorts, staring out at the horizon. It's dawn, and the sky's violet is giving way to oranges and pinks.

I throw his t-shirt overhead and cross the room, wrapping my arms around him from behind, smiling as my face rests against his bare back. "Go ahead and surf. I know you want to."

He turns, pulling me to his chest. "I had a thought." He tucks a lock of hair behind my ear. "Have you tried surfing again, since that day in Malibu?"

I stiffen.

Malibu. We were so happy yet so miserable. And so *innocent*, though neither of us would have thought it at the time. What might have happened if I'd just left with Luke then? If the two of us had walked out of the water together, gathered our stuff, and silently driven away? Danny would have hated me, but he'd still be alive. And I wouldn't have hurt Luke.

But we can't fix it. All we can do is start over, and never let anything come between us again.

"Surfing? No." I slide my fingers through his. "But there are a ton of people staying in the hotel this weekend. We'd attract so much attention out there together. There'd be photos of it everywhere tomorrow."

His spine draws straight and he steps away. "Maybe we needed to talk more yesterday than I thought." His eyes grow cold. "Is there a reason you still don't want people to know?"

I close the distance between us, pressing my mouth to the center of his sternum. "You can fly a plane over LA announcing it, for all I care. It has nothing to do with that. But you're a pro surfer and I'm a shitty beginner. Everyone on the beach will be laughing at me and feeling sorry for you."

His shoulders relax. His arms come around me again and he presses his lips to the top of my head in silent apology. I guess it's going to take a while for him to get over how bad things were. It'll take a while for me too.

"I can assure you that no straight male will be feeling sorry for me, and you did just fine last time, but there'll be almost no one outside for a few hours. We could go now."

The water will be cold and the waves here are larger than they were in Malibu. "I don't have a wetsuit," I argue weakly. "I'll freeze."

He gives me a sly smile. "I had one delivered for you yesterday. It's at the front desk."

I laugh. "I guess I was kind of a sure thing, then?"

"Juliet Cantrell," he whispers, tugging me tight against him, "you've *never* been a sure thing."

My nipples tighten under the borrowed t-shirt.

I raise my eyes to his. "I'm a pretty sure thing right now."

He lifts me up so quickly I gasp, pulling my legs around his hips as he starts walking toward the bed. He grins. "You're not getting out of surfing. But I guess it can wait."

An hour later we arrive at the beach. The sun is fully up now, the sky striped pink and blue. Aside from a few surfers in the water and an old guy with a metal detector, we've got the place to ourselves.

He tows me out until we reach the break. Even with a wetsuit on, the water's cold as hell, but the sun's out and Luke's smile is as young and untroubled as it was seven years ago.

With his help, after several failed attempts, I manage to catch a wave.

The last time I did this was in Malibu, and now, just like then, he's smiling, but there's something deeper in his gaze. Something serious.

I start paddling toward him, but for some reason, he's paddling toward me as well. He reaches me and grabs the front of my board, tugging it so our faces are close.

"Marry me," he says.

This time, he'll get no argument. If I'm willing to brave cold water and huge waves to stay near Luke Taylor, I'm sure not going to complain about this. "Name the date. And we'll need to buy a hammock."

He leans over my board and presses his lips to mine for a long moment. "As soon as possible. And I ordered the hammock yesterday."

We're getting our happy ending after all. I'd have waited for it forever, but I'm so glad I didn't have to.

EPILOGUE

It's summer, and the sun is starting to rise. I wake, feeling guilty that I've slept in, though a year ago I'd have considered dawn *bedtime*, not an indulgent night's sleep.

No one would fault me for sleeping in, my husband least of all, but I am still superstitious. When he leaves to surf in the mornings, I like to remind him to be careful, though the warning is probably unnecessary now. The waves on Oahu's North Shore are daunting year-round, but ever since we found out I was pregnant, he takes fewer risks.

I brush my teeth and splash water on my face, reading a text from Libby as I move toward the back deck.

She's sent a picture of George, her son—his face absolutely covered in purple yogurt.

LIBBY

Just preparing you for what you'll be facing in a couple months

I laugh. It's possible her life has changed even more than mine: she's a single mother now—Grady left the state entirely after he was removed from his position—and she now oversees Danny's House, which looks poised to go national.

In the end, the article in *The New York Times* was simply a glowing story about triumph in the face of tragedy, which might have been related to the sheer number of publicists and agents—mine, Drew's, and Luke's—who called to complain about the reporter's bias.

I reach the deck and peer into the distance, surveying the guys in the water. It's impossible to tell which one is my husband until the moment I see him drop into the wave, gliding down its face effortlessly. He carves along the surface and then enters the barrel, disappearing for a moment. My breath holds, and doesn't release, until he reappears. This is the price for loving Luke—the fear, these moments of waiting. After so many years apart, I pay them gladly.

Who would we have turned out to be, in another life? If we'd followed the paths others would have chosen for us? He might have taken that business degree and gone into marketing or sales. I might be a pastor's wife, hiding every true part of myself, or a music teacher hitting the snooze button repeatedly every morning because she didn't want to go into work.

Instead, Luke fills his day with the things he loves, and I'm doing my best to follow suit. We put a recording studio in the house, and the album I'm writing now is better and more personal than anything I've ever done. I'd begun to think I was empty, depleted, that there was nothing I cared about enough to put it to music, when really I'd just buried it so deep I'd nearly forgotten it was there.

I wish Donna would be around to hear it, but at least she lived long enough for other things. She saw us get married—on the beach, at sunset, with only a handful of guests—and she saw Danny's House operating at full capacity.

The end came shortly after their first Christmas, which we

were there for. She told me, on the day before she died, that she wasn't scared. "I'm about to see Danny again," she said. "What's there to be scared of?"

I hope, for her sake, she was right.

Luke drops into another wave, then starts paddling toward the shore. He's not even smiling, but I know what I see on his face is unadulterated joy.

He unzips the wetsuit, letting it hang off his lean hips as he shakes out his hair. All day, every day, I am surrounded by men with virtually no body fat and muscles most guys don't have, and yet it's only Luke's beauty that still takes me by surprise, that I can't quite get used to. He starts toward me while I head down the steps from the deck to bring him a towel.

"Babe," he growls, "I thought we talked about you walking onto the beach in your pajamas."

I laugh. "I'm eight months pregnant and this is hardly sexy. All I'm going to do is scare these guys away from marriage."

"You have no idea how wrong you are," he says, pulling me close. He's damp, but I don't care. His mouth hovers over mine. "As for the pregnancy thing, I've heard a rumor that sex can sometimes move things along."

I laugh. He mentions this *"rumor"* several times a day. "I feel like I've heard that somewhere too."

I pull him to the hammock he hung between two trees and he lets me climb in first, awkward now, before he joins me, sliding an arm beneath my head. We sway in the breeze, watching the sun paint the world with color. In a moment, I'll take him upstairs so he can make us pancakes. Perhaps we will check out that rumor he's heard one more time. But not just yet.

I don't want to be anywhere else.

THE END

Can't get enough of Elizabeth O'Roark?

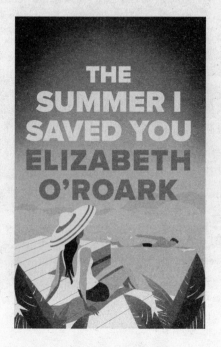

Keep reading now for a sneak peek of Caleb's story in *The Summer I Saved You*.

THE SUMMER I SAVED YOU

HOPE
2004

My aunt wasn't happy.

I'd only met her once before, this woman who'd raised my father, but as she waited on her front porch, watching me tug a beat-up suitcase behind me, she looked no more impressed than she had the first time.

I wasn't all that happy either. I'd thought she might live in a mansion, like my father did. I'd hoped to go back to school with photos to rub in Krystal Duncan's face. But this place wasn't going to do me any good at all.

"I still don't understand why this is necessary," my aunt said to my mom. "He paid you a settlement. What did you do with the money?"

My mother's eyes narrowed. "Kids are a lot more expensive than you think."

I'd seen my father before, in magazines or on TV, standing beside his pretty wife and their son. I couldn't fault my dad for choosing them over us: he'd met them first, and they were always smiling and wore much better clothes. I guessed I'd have picked them too.

"And how long is this *work emergency* of yours going to take?" demanded my aunt.

My mother's gaze jerked to mine—a warning to keep my mouth shut. "A couple weeks. We're busy, so I might not be able to answer when you call—speaking of which, I need to head back. This drive took forever. Be good, Hope." And then she was hustling back to the car as fast as she possibly could.

"Didn't even shut the engine off," my aunt muttered, before she turned to me with a mix of disdain and pity on her face. "It's going to be very dull for a seven-year-old, you realize. You'll need to stay inside. I can't have your father knowing you're here."

I nodded. My mom had been paid to keep my existence silent, so I was used to it. "I'm very good at keeping secrets."

She raised a brow at that and I wondered if she knew I was keeping a secret from her too. My mom didn't have a work emergency—she didn't even have a job. She was going to Disney with her boyfriend, and if I kept it to myself, they'd take me with them next year.

My aunt sighed, grabbing my suitcase. "Well, come on, then," she said, leading me into a house with peeling wallpaper and a damp smell, like wet dog or the sink at school.

Krystal Duncan had gotten a full princess makeover when she went to Disney—Ariel dress, the hair, everything. Her birthday invitations used the photos she'd had taken.

Maybe I could get a picture dressed like Ariel when I went, use *my* photo on a birthday invitation. My mom would need to get a house first, but she said that might happen soon if we *"played our cards right."*

"If I send out the same birthday invitations as Krystal Duncan, will she say I was copying her?" I asked as we walked up the stairs.

My aunt frowned. "You've got bigger things to worry about than birthday invitations. You're in here."

The room she referred to faced the neighbors' house, but I could see the lake to the left, with a dock jutting out onto it and a bunch of older boys standing on its edge. I walked to the window and watched as they flipped into the water, one after the other, howling and yelling and so...free.

"You can watch, but don't open the window and don't even think about going out there," my aunt warned. "Your father would kill me if he knew I was doing this. I need to get back to work. Stay here and be quiet."

I nodded. It was something I heard often enough at home, too. "I'm very good at keeping quiet."

My aunt's shoulders sagged. "I'll just bet you are," she said, walking to the door.

I turned to watch the boys again. They were all happy, all lean and tan and glowing with good health, but for some reason my gaze landed on just one of them and refused to stray.

The sight of him called to me. As if he was saying, "Hope, find me, I'm yours," though he had no clue I existed.

I decided to watch him carefully, whenever I could. If he was drowning, I'd go save him, like Ariel saved Prince Eric.

I was weirdly certain that one day he'd need me to do it.

ACKNOWLEDGMENTS

Thanks so much to my amazing beta readers: Entirely Bonkerzz, Michelle Chen, Katie Foster Meyer, Nikita Navalkar, Jen Wilson Owens and Tawanna Williams. Love you guys to the moon and back.

Thanks to the editing gurus: Sali Benbow-Powers, KM Golland, and Julie Deaton, and all the other people who helped get this book off my laptop and into the world: Christine Estevez, Valentine PR, Lori Jackson, Samantha Brentmoor, and every person who's shouted their encouragement on Instagram, Facebook and TikTok.

The bike incident in this book was actually somewhat auto-biographical. When I was in middle school, a group of guys grabbed me through the open window of a car in broad daylight and tried to pull me off my bike. I ran and hid until they were gone, and I never told a soul because I was certain I'd somehow be blamed for it and thought I might be at fault. Much later, working as a child therapist, I'd discover just how often kids kept *far* more traumatic events to themselves because they thought, perhaps, they were at fault and knew telling would only make things worse—which it often did.

So for everyone out there who, like Juliet, suffered something terrible in silence out of self-preservation...I'm so sorry that happened.

Can't get enough of Elizabeth O'Roark and the Summer Series?

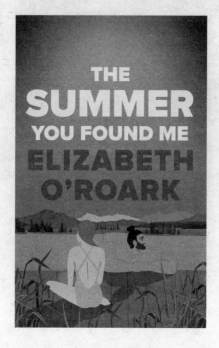

Meet Kate and Beck in
The Summer You Found Me today!